ALSO BY DAVID MOODY

HATER

YOU MAY CONTACT THE AUTHOR AT:

davidmoody@djmoody.co.uk

OR www.davidmoody.net.

DOG BLOOD

DAVID MOODY

THOMAS DUNNE BOOKS
ST. MARTIN'S GRIFFIN 🅜 NEW YORK

THOMAS DUNNE BOOKS.
An imprint of St. Martin's Press.

DOG BLOOD. Copyright © 2010 by David Moody. All rights reserved. Printed in the United States of America. For information, address St. Martin's Press, 175 Fifth Avenue, New York, N.Y. 10010.

www.thomasdunnebooks.com
www.stmartins.com

Design by Greg Collins

The Library of Congress has cataloged the hardcover edition as follows:

Moody, David, 1970–
    Dog blood / David Moody.—1st ed.
        p. cm.
    ISBN 978-0-312-53288-8
    1. Life change events—Fiction. 2. Survival skills—Fiction. 3. Fathers and daughters—Fiction. I. Title.

    PR6113.O5447D64 2010
    823'.92—dc22

                                                                    2009045770

ISBN 978-0-312-57741-4 (trade paperback)

First St. Martin's Griffin Edition: May 2011

10 9 8 7 6 5 4 3 2 1

TO THE MEMORY OF
Dr. Brian Barnes
(1942–2006)

ACKNOWLEDGMENTS

I'd like to thank a number of people for their help and support.

First, and perhaps most obviously, to John Schoenfelder at Thomas Dunne Books in New York and Jo Fletcher at Gollancz in London; thank you both for your tireless enthusiasm, observations, recommendations, guidance, and suggestions.

To my family and friends, thank you for your patience, tolerance, and unwavering belief and support over the last few years as I've negotiated this particularly crazy section of my haphazard and largely improvised "career path." Particular thanks to my long-suffering wife, Lisa, who never questions why she regularly catches me researching subjects as diverse and unsavory as genocide, germ warfare, secret underground bunkers, torture techniques, and countless other topics!

Finally, and most important, to those of you who've read and enjoyed my previous books, thank you for coming back for more! Particular thanks to those readers who've been with me since the very early days of giving away thousands of free downloads of *Autumn* and all my subsequent adventures with "Infected Books." Some of you read *Hater* when it was self-published in the summer of 2006, and you've been waiting since then for this sequel to arrive. It's finally here and I hope you enjoy it. I promise, you won't have to wait anywhere nearly as long for the conclusion to the trilogy!

To everyone I've listed above and to anyone else I should have mentioned but didn't, thank you.

THE CAUSE OF THE Hate (as it had come to be known on both sides of the uneven divide) was irrelevant. At the very beginning, when the doubters had been forced to accept that something was really happening and that the troubles weren't just the result of media-fueled, copycat mob violence, the usual raft of baseless explanations were proposed; scientists had screwed up in a lab somewhere, it was an evolutionary quirk, it was a virus, a terrorist attack, aliens, or worse . . . Thing was, people were quickly forced to realize, *it didn't matter.* You could bullshit and postulate and hypothesize all you wanted—it wouldn't do you any harm, but it wouldn't do you any good either. Within days of the belligerent population finally beginning to accept that the shit had indeed hit the fan with almighty force, no one talked about the cause of the Hate anymore.

Hardly anyone wasted time even thinking about it. The only thing of any importance to the non-Hater section of the populace now was survival. And the so-called Haters? The one-third of society who *had* changed? Those previously "normal" people who, without warning, had each become savage, brutal, and remorseless killers? The only thing that mattered to any of them was destroying every last one of the Unchanged (as they labeled their enemy) until none remained alive.

Before it had actually happened, the popular assumption in most apocalyptic films and books was that the population as a whole would immediately bind together against their common enemy and either stand united and fight back or take cover and hunker down when it became clear that something of Armageddon-like proportions was looming on the horizon. They didn't. Whether it was because many of them simply chose to bury their heads in the sand through fear or denial until it was too late, or whether it was instead just their stubborn refusal to abandon their homes, material possessions, and daily routines, no one knew. No one cared. A cynic might suppose that the effects of the Hate had been camouflaged by an inherently bad-tempered, mistrusting, selfish, and greed-driven society, but the exact reasons for society's lack of reaction were neither clear nor important. The bottom line was that the extent and implications of what was happening weren't fully appreciated until it was far too late, and the repercussions were devastating. This, it was painfully apparent, was no ordinary war.

In many ways the situation the Unchanged found themselves facing was indefensible. This conflict wasn't faction versus faction or army against army; it was individual versus individual, more than six billion armies of one. Beyond that, the Hate didn't care who you were, where you were, or what you were. You were simply on one side or the other, your position in this new, twisted, fucked-up world decided without your involvement by unknown variables and fate.

Within weeks command structures at every level were compromised. Organizations fell apart. Families crumbled. The Haters were everywhere and everyone, the whole world beaten up from the inside out.

The ratio of Unchanged to Haters was generally thought to have settled somewhere between 2:1 and 3:1. In spite of their enemy's ferocity and apparently insatiable bloodlust, their greater numbers and preexistence gave the Unchanged an early advantage that was quickly squandered. With no time or inclination to look for a cure (could the condition even be reversed?), separation and eradication soon became the only viable option for survival. Conveniently ignoring lessons learned through history and any moral arguments, a halfhearted attempt to cull the Haters failed dramatically. Almost overnight the Unchanged plan of attack was forced to become a plan of *defense*, and their first priority was to make their people defendable. Civilians were herded together, major city centers quickly becoming swollen, overcrowded, undersupplied, understaffed refugee camps. Once they'd successfully separated "us" from "them," the Unchanged theory went, they'd head back out into the wastelands and hunt the fuckers out.

Less than four months ago, when the last frosts of winter had finally thawed and the first green buds of the year's new growth had tentatively started to appear, this public park had been a frequently empty and underused oasis of lush greenery buried deep within the drab gray concrete heart of the city. It was a place office workers used to escape to during lunch breaks or take a shortcut through on their way to or from work. A place where kids playing hooky from school would hide and drink stolen alcohol and smoke cigarettes and carve their names on wooden benches and tree trunks. A place where elderly shoppers with too much time and too many memories would sit and talk to anyone who'd listen about how the country had gone to ruin and how things used to be so much better back in their day . . . and it had to be said, they were right.

Tucked away in the long shadows of office buildings, shopping malls, convention centers, and multiplex cinemas, what used to be a vast and open expanse of grass was now covered in cramped rows of ragged, refugee-filled tents. Two soccer fields had become helicopter landing pads, constantly in use. The patch of soft asphalt where children's swings, merry-go-rounds, and slides used to be had been commandeered to house heavily guarded and rapidly dwindling stockpiles of military equipment and supplies. The changing rooms on the far side of the park were now a hopelessly inadequate field hospital. Next to the small, square redbrick building, a tall wooden fence had been erected all the way around the park's four concrete tennis courts. They had, until three weeks ago, been used as a makeshift morgue, but by then the number of stacked-up corpses awaiting removal had reached such a level that the cordoned-off area had become a permanently lit funeral pyre. There was no longer any other way of hygienically disposing of the dead.

Before his mother had tried to kill him and he'd been dragged screaming into the war he'd desperately tried to isolate himself from, Mark Tillotsen had sold insurance in a call center. He'd worked hard and had enjoyed (as much as anyone enjoyed selling insurance in a call center) the job. He'd liked the anonymity of the role, and he'd taken comfort from the safety of the daily routine, the procedures and regulations he hid behind, and the targets he worked toward. In his last development review, just a month or so before the Hate, his manager had told him he had a bright future ahead of him. Today, as he trudged slowly through the afternoon heat toward a convoy of three battered trucks bookended by heavily armed military vehicles, he wondered whether he, or anyone else for that matter, had *any* kind of future left to look forward to.

Mark hauled himself up into the cab of the middle truck and acknowledged the driver. His name was Marshall, and they'd traveled outside the city together several times in recent weeks. Marshall was a stereotypical trucker, more at home behind the wheel of his rig than anywhere else. His arms were like tree trunks, with fading tattoos hidden beneath a thick covering of gray hair. He gripped the steering wheel tight in his leather-gloved hands even though they weren't moving. His head remained facing forward, his expression sullen and serious. To show no emotion at all was better than letting Mark see how nervous he really was. This wasn't getting any easier.

"All right?"

"Fine," Mark replied quickly. "You?"

Marshall nodded. "People today, not supplies."

"How come?"

"Helicopter spotted them on infrared, about three miles outside the zone."

"Many?"

"Don't know till we get there."

That was the end of their brief, staccato exchange. Nothing more needed to be said. Although it was widely believed that the Change was over and by now you'd know whether the person standing next to you was going to rip your fucking head off or not, conversations between strangers remained brief and uncomfortable and only happened when necessary. You constantly trod a fine line; to ignore someone was dangerous, to overreact was worse. You didn't want to give anyone reason to believe you might be one of *them*. All that Mark knew about Marshall was his name, and that was how he wanted to keep it.

Time to move. Marshall started the engine of the truck, the sudden rattle, noise, and vibration making Mark feel even more nauseous and nervous than he already was. *Remember why you're doing this,*

5

he repeatedly told himself. Apart from the fact that going outside the so-called secure zone allowed him to escape the confines of the shitty, cramped hotel room where he, his girlfriend, and several other family members had been billeted, willing militia volunteers like him were paid with extra rations—a slender additional cut of whatever they brought back. More importantly, going out into the open and watching those evil bastards being hunted down and executed was as close to revenge as he was ever going to get. And Christ, he needed some kind of revenge or retribution. Through no fault of his own his life had been turned upside down and torn apart. Like just about everyone else, he'd lost almost everything and he wanted someone to pay for it.

The truck lurched forward, stopping just inches short of the back of the vehicle in front, then lurched forward again as the convoy began to move. Mark glanced back across the park as a helicopter gunship took off from its soccer-field landing pad before taking up position overhead, their escort and their eyes while they were outside the city.

A single strip of gray pavement weaved through the park from a central point, running through a large, rectangular parking lot (now filled with military vehicles), then continuing on as a half-mile-long access road with copses of trees on either side. As the track curved around, Mark shielded his eyes from the relentless afternoon sun and looked out across this bizarre militarized zone. How could it have come to this? He'd played here during school vacations as a kid; now look at it. The village of tents and trailers made it look more like a third-world slum than anything else. Or perhaps a badly organized humanitarian response to some devastating natural disaster—the aftermath of a hurricane, tsunami, earthquake, or drought?—although nothing like that ever happened here. He forced himself to look up from the never-ending crowd of refugees that seemed to cover every visible square yard of land, forced himself to shut out their constant cries and moans that were audible even over the rumble of the truck, and forced himself to ignore the foul, rancid smell that filled the air. He concentrated instead on the tops of the trees that swayed lightly in the lilting early summer breeze. That was the only part of the world that looked like it used to in the days before the Hate.

It was a relief when they reached the access road and Marshall followed the other vehicles around to the right. Even here, though, there were people everywhere, crowded in and around the trees, desperate to find shelter and shade. There were more of them here than when he'd last been out with Marshall. He focused on one particular woman who sat cross-legged on the grass, desperately trying to hold on to a hysterical, squirming, screaming child. Surrounded by her few remaining possessions gathered up in plastic bags, she gently rocked her terrified, inconsolable little girl. He found himself wondering what had happened to this woman to bring her here. Had she had a partner? Had they turned against her? Had there been more kids? She looked up and caught his eye, and he quickly looked away. He forgot her almost immediately, suddenly preoccupied with his own insurmountable problems instead. Mark's girlfriend, Kate, was pregnant. Much as he tried to deny it, he wished she weren't.

The convoy moved away from the densely occupied heart of the city and out through the exclusion zone. This was a bizarre and unsettling place. In the wake of the panic and terror caused by the onset of the Hate, under military orders the authorities in cities like this had pulled the remaining population inward, housing them temporarily in stores, office buildings, high-rises, and anywhere else that space could be found. The exclusion zone (which was generally between half a mile and two miles wide) was an area of dead space, a desolate strip of no-man's-land wedged between the hordes of overcrowded refugees and the city border, which was patrolled from the sky. It was a place that had been abandoned rather than destroyed and that now stood like a vast and dilapidated museum exhibit. They drove past the front of a modern-looking school, its buildings empty when they should have been filled with students, the knee-high grass making its athletics track look more like a field of crops overdue for harvest. At the front of the convoy a military vehicle that had been fitted with a makeshift snowplow-like attachment cleared the road of a number of abandoned cars that had been stuck in a frozen, unmoving traffic jam for weeks.

The closer they got to the border, the worse Mark began to feel. Desperate not to let his anxiety show (for fear of Marshall misreading his reaction), he leaned against the window and forced himself to breathe in deeply, frantically trying to remember the relaxation and stress-control techniques he'd been taught in the "Dealing with Customer Complaints" workshop he'd been sent to last December. Christ, it didn't matter how many times he did this, he still felt woefully underprepared. No amount of relaxation methods and calming techniques would prepare him for what he was about to face.

"Couple of miles," Marshall said, startling Mark. He sat up straight and readied himself, his heart thumping ten times faster in his chest than it should have been. They were well outside the exclusion zone now, and even though there were no signposts, physical boundaries, or other warnings marking the Change, he suddenly felt a hundred times more vulnerable and exposed.

"Did you say we're out here for people today?" Mark asked, remembering their brief conversation when he first got into the truck.

"Yep."

"Great."

A double pisser. Excursions outside the city were always more risky and unpredictable when civilians were involved. More importantly, if they weren't out here collecting supplies, there'd be nothing for them to take a cut from when they got back.

"Look on the bright side," Marshall said under his breath, sharing Mark's disappointment and almost managing to smile. "Loads more of those cunts die when the public are involved."

He was right. As soon as the first civilians took a step out of their hiding place, hordes of Haters would inevitably descend on them from every direction. Maybe that was the plan? Easy pickings for the helicopter and the forty or so armed soldiers traveling with them in this convoy. He wondered what kind of state the survivors they rescued would be in. Would they even be worth rescuing? He couldn't imagine how they'd managed to last for so long out here. Christ, it had been hard enough trying to survive back in the city. If these people thought their situation was going to get better after they were rescued, they were very wrong.

The road they followed used to be a busy commuter route into town, permanently packed with traffic. In today's baking afternoon heat it was little more than a silent, rubbish-strewn scar that snaked its way between overgrown fields and run-down housing projects. Sandwiched between the first military vehicle and the squat armored troop transport bringing up the rear, the three empty, high-sided wagons clattered along, following the clear path that had been snow-plowed through the chaos like the carriages of a train following an engine down the track. Still bearing the bright-colored logos and ads of the businesses that had owned them before the war, they were conspicuously obvious and exposed as they traveled through the dust-covered gray of everything else.

Mark stared at the back of a row of houses they thundered past, convinced he'd seen the flash of a fast-moving figure. There it was again, visible just for a fraction of a second between two buildings, a sudden blur of color and speed. Then, as he was trying to find the first again, a second appeared. It was a woman of average height and slender build. She athletically scrambled to the top of a pile of rubble, then leaped over onto a parched grass verge, losing her footing momentarily before steadying herself, digging in, and increasing her pace. She sprinted alongside the convoy, wild hair flowing in the breeze behind her like a mane, almost managing to match the speed of the five vehicles. Mark jumped in his seat as a lump of concrete hit the truck door, hurled from the other side of the road and missing the window he was looking through by just a few inches. Startled, he glanced into the side mirror and saw that they were being chased. His view was limited, but he could see at least ten figures in the road behind the convoy, running after them. They were never going to catch up, but maybe they sensed the vehicles would be stopping soon. They kept running with a dogged persistence, the gap between them increasing but their speed and intent undiminished. He looked anxiously from side to side and saw even more of them moving through the shadows toward the road. Their frantic, unpredictable movements made it hard to estimate how many of them there were. It looked like there were hundreds.

Marshall remembered the place they were heading to from before the war, a modern office building in the middle of an out-of-town business park; as part of his job in his former life he'd made deliveries to a depot nearby on numerous occasions. He was glad he was following and not leading the way today. It was getting harder to navigate out here, and he'd convinced himself they had farther to go than they actually did. Everything looked so different out here beyond the exclusion zone, the landscape overgrown and pounded into submission after months of continuous fighting. A reduction in the number of undamaged buildings was matched by a marked increase in the level of rubble and ruin. There were more corpses here, too. Some were heavily decayed, sun-dried and skeletal; others appeared fresh and recently slaughtered. Christ, he thought to himself, not wanting to voice his fears and observations, what would this place be like a few months from now? There were already weeds everywhere, pushing up through cracks in the pavements and roads and clawing their way up partially demolished buildings, no municipal workers with weed-killer sprays left to halt their steady advance. Recent heavy rainstorms and the relative heat of early summer had combined to dramatically increase both the rate of growth of vegetation and the rate of decay of dead flesh. Everything seemed now to have a tinge of green about it, like mold spreading over spoiled food. The outside world looked like it was rotting, and the stench that hung heavy in the air was unbearable.

High above the line of trucks, the helicopter suddenly banked hard to the right and dropped down. Mark leaned forward and watched its rapid descent, knowing that the sudden change in flight path meant they'd reached their destination. Despite an irrational fear of heights, at moments like this he wished he were up there picking off the enemy from a distance rather than trying to deal with them down at ground level. Not that he was expected to fight unless he had to, of course. His role was simply to get as much food, supplies, civilians, or whatever they were out here to acquire into the trucks in as short a time as possible. He wasn't stupid, though. He knew that these missions were often little more than thinly veiled excuses to stir up as many of the enemy as possible, draw them into a specified location, and blow the shit out of them. Their uncoordinated, nomadic behavior and apparently insatiable desire to kill made them surprisingly easy to manipulate and control. Any activity outside the exclusion zone would inevitably cause most of them within an unexpectedly wide radius to surge toward the disturbance, where they could be taken out with ease. And if civilians, soldiers, or volunteers like him got hurt in the process? That was an acceptable risk he had to get used to. Anyone was expendable as long as at least one Hater died with him.

The convoy swung the wrong way around a traffic circle, then joined the road that led into the business park. Once well maintained and expensively landscaped, it was now as run-down and overgrown as everywhere else. The snowplow truck smashed through a lowered security barrier, then accelerated again, bouncing up into the air and clattering heavily back down as it powered over speed bumps. Mark could see the office building up ahead, the sun's fierce reflection bouncing back at him from its grubby bronzed-glass fascia. He tried to look for an obvious entrance, but at the speed they were approaching it was impossible. He clung to the sides of his seat and lurched forward as Marshall, following the lead of the driver in front, turned the truck around in a tight arc and backed up toward the building. He slammed on the brakes just a couple of yards short of the office, parallel with the other vehicles.

Mark didn't want to move.

Marshall glared at him. "Go!"

He didn't argue. The tension and fear suddenly evident in Marshall's voice were palpable. Mark jumped down from the cab and sprinted around to open up the back of the truck. He was aware of sudden noise and movement all around him as soldiers poured out of their transports and formed a protective arc around the front of the building and the rest of the convoy, sealing them in. More soldiers, maybe a fifth of their total number, ran towards the office building's barricaded entrance doors and began to try to force their way inside. A burned-out car surrounded by garbage cans full of rubble blocked the main doorway.

"Incoming!" a loud voice bellowed from somewhere far over to his left, audible even over the sound of the swooping helicopter and the noise of everything else. Distracted, he looked up along the side of the truck toward the protective line of soldiers. Through the gaps between them he could see Haters advancing, hurtling forward from all angles and converging on the exposed building with deadly speed. Like pack animals desperately hunting scraps of food, they tore through holes in overgrown hedges, clambered over abandoned cars, and scrambled through the empty ruins of other buildings to get to the Unchanged. Mark watched transfixed as many of them were hacked down by a hail of gunfire coming from both the defensive line and the helicopter circling overhead, their bodies jerking and snatching as they were hit. For each one that was killed, countless more seemed to immediately appear to take their place, all but wrestling with each other to get to the front of the attack. Some of them seemed oblivious to the danger, more concerned with killing than with being killed themselves. Their ferocity was terrifying.

Mark heard the sound of pounding feet racing toward him. He spun around, ready to defend himself, but then stepped aside when he saw it was the first of a flood of refugees who were pouring out of a smashed first-floor window. He tried to help them up into the back of the truck, but his assistance was unwanted and unneeded. Sheer terror was driving these people forward, every man, woman, and child fighting with every other to get into one of the transports, desperate not to be left behind. After weeks of living in unimaginable squalor and uncertainty, and with their hideout now open and exposed, this was their last chance—their only chance—of escape.

The relentless gunfire and the thunder and fury of the helicopter overhead continued undiminished. Mark tried to block out the noise and concentrate on getting as many people as possible into the truck. Ahead of them, the soldiers were being forced back. Marshall revved the engine, his only way of letting Mark know he was about to leave. Terrified of being left behind, he ran forward and hauled himself up into his seat, leaving more refugees to try to cram themselves into the truck.

"This is getting shitty," Marshall said, nodding over toward a section of the defensive line of soldiers that appeared dangerously close to being breached. "We're going to—"

Before he could finish his sentence, a gap appeared in the line where a Hater woman took out a soldier as he reloaded. She knocked the soldier to the ground, leaped onto his chest, and caved his head in with a soccer-ball-sized lump of concrete. As the soldiers on either side tried to react and defend, one gap became two and then three and then four. In disbelief Mark watched as a huge beast of a Hater manhandled another soldier out of the way and smashed him up against a wall. The soldier continued to fire at his attacker, but the Hater seemed oblivious to the bullets that ripped into his flesh, continuing to move and fight until he finally dropped and died.

The speed and strength of the enemy were bewildering and terrifying. Marshall had seen enough. Following the lead of the truck to his right, without waiting for order or instruction, he accelerated. Unsuspecting refugees fell from the back of the truck and immediately began sprinting after the disappearing vehicle, but they didn't stand a chance. Haters rushed them from either side, taking them out like animal predators preying on plentiful, slow-moving game on the savannah. In the distance the last few civilians spilled out of the building like lambs to the slaughter.

The third truck—the one that had been parked immediately to Marshall's left—hadn't moved. Mark watched in the side mirror as Haters yanked the doors of the truck's cab open and dragged the driver out, swarming over him like maggots over rotting food. Within seconds they'd enveloped the entire vehicle and were massacring the refugees who'd fought to get in the back to be driven to safety. As the distance between the truck he was in and the building behind him increased, all Mark could see was more refugees and stranded soldiers being wiped out in countless brutal, lightning-fast attacks. Above them all, the helicopter continued to circle and attack, its gunner's orders now simply to destroy anything on the ground that still moved.

Those Haters who had escaped the carnage outside stormed into the building, looking for more of the Unchanged to kill. More than twenty of them moved from room to room, sweeping over every last square foot of space, desperate to kill and keep killing. One of them sensed something. In a narrow corridor he stopped beside an innocuous doorway that the rest of them had ignored. There were dirty handprints around the edges of the door, and he was sure he'd heard something moving inside. It was the faintest of noises, barely even audible amid the chaos of everything else, but it was enough. He grabbed the handle and pulled and pushed and shook it, but the door was locked. He took a hand axe from an improvised holster on his belt and began to smash at the latch. One of them was still in there, he was certain of it. He could almost smell them . . .

The short corridor was empty, and the noise of his axe splintering the wood temporarily drowned out the sounds of fighting coming from elsewhere. Ten strong strikes and the wood began to split. He hit the door hard with his shoulder and felt it almost give. Another few hits with the axe and another shoulder shove and it gave way. He flew into the dark, foul-smelling room and tripped over a child's corpse that had been wrapped in what looked like an old, rolled-up projector screen. An Unchanged woman—the dead child's mother, he presumed—ran at him from the shadows. Instead of attacking, she dropped to her knees in front of him and begged for mercy. He showed her none, grabbing a fistful of hair, then chopping his axe down into the side of her neck, killing her instantly. He pushed her body over. She collapsed on top of her child, and he looked down into her face, her dead, unblinking eyes staring back at him. He felt a sudden surge of power and relief, the unmistakable, blissful, druglike rush of the kill.

The room was filled with noise again as the circling helicopter returned. Taking cover behind a concrete pillar, he peered out through a small rectangular window and watched as more of the fighters still out in the open were taken out by machine-gun fire from above. Then, without warning, the helicopter turned and climbed and disappeared from view. He listened as its engines and the thumping of its rotor blades faded into the distance.

Danny McCoyne knew he had to get out of the building before they came back. He'd seen them use these tactics before. He knew what was coming next.

HAVE TO GET AWAY from here. It's too dangerous to stay. If there's one thing I've learned about our piss-weak, cowardly enemy, it's that they always deal their deadliest blows from a distance.

The leaden feet of the woman's corpse are blocking the door and stopping me from getting out. I drag her out of the way, then shift the kid's body, kicking it back across the cluttered floor. The kid's bloodstained projector-screen shroud unrolls, revealing his lifeless face. Jesus, he was one of us. I uncover him fully. His wrists and ankles are bound. Can't see how he died, but he hasn't been dead long, a few days at the most. Probably starved. Another pitiful example of an Unchanged parent refusing to accept their kid's destiny and let go. Did she think she'd be able to tame him or find a "cure" or something? Dumb bitch.

Back out into the corridor. Most people have gone now, but I can still hear a few of them moving about, hunting down the last kills before they move on. I automatically head toward the back of the building, hoping I'll find more cover going out that way. A small kid darts past me, moving so fast that I can't even tell if it's a boy or a girl, then doubles back when it can't get out. I keep moving forward until I reach a T-intersection. There's a fire door to my left, but it's been blocked and I can't get through. I follow three men and a woman the other way into a dank toilet that smells so bad it makes my eyes water. The sudden darkness is disorienting, and the man in front of me takes the full force of a clumsy but un-expected attack from an Unchanged straggler who's hiding in the shadows under a sink. There's hardly room to swing a punch in here, but between the five of us we get rid of him quickly. I smash his face into a cracked mirror with a satisfying thump. He leaves a bloody stain on the glass, just another mark among many.

In a wide, rectangular handicapped cubicle there's a narrow win-dow high on the wall above the dried-up, mustard-brown-stained toilet bowl. One of the men, a small, suntanned, wiry-framed guy, climbs up onto the toilet, then uses the pipework to haul himself up. He opens the window and squeezes out through the gap. We take turns to follow him, impatiently standing in line like we're waiting for a piss. The fighter in front of me has a wide belly and backside, and I can't see him getting through. I'll be damned if I'm going to get stuck in here behind him. I push him to one side and climb past, knowing I'll be long gone before he gets outside, if he gets out at all. I throw my backpack down, then force myself through the narrow window frame and drop down into a flower bed overrun with brambles and weeds. A pile of waste and emaciated corpses cushions my fall. I quickly get up, swing my pack back onto my shoulders, and start to run. Won't be long now before they . . .

"Oi, Danny!"

Who the hell was that? My heart sinks when I look back and see Adam hopping after me with his ski-pole walking stick, his useless, misshapen, badly broken left foot swinging. I found this poor bastard trapped in his parents' house a few days back, and I haven't been able to shake him yet. He can hardly walk, so I could leave him if I wanted to, but I stupidly keep letting my conscience get the better of me. I tell myself that if I get him away from here he'll be able to kill again, and anyone who's going to get rid of even one more of the Unchanged has got to be worth saving. I run back, put my arm around his waist, and start dragging him away from the building.

"Thanks, man," he starts to say. "I thought I—"

"Shut the fuck up and move."

"Oh, that's nice. What did I ever—"

"Listen," I tell him, interrupting him midflow. "They're coming back."

I pull him deep into the undergrowth behind the office building. Even over my hurried, rustling footsteps and although the canopy of leaves above us muffles and distorts the sound, I can definitely hear another aircraft approaching. Whatever's coming this time is larger, louder, and no doubt deadlier than the helicopter that was here before.

Adam yelps as his broken ankle thumps against a low tree stump. I ignore him and keep moving. His leg's already fucked; a little more damage won't matter.

"Sounds big," he says through clenched teeth, trying to distract himself from the pain. I don't respond, concentrating instead on putting the maximum possible distance between me and the office. Other people run through the trees on either side of me, illuminated by shafts of sunlight that pour through the odd-shaped gaps between leaves, all of them passing us. The noise is increasing, so loud now that I can feel it through the ground. It must be a jet. Christ, what did I do wrong to end up saddled with a cripple at a time like this? Maybe I should just leave him here and let him take his chances? I look up, and through a gap in the trees I catch the briefest glimpse of the plane streaking across the sky at incredible speed, so fast that the noise it makes seems to lag way behind it.

"Keep moving," I tell him. "Not far enough yet—"

I stop and hit the deck as soon as I hear it: the signature whoosh and roar of missiles being launched. Adam screams in agony as I pull him down, but we'll be safer on the ground. There's a moment of silence—less than a second, but it feels like forever—and then the building behind us is destroyed in an immense blast of heat, light, and noise. A gust of hot wind blows through the trees, and then dust and small chunks of decimated masonry begin to fall from the sky, bouncing off the leaves and branches above us, then hitting the ground like hard rain. The thick canopy of green takes the sting out of the granite hailstones. The shower of debris is over as quickly as it began, and now all I can hear is the plane disappearing into the distance and both Adam's and my own labored breathing. He sits up, struggling with his injuries. Crazy bastard is grinning like an idiot.

"Fuck me," he says, "that was impressive."

"Impressive? I could think of other ways to describe it. If you'd been any slower we'd have had it."

"Whatever."

He leans back against a tree, still panting heavily. We should keep moving, but the idea of resting is appealing. The Unchanged won't come back here for a while. Even here in the shade the afternoon heat is stifling, and now that I've stopped, I don't want to start walking again. I give in to temptation and lie back on the ground next to Adam and close my eyes, replaying the memory of today's kills over and over again.

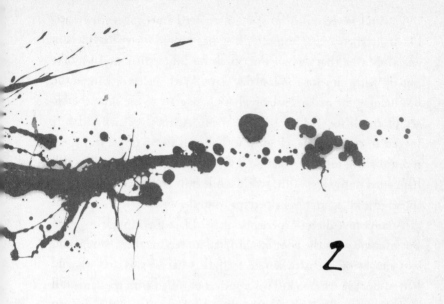

2

WE KEEP WALKING AS the daylight slowly fades, the darkness finally bringing some respite from the heat.

"What time is it?" Adam asks.

"No idea."

"What day is it?"

"Don't know that either."

"Don't suppose it matters," he grumbles as we limp slowly down a long dirt track that curves around the edge of a deserted farm. He's right—the time, day, date, temperature, position of the moon . . . none of it really matters anymore. Life is no longer about order and routine, it's about the hunt and the kill and just getting through each day unscathed. When the war began, killing was all that mattered, but things feel like they're changing now.

I would never tell him, but I've enjoyed traveling with Adam. Having someone like him to talk to has proved unexpectedly beneficial. Maybe that's why I went back for him earlier, and why I've put up with him for the last few days. Without even realizing it, he's helping me make sense of what's happened to me since the onset of the Hate. Before I killed them, Adam's parents had him locked in their garage, chained to the wall like a dog. He'd spent months there in total isolation. I've had to explain everything that happened to the rest of the world while he'd been locked away. Going over it all again has helped me to understand.

Adam's first direct experience of the Hate was similar to mine, but in some ways the poor bastard had it even tougher than me. He was caught off guard when he realized what he was and what he had to do. He tried to kill his family, but, filled with the same fear and disorientation that I remembered feeling after I'd killed my father-in-law, his father managed to fight back and smashed his right hand and left ankle with a small sledge hammer. Rather than finish him off or turn him over to the authorities, though, Adam's parents locked him up and locked themselves down. They didn't have the strength to kill him, even though they knew he'd kill both of them in a heartbeat. I understand why they did it. It's like the tied-up kid I found earlier today. The Unchanged just can't let go. They hold on to the people that used to matter to them in the vain and pointless hope they'll somehow be cured or change again. But how can we be cured? We're not the ones who are sick. Adam's parents had the whole thing planned out. They starved the poor fucker for days, then fed him drugged food to keep him subdued and under control. Finding him was like something out of a fucked-up Stephen King book. Wonder if Stephen King's like us or like them . . . ?

"Can we stop soon?"

"Suppose."

"You got any idea where we are?" Adam asks. His voice is weak. I glance across at him. His face is white and his skin clammy.

"Roughly," I answer. Truth is I'm not exactly sure, but for the first time in ages I actually do have a fair idea of where I am. For weeks I've traveled everywhere on foot. Like most people I've shunned cars and other similar means of transport—they make me feel conspicuous when all I want to do is disappear, and anyway, most roads are blocked and impassable now. I knew we were getting close, but it was yesterday afternoon, after we'd spent almost an hour waiting on the outskirts of a vicious battle for a kill that never came, when I caught sight of the Beeches on the horizon—a distinctively shaped clump of ancient trees perched on top of an otherwise barren and exposed hill. The trees are a natural landmark I used to pass on the highway traveling back home from rare day trips out with Lizzie and the kids. My best guess was that we were three or four miles short of them, and from memory they were another five miles or so from the edge of town.

"So where are we?"

"Close to where I used to live."

"So why do you want to go back there?"

"What?" I mumble, distracted.

"Back home? Why do you want to go home?"

"I lost my daughter, and I want to find her again," I tell him. "She's like us."

He nods his head thoughtfully. Then, from out of nowhere, a huge grin spreads across his tired, sweat-streaked face.

"So how many did you kill today, Dan?"

"Two, I think. You?"

"Beat you! I got three. You should have seen the last one. Speared the fucker on my stick. Took more effort to pull it out again than it did to skewer him!"

"Nice."

"I tell you, man," he continues, the tiredness gone and his voice suddenly full of energy and enthusiasm, "it's the best feeling. When I first see them they scare the hell out of me, but as soon as I'm ready and I've got my head together, all I want to do is kill. Does that feeling ever go? Tell me it doesn't . . ."

Adam's still living off the buzz of sudden power and freedom that comes with understanding the Change and experiencing your first few kills. I felt the same when it happened to me. It'll be a while before he comes down again. It's like a drug, and we're like junkies. I don't get the same highs I used to anymore, just the cravings. The euphoria has faded, and life's more of a struggle now. It's getting harder to find food, and I'm tired. The gap between kills is increasing, and all that's left to do in those gaps is think.

"The feeling doesn't go," I answer. "It just changes."

"Wish I'd been there at the start . . ."

For a few seconds he's quiet again, daydreaming about all the opportunities he's convinced he's missed. The silence is only temporary while he thinks of the next question to ask.

"So what are we?"

"What do you mean?"

"All I want to do is kill, man. I'm addicted. Am I some kind of vampire?"

"Don't be stupid."

"I'm not, think about it . . ."

"Believe me, I have thought about it. We're not vampires. We don't drink blood, we just spill it. I like garlic in my food, I'm okay with sunlight, and I can see my reflection in mirrors."

"You sure? You seen the state of yourself recently?"

I ignore his cheap jibe. He's right, but he looks no better. It's months since I cut my hair and weeks since I last shaved. I did manage to wash in a stream yesterday—or was it the day before . . . ?

"What are we, then? Werewolves?"

I shake my head in disbelief. This guy's relentless. What's even more disturbing is the fact I've already had this conversation with myself and I've got my answers prepared. Truth is, at the beginning, there were times I felt more like an animal than a man. In some ways I still do, but now I scavenge more than hunt. Less like a wolf, more like a rat.

"We're not werewolves. We don't change when the moon comes out."

"I know that, you prick," he says, catching his breath as the toes on his broken foot drag on the ground. I stay quiet for a moment, wondering if I should tell him what I really think or whether it's just going to pointlessly prolong this stupid conversation.

"Here's what I reckon," I say, deciding just to go for it. "You want to compare us to a type of monster? Look at the evidence—"

"What evidence?"

"Look at how we live and what we do."

"I don't get you . . ."

"We drag ourselves around constantly, looking for Unchanged to kill. It's almost like we're feeding off them. When you're killing you feel alive, like you can do anything, but the rest of the time it's like you're in limbo. Just existing. Not really living, but not dead either . . ."

"So what are you saying?"

"I'm saying we're like zombies," I finally admit. "Being out here is like being one of the undead."

He doesn't react. For a minute everything is quiet and deceptively peaceful, the only sound our slow, uneven footsteps on the dirt track.

"Do you know what I always used to wonder?" he eventually asks.

Do I really want to know?

"What?"

"I used to wonder what happened to the zombies after the end of the film. You know what I'm saying? When all the living have been infected and there's no one left to kill, what happens next? Does the hunger ever go away, or is rotting all that's left for them?"

ADAM IS STRUGGLING, HIS battered body a wreck, but he keeps moving. The light's almost completely gone, and we need to stop. Apart from a single helicopter in the distance and a fast-moving truck a few miles back, we haven't seen or heard anyone for hours. Things have changed—when the fighting first started there were people everywhere. Maybe it's because I'm moving at a fraction of my normal pace that the world seems empty? Part of me still thinks I should just dump Adam and go on alone. We'll find somewhere to stop and rest for the night. When I'm ready to get moving again I'll decide whether I'm going to take him with me.

"Over there."

"What?"

"There," he says, pointing across the road with his badly broken hand. His fingers jut out at unnatural angles, and I can't see what he's gesturing at. "Look . . . through the trees . . ."

On the opposite side of the road we're following is a dense forest. I squint into the semidarkness to try to see whatever it is he thinks he's spotted. He shuffles around and hops away from me, moving toward a gap in the trees that stretches farther into the gloom. I look down and see that there are muddy tire tracks curving onto the road from the mouth of a barely visible track.

"What do you reckon?" he asks.

"Got to be worth a look. There wouldn't be a track if it didn't lead somewhere."

"Might be more of them down there . . ."

He tries to speed up again, eager to kill, but I pull him back. I'm not sure. This doesn't feel right. I can see the outline of a large building up ahead on the edge of a clearing, and I cautiously edge closer. The building is huge and box-shaped, like a warehouse—but why here out in the middle of nowhere? I take another few steps forward, and realization slowly begins to dawn. Shit, I know what this place is.

"What's the matter, Dan?"

I don't answer. Can't answer. My mouth's suddenly dry, and my legs feel like lead. I should turn around and walk away, but I don't, and I keep moving forward on autopilot, my mind racing. We enter a dusty, gravel-covered yard, lines of mazelike wooden barriers making it look like a deserted, out-of-season tourist attraction. Up ahead the building's doors hang open like a gaping mouth.

"What is this?"

"You don't know?"

He shrugs his shoulders.

"Should I?"

"Slaughterhouse."

Adam leans against the nearest barrier and works his way along it toward the open door.

"You told me about these places, but I . . ."

"What? You didn't believe me?"

"It's not that . . ."

He stops talking and I stop listening. Like a character in a bad horror movie, I walk into the building. It's almost pitch black inside, but I can see enough to know that we're in a narrow corridor with a set of heavy double doors directly ahead. It's musty and damp in here, the faint scents of the forest and wood smoke mixing with the heavy, acrid stench of chemicals and decay. I wish I had a flashlight. The gloom makes it too easy to remember the night I almost died in a place like this. Standing here in the dark I can still see the helpless, terrified faces of the people crammed around me as we were herded like cattle toward the killing chamber. I remember their lost and desperate expressions, the confusion, frustration, and pain so evident. I remember my own terror, convinced I was about to die . . .

"You okay?" Adam asks, finally catching up and nudging into me from behind. I hadn't even realized I'd stopped walking. I feel like I've stepped out of my body and now I'm watching from a distance. It's a nauseous, unsettling feeling, like the nervous relief you feel when you walk away without a scratch from a crash that's just written off your car. You're thinking, *How did I get away with it? How close was I to biting the bullet?* and then your mind starts with the "what ifs" and "if onlys" . . . I know that if I'd have been another hundred or so people farther along the line that night, I'd be a dead man now.

I lean up against one of the doors in front of me. It moves freely, and I shove it open and walk into what must have been the gas chamber. The dark hides the details of what I know is all around me. There are bodies here. I have no idea how many, but I can see their shapes stacked up in featureless piles. The cavernous room is filled with the buzzing of thousands of flies gorging on dead flesh, and I keep looking up to avoid looking down. There's a hole in the roof three-quarters of the way down the length of the room, and I can just about make out metal gantries and walkways high up on either side. Wide-gauge pipework weaves in and out of the walls of the building, and an enormous exhaust fan has been mounted at the far end of the room, its blades still turning slowly in the gentle evening breeze.

"Let's get out," Adam whispers from somewhere close behind me. "Fucking stinks in here."

I move forward again, dragging my feet along the ground so I don't trip over anything I can't see, convinced that the entire floor is covered with gore and bits of bodies. I kick bits of wood and twisted chunks of metal out of the way—remnants of the fallen section of roof—and finally reach the far wall, my pace almost as slow as Adam's. I work my way along, trying to find a way out. In the farthest corner, hidden from view by another unidentifiable pile of rubbish, is a wide door that's hanging off its hinges, half open. I duck underneath it, then turn back and prop it open fully so Adam can get through. His uneven footsteps and grunts and moans of effort make him sound like a monster in the shadows.

"We can't stay here," he says.

"Might be some other buildings around."

As soon as he's completely outside, I put my arm around him and support his weight. We've only taken a few steps when he stops.

"Fuck me," he mumbles. "Would you look at that . . ."

At the side of the long, narrow building is another clearing, out of sight until now, and the ground is almost completely covered with bodies for as far as I can see. There are hundreds of them, thousands probably, stacked up in massive piles. I leave Adam again and move toward the nearest one. From a distance the gloom makes it look like a single, unidentifiable mass, only distinguishable as human remains because of the countless hands, arms, and legs that stick out from it at awkward angles. As I get closer, however, a level of sickening detail is revealed. These bodies have been dumped—not even laid out—and those at the bottom have been crushed by the weight of the rest, leaving them unnaturally thin, almost like they've been vacuum-packed. Higher up, countless squashed, frozen, waxy faces stare back at me unblinking. Their discolored flesh, hollow cheeks, and sunken eyes give each of them grotesque, nightmarish, masklike expressions. Seeing them makes me think about my own mortality. I don't feel anything for any of the people here—they're just empty shells now, each of them a spent force—but I swear I won't end up like this.

"Look on the bright side," Adam shouts across the clearing.

"There's a bright side?"

" 'Course there is. You got away. That could have been you, that could. Could have been me . . ."

I ignore him and keep walking farther into the clearing, following a narrow pathway between another two fifty-yard-or-so-long piles of death. Distracted, I lose my footing when I reach the end of the rows, and the ground suddenly starts to crumble beneath my boots. I fall back and find myself sitting on my backside on the edge of a vast hole, at least twenty yards square and deep enough for me not to be able to see the bottom in some parts. I know immediately what it is—a mass grave filled with an incalculable number of people like Adam and me. I get up and carefully walk around the edge. There's a bulldozer up ahead with a massive metal scoop. At first I think they must have used it to dig the pit, but then I see there's a scrap of clothing caught on the teeth of the scoop and I realize they were using it to fill it. Directly below me there are corpses reaching almost all the way up to the surface, piled up where they were tipped out. They look like they're climbing over each other to get out.

I jog back over to Adam, forcing myself to look away from the dead. How many sites like this were there, and are any still in operation? Even now as I'm wasting time here, are more of our people being killed elsewhere? Then another thought crosses my mind that makes me go cold: my daughter, Ellis. Did she end up in a place like this? Is she there now, waiting to die? Is she *here*? For a few desperate seconds I turn back toward the corpses and start looking through them, terrified the next face I see will be my little girl's. Then, as quickly as sudden panic just took hold, common sense takes over again. If she's here there's nothing I can do. I have to believe she's still alive. She's all I've got left.

"So where are they all?" Adam asks.

"Who?"

"The fuckers who did this. Where'd they go?"

"I don't know," I answer as I lead him out behind the main building toward a group of three square-shaped, light-colored, prefabricated huts that look new in comparison to everything else. "Just abandoned the place, I guess. Maybe they were attacked?"

"Hope the bastards got what they deserved."

Two of the almost identical shedlike buildings are locked. The corrugated metal roller door on the front of the third, however, is not. I open it fully and go inside. It's small, cramped, and half full of bags of chemicals. Doesn't matter. It'll do for tonight. No one with any sense will come here, and even if they do, we'll just play dead. I'd have fought side by side with any of the thousands of people who died here, but they're just rotting meat now, and we'll use them as cover.

Adam sits down on a pile of sacks, struggling to get comfortable and still talking nonstop about nothing of any importance. I close the door, then find myself a scrap of space in the far corner of the hard concrete floor and try to sleep, resting my head on another plastic sack full of Christ-knows-what. It could be poisonous or corrosive, but it doesn't matter. I cover it with my coat and close my eyes, too tired to care.

4

I'M WOKEN BY A crash and a muffled cry of pain. I sit up quickly and look around the dark room, struggling for a second to decide where I am. The combination of the acrid chemical smell and the stench of decay helps me remember. Where's Adam? I catch a momentary glimpse of him outside through the open door, hobbling back toward the main building. I grab a knife from my backpack and run after him. I've barely taken two steps out of the chemical storeroom when I hear other voices up ahead. There are people around the front of the cull site. I drag Adam out of the way, stopping only when we're both pressed up tight against the outside wall at the back of the main killing chamber.

"It's Unchanged," he whispers, voice full of nervous excitement. "I saw them."

"How many?"

"Don't know. Heard engines."

What the hell do I do now? Despite what Adam probably thinks, we can't risk taking them on until we know how many we're facing. There could be hundreds of them here, and if they've dared come out into the open like this then they're probably armed to the teeth and ready to fight. What do they want? Maybe they've come to try to get this place restarted? Shit, maybe they're here looking for us?

"Wait here," I tell him, pushing him toward an alcove. "Keep yourself under control and don't do anything until I come back, okay? I'll try to get a better look."

Adam nods and does as I say. I take a couple of steps away from the building and see that there's a metal ladder running from ground level to an access hatch up high. Before I can talk myself out of it I start climbing, trying to limit the sound of my heavy boots on the metal rungs. I pause when I'm two-thirds up and lean over to one side to peer in through a grubby window. The early morning sun is blazing through the windows along one side of the slaughterhouse and the hole in the roof, filling it with light, uncovering every grue-some detail that was hidden in the darkness last night. The Un-changed are inside the building now. I can see a couple of them slowly picking their way through the bodies and debris.

At the top of the ladder I open the hatch and carefully ease my-self inside. I'm on one of the narrow gantries running around the edge of the vast room, and I know I'm all too visible up here through the metal grilles. I move toward the side of the room that is still in shadow. I'm right above one of the intruders now. Looks like he's wrestling with a corpse, trying to pry a rifle from the death grip of a decaying soldier. Fortunately he's preoccupied, and I keep moving toward the front of the site undetected. Farther ahead I notice that this walkway's loose. Several brackets and supports have come away from the wall, and it's already feeling less secure. I'm less worried about my safety and more concerned that the creaking and groaning of the metal will cause one of the scavengers below to look up. They don't look like typical Unchanged military or militia. They're wearing odd, mismatched clothing, and they're both weighed down with weapons, far more than they need. They look more like mechanics than soldiers.

A sudden noise makes me catch my breath. I look back over my shoulder and stare down, worried they've found Adam. It's nothing, just another Unchanged helping himself to a dead man's gun.

I turn around to try to get off this unstable walkway, but stop when I glimpse something happening through the large dust- and cobweb-covered window at my side. The reason for the enemy being here has suddenly become painfully apparent. Outside, under the protective gaze of five armed militia fighters, two young women and a white-haired, elderly man are working their way along the nearest pile of corpses, stripping them of anything of value. Inhuman bastards. There must be a hell of a black market somewhere for them to risk doing this, but the fuckers look well organized, and they know what they're doing. Wearing yellow dishwashing gloves, the three of them move along the bodies at speed, each of them working at different heights, snatching rings and watches from the dead hands that stick out of the massive mound of rotting flesh, filling buckets with their stolen booty. A teenaged boy grabs each bucket when it's full, replacing it with an empty one and carrying the stash away out of sight. What I'm watching makes me seethe with hate and anger, but what can I do? There are too many of them to risk taking on alone (and even though Adam's with me, in terms of fighting I still think of myself as being alone). All I can do is wait for them to disappear.

Hang on, something's caught the attention of the grave-robbing bastards below me. One of them stops scavenging and calls to his pals. Carrying several weapons each, they head toward the door in the corner we exited through last night. I run back along the gantry, but before I get to the hatch I know it's Adam. I hear the stupid kid before I see him through the window. Should have known he'd struggle to keep himself under control. The Unchanged are outside now, heading straight for him as he limps aggressively toward them, the sharp tip of his ski-pole walking stick held out like a bayonet. Fortunately the rest of this gang are either unaware or too interested in their haul to get involved. I climb back out through the door and down the ladder. Adam and the Unchanged are out of sight now, but I can still hear them fighting. With half a dozen rungs left I jump down and run around the corner to help, knife in hand. Adam's on the ground, taking a heavy beating from two of them. To his credit he's already taken the other one out. The scrawny little fucker is slumped up against the side of the building, impaled with Adam's metal stick.

I grab the shoulders of one of his attackers and slam him down onto the dusty ground. His body rattles with the impact, and the look on his face is one of surprise more than anything else. Before he realizes what's happening I stab my knife into his chest, aiming for his heart. The blade's stuck in his breastbone. No time to pull it out. I run straight at the other one, punching the side of his head with enough force to knock him over. He scrambles back up, shakes his head clear, and rushes at me, holding a rifle by the barrel and swinging it around like a club. I duck his first clumsy strike, then, while he's still off balance, thump my axe into the base of his spine. I shove his face down into the dirt to muffle his screams until I'm sure he's dead.

Need to get under cover. We're out of sight and there's no sign of them yet, but the others will come looking for their people before long. Adam's out cold, and my already slim chances of winning this one-sided fight have just been slashed even further. All I can do now is get out of the way and wait for the rest of these fuckers to move on. Trouble is, I realize as I shove my arms under Adam's shoulders and start dragging him back toward the chemical store-room, when they find the bodies of three of their own they're not going to go anywhere. Then, as I reverse through the door and look back, I realize the tracks Adam's feet have left in the gravel and dust will lead them straight to us.

I dump his useless, groaning bulk in the space on the floor where I slept last night. There's a dribble of blood running from the corner of his mouth, but I can't tell if it's just his mouth that's cut or whether his injuries are more serious. The way they were laying into him, I wouldn't be surprised if his insides were well and truly fucked.

I stand up to lower the roller door back down, but it's too late. There's already another one of them standing over the bodies, and this one looks like he actually knows how to use the powerful rifle he's carrying. He's calling for reinforcements, but he hasn't seen me. I duck down behind more of the acidic-smelling chemical sacks and watch him through a narrow gap between two waist-high piles. All I can see is his boots. As I'm watching, another two pairs of feet approach. I don't think they've seen the tracks in the dirt yet, but it's only a matter of time. It's not like there's anywhere else around here I'd be hiding. I try to stay calm and prepare myself mentally for the fight, working out which one I should attack first and which way I should run. Maybe running is the only option? Sorry, Adam, I think this is where we say our good-byes. Can't see any way of getting him out of here now. Poor bastard's three-quarters dead anyway.

Another two of them join the first three. Five to one—those are bad odds in anyone's book. I'd have been better off taking my chances and lying flat on a pile of corpses. Wish I'd thought of that sooner. Perhaps I can still get over to that open grave . . . ?

Here they come. One of them starts to walk toward this building. Christ, I don't even have my knife with me. It's still buried to the hilt in the gut of one of them. Maybe I can reach my backpack from here . . .

Wait. They've stopped.

Something's distracted them. Figuring I've got nothing to lose, I slide across the floor to try to get a better view of what's happening. They're starting to move back toward the front of the building now. Can't see why, but their weapons are raised. This is my chance to make a break for it. I get up, grab my backpack, and run back outside, then stop when one of the enemy scavengers goes flying past the front of the chemical storeroom. He skids along the ground, thrown like a rag doll, eventually landing in a heap in the dust a few yards from my feet. Another one of them reappears, this one running backward, trying to fire his rifle and at the same time retreat and defend himself from whatever it is that's attacking. I'm right out in the open again now, my curiosity and bewilderment forcing common sense to take a backseat, and I can finally see what's happening. The cavalry have arrived. Halle-fucking-lujah. At precisely the right moment a van full of our people has turned up at the site, and they've got two powerful and incredibly aggressive fuckers in tow who are making short work of any of the Unchanged stupid enough to stand in their way. The way these two are fighting is savage and brutal in the extreme, and it's awe-inspiring to watch. They move with an agility and speed that belie their otherwise ordinary appearance. Totally focused on the kill, they are oblivious to everyone and everything else around them.

The old man I saw stripping corpses is hobbling toward me, a look of absolute fear plastered across his weathered face. He runs straight at me, yelling for help, too terrified to realize I'm going to kill him.

"Get out of here," he tries to warn me, barely able to breathe. "They'll—".

I end his sentence before he has a chance to. I grab his shock of white hair, yank his head back, and punch him hard in the throat. He collapses at my feet, choking. I snatch a knife from my backpack and finish him off. Suddenly feeling fired up and alive, I sprint down toward the battle that's raging at the front of the building, desperate to kill again.

By the time I get there it's over, the suddenly one-sided fight ended with incredible speed, force, and brutality by seven other people like Adam and me. None of them questions me. There's an immediate, unspoken trust between us, and within minutes I'm helping them dump the bodies of the Unchanged with the thousands of others already here.

5

THESE PEOPLE ARE SURPRISINGLY well coordinated. There are seventeen of us here now including me and Adam, another group having just arrived on foot through the trees to the east of the cull site. I've stumbled into the middle of a preplanned rendezvous, and I'm going to take advantage of it while it lasts. They won't be here long. Sticking together in large numbers is dangerous. It leaves us exposed.

They work quickly, hiding their vehicles in the shadows of the building and stripping the site of weapons and anything else of value. Guards patrol the perimeter constantly; others watch from the roof. The two most aggressive fighters are positioned one at either end of the building. As I walk toward the chemical storeroom with a short, stocky man, I notice that the fighter out back is shackled. She has a heavy-duty chain padlocked around her waist that's anchored to a metal stake driven deep into the ground.

"What's all that about?" I ask quietly, not wanting her to hear. He takes off his glasses and cleans the one remaining lens on the bottom corner of his shirt.

"You've not come across Brutes before?"

"Brutes?"

"That's what we call them."

"Them? You make it sound like they're different from us."

"Not really," he sighs, like it's an effort having to explain. "They're the same as us, but extreme."

"Extreme?"

"Are you the guy who was hiding here?"

"I wasn't hiding, I just—"

"Why didn't you attack?"

"What?"

"When those thieving bastards first turned up this morning, why didn't you attack them?"

"Because I didn't know how many of them there were. I didn't know what weapons they had and—"

"Exactly," he interrupts, replacing his glasses. "You knew there was a good chance you'd have been killed if you'd tried anything."

"It wasn't worth the risk."

"Don't blame you," he says, leaning up against the side of the chemical storeroom and shielding his eyes from the climbing sun. "I'd probably have done the same."

"So what's your point?"

"The point is a Brute wouldn't have held back. They can't. They catch a scent of Unchanged and they'll hunt them down and attack, no matter what the odds are."

"Bloody hell . . ."

"Useful, though. They make good guard dogs! Always on the lookout. Just look at her."

He nods over in the direction of the woman tied up at the back of the killing chamber. She's almost constantly straining against her shackles, trying to break free and go after the enemy she knows is still out there somewhere. I'm transfixed by her face, flushed red and full of rage, and yet, in a different light, she doesn't look like a killer at all. When she relaxes, her features are surprisingly soft, gentle, and feminine.

"She could just be someone's mother."

"She was. Her name's Pat. She had someone with her when we first found her, someone who knew her before the change. She was a teacher in an elementary school. Hard to believe, isn't it? A well-respected pillar of society, cornerstone of the community, great with kids, wouldn't hurt anyone . . . you get the picture."

"Incredible . . ."

"My brother was a Brute," he continues. "From sheet metal worker to a killer like that overnight."

"What happened to him?"

"We lost him."

"Sorry, I . . ."

"Oh, he's not dead, I don't think. When I say we lost him, I mean we *lost* him. Clever bastard slipped his chains and got away. Christ knows where he is now. Don't suppose it matters as long as he's still killing. Your friend in here, is he?"

He slaps the wall of the chemical storeroom.

"What?" I mumble, still thinking about this guy's missing brother and forgetting what we came out here for. "Yeah, sorry. He's in the back."

By the time we clear the doorway and are ready to move him out,

Adam's just about regained consciousness. He's still in a bad way—pale, clammy, and barely able to move. We fashion a stretcher from wood stripped from the walls of the main building, and between us we carry him back to the others.

6

MY NAME'S PRESTON," A disarmingly confident, oily man says, grabbing my hand and shaking it vigorously. I already know I don't like him. He's too loud and in-your-face. He reminds me of the senior managers I used to despise at work; the higher up the corporate ladder they managed to climb, the more arrogant, obnoxious, and smarmy they became. He's wearing a bizarre combination of military garb and civvies. His clothes make him look like someone's dad going to a costume party as a World War II general.

"Danny McCoyne."

"Good to meet you, Danny. You had some food?"

"Yes, I—"

"Excellent. Have you been introduced to anyone?"

"I've met a few people. I don't know if—"

"Great," he says, interrupting me again. Irritating little shit. Apparently he's the self-appointed leader of this cell and I've been granted a personal audience (as, I've learned, are all new "recruits"). We're sitting in the back of a beaten-up van, just him and me. The heat is suffocating. He's propped the doors open.

"Look, I—" I start to say.

"So what have you been up to, Danny?" he asks, his hat trick of interruptions complete.

"What?"

"Since the war started. What have you been doing with yourself?"

Is this a trick question? What does he think I've been doing? I've fought whenever I've been able, done all I can to get rid of the maximum number of Unchanged. Does this guy think I'm just some lazy shyster, hiding out here in the middle of nowhere, waiting for the war to end?

"Fighting."

"Good. On your own?"

"Generally traveling on my own, fighting with others whenever I've had the chance. Look, what's all this about?"

"You killed many?"

Now he's beginning to annoy me. Idiot. I've a good mind just to leave. His questions make me feel uneasy, inadequate almost. I don't think I could have fought any harder, but how does that stack up against everyone else? For the first time it occurs to me that I don't know how "good" a fighter I actually am. Is my tally of victims higher or lower than average? Does it matter? As long as we're all killing, does anyone care how quickly, enthusiastically, or effectively we do it? I suddenly feel like I'm in one of those pointless personal progress review meetings I used to have at work. Have I hit my agreed Unchanged corpse target for this month?

"Plenty," I answer, "but I haven't been keeping count."

"Too many to keep track of, eh?" He grins. Patronizing bastard.

"Something like that."

"Have you noticed their numbers are dropping off? That there's fewer of them around to kill?"

"Yes."

"And do you know why that is?"

I shrug my shoulders. "Could be any one of a number of reasons," I reply, suddenly feeling like a little kid put on the spot in class. I'm being deliberately vague, not wanting to give this joker an opportunity to make me look stupid, playing cat-and-mouse games with the truth like I used to with my supervisor and managers back at the council. "I know it's not because we've killed them all."

"If only that was the case. The real reason is that they're continuing to concentrate themselves together, completely pulling out of areas like this. Tell me, have you heard of Chris Ankin?"

I stop and think. The name sounds familiar. Then I remember, Chris Ankin was the politician who recorded the message I heard when the war first began. After I got away from the slaughterhouse that night, his was the voice that finally explained what was happening to me and why. I kept a copy of that message on a phone I found and replayed it again and again until the battery died and I threw it away.

"I know him. I thought he was dead."

"He wasn't last time I saw him."

"And when was that?"

"About ten days ago. Have you been following his messages?"

"Haven't heard anything for weeks."

Preston turns around and searches behind him. He pulls out a laptop from under one of the front seats and turns it on. I watch as it boots up, staring at the start-up screen graphics and messages as if I were watching a Hollywood blockbuster. It makes me feel unexpectedly nostalgic and empty, remembering things I haven't seen or thought about since my old life ended. After several minutes the machine is ready. With the speed of a computerphobic two-fingered typist, he logs on and opens a video file. At the bottom of the screen a number of small icons and speech bubbles appear, then disappear, as programs try pointlessly to search for updates via networks that no longer exist. A haggard and tired-looking, pixelated face (Chris Ankin, I presume) appears in a small window, which, after much cursing, Preston manages to enlarge to fill the screen. By the time he passes the laptop over to me, the politician's already in full flow. His voice is distorted by the tinny speakers but is still recognizable and strangely reassuring.

"When your enemy's tactics change, you have to reassess your own tactics, too," he explains. "From the earliest days of this war, fate and circumstance have combined to make us underdogs. We are, however, underdogs in numbers only."

I glance across at Preston, but he doesn't look back. His eyes are glued to the screen. Even though he's probably heard this a hundred times already, he's still hanging on Ankin's every word.

"Since day one, our enemies have been retreating. The way we've fought this war put them on the back foot from the beginning, and it's a position from which they've struggled to recover. The fact that our two opposing sides were so closely intertwined before we realized we *were* two opposing sides has made it all but impossible for them to isolate themselves and defend against us. We're practically invisible to them, and that has strengthened our hand dramatically. But now, now that we're months into this campaign, the position is beginning to change.

"With every day that passes, our people have become more and more diffuse. We each move from fight to fight, from battle to battle, going wherever we're needed. As a result our numbers are increasingly spread out, and the enemy has taken advantage of this."

"What's he talking about?"

Preston glares at me. "Just shut up and listen."

"They've pulled back into the hearts of their remaining cities, pulling their people closer together and drawing them in from the outside. There's strength in numbers, and we need to do something similar. We need to stop fighting as individuals and form a coordinated attack force, an army if you will."

"But they'll hunt us out. If we start grouping together in large numbers, they'll find us and—"

Preston sighs and pauses the video. He rubs his eyes and shakes his head.

"This is so much bigger than you and me, Danny," he says. "We're just cogs in a machine, and we're expendable. Ankin's not talking about setting up a military force with sergeants and captains and the like. He's just trying to get us to work together and coordinate our efforts."

"I understand that, but—"

"We have to start making better use of the people and resources we've got, and start hitting the enemy where it hurts. If we can do enough damage to start them off, they'll destroy themselves. You heard about London, didn't you?"

"No. I haven't heard anything for weeks."

"It happened incredibly quickly. We lost thousands that night but they lost many, many more."

"How? What happened?"

He seems surprised that I don't know.

"The mother of all battles," he explains. "We came at them from all angles, caused so much panic and confusion that they lost control. In the end the only option left for them was to destroy it completely."

"Jesus . . ."

"And we can make the same thing happen again and again if we learn to fight smarter. We don't have any choice. Our only alternative is to wait out here in the wastelands until they decide to come out into the open again and hunt us down, but by then it'll be too late. We have to act now."

"So what do you want from me?"

He looks straight at me and puts down the laptop, giving up on the video. This feels ominous. He's going to ask me to sign up and join his happy brigade of killers, I know he is. Thing is, apart from Adam, I've spent weeks fighting alone. Do I really want to go back to being one face in hundreds again? I've never been any good at taking orders.

"We want you to fight with us," he says, unsurprisingly. I bite my tongue. "The more of us there are, the better our chances will be. Tell me about yourself, Danny. What your skills are, where you're heading . . ."

"Don't know where to start."

For a moment I truly am flummoxed. No aspect of my former life has any bearing on me today, and as far as skills are concerned, what does he expect me to tell him? That I've got a Certificate in Dismemberment? A PhD in Asphyxiation Techniques? The sudden protracted silence is uncomfortable.

"Well, what did you do before all of this?"

"I worked in an office."

"Okay, what line of business?"

"Processing parking fines."

Preston pauses to try to get his head around the banality of my prewar existence.

"Not much call for that these days," he sighs without a hint of sarcasm in his voice. "Any special skills? Military or police experience?"

I feel suddenly inadequate. What we do is instinctive, not taught. My answer is automatic and stupid.

"I was in the Scouts for a while."

"Don't screw around," he warns. "I'm serious."

"No, nothing."

"So now you're just drifting without a purpose? Spending your time hiding behind the corpses of our people?"

"I wasn't hiding," I snap quickly, annoyed by his tone. "We were just passing through."

"That's what they all say."

Truth is, I have been as directionless as he's implying—but now I've got a reason to keep moving.

"Actually," I announce, "I'm heading home."

"Home? Why the hell would you want to do that? What possible reason could you have for wanting any connection with your past life?"

"I want to find my daughter."

He looks up, his interest suddenly piqued.

"Why?"

What do I tell him now? Have I made a mistake admitting I want to look for Ellis? Does he think I'm less of a man because of it? A weaker fighter? That I'm in league with the enemy even? Do I even know why I want to find Ellis? What am I hoping to achieve? Life with her could never be like it used to be again, so why am I bothering? As much as the thought of who and what I used to be now disgusts me, I wonder if that's the real reason I want to be with her again. Maybe I'm just trying to bridge the gap between today and all that happened in the years before now. This uncomfortable silence seems to last forever. I open and close my mouth to speak, but no words come out. Then Preston speaks for me.

"She's like us, isn't she?"

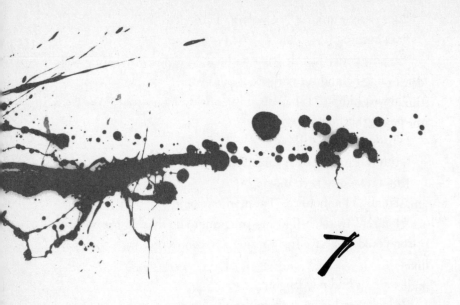

7

PRESTON STARES AT ME intently. What the hell is he thinking? So he knows that Ellis is one of us, so what? Why should that make any difference to him? Whatever the reason, his tone has definitely changed. He's suddenly more serious and direct. He left the van momentarily to speak to someone, then came back and pulled the door shut. It's suffocatingly hot in here now.

"Tell me about her, Danny."

I don't like this. I'll drip-feed him information and find out why he wants to know. Years of living in the old world have taken their toll, and my guard is up. Part of me can't help wondering whether I've managed to stumble on the last remaining pedophile ring in existence. When I don't answer he asks another question.

"How old?"

"Just turned five."

"And you think you know where she might be?"

"Possibly," I answer quickly. I can afford to give him some vague details. Even if I knew exactly where Ellis was, I could tell him anything. He doesn't know anything about her. He doesn't know what she looks like. Christ, I haven't even told him her name.

"She somewhere near here?"

"Might be."

Preston leans over to the front seat and picks up a map, which he unfolds.

"Show me."

"I'm not telling you anything until you tell me why you're so interested in my daughter. What are you, some kind of pervert? A kiddie-fiddler?"

His face remains impassive and serious. There's not a flicker of emotion.

"It's not just your daughter we're interested in," he finally starts to explain. "Our belief is that children are key to our future. They're important now, and they'll be even more crucial when this war's won."

"Go on."

"Have you ever seen a child fight? They're fast, strong, agile . . . completely uninhibited. They're not burdened with years and years of memories of the old way of things; all they know is now. They accept what they see and experience today, and they accept it without question. *This* is their normality."

What he says makes some kind of sense, but I don't trust this guy. His slimy, slick way of speaking immediately gets my back up. He comes across like a politician, a subpar spin doctor. I know we're both fighting on the same side, but how different are our aims and objectives?

"You talk a lot, but you're not actually *saying* anything. Why should I tell you anything about my little girl?"

"Kids are true fighters, Danny, perfect fighters even. Brutes are strong and aggressive, but children are something else entirely. I think—"

He stops speaking suddenly, almost as if he's not sure I can be trusted. I press him, keen to hear what he has to say. He runs his fingers through his greasy, slicked-back black hair.

"I think the line between us and the Unchanged starts to blur when you're looking at very young children. Like I said, they don't carry the baggage and the memories we do. Given the right stimulation and provocation, I think even an Unchanged kid could be taught to fight like us."

There's another silence as we both think about what he's just said. My initial reaction is that it's probably bullshit, but he might just have a point. A young kid growing up surrounded by all this madness wouldn't know any different. They'd have to learn to fight to survive, whatever their initial allegiance.

"I got separated from my family when the Change happened to me," I tell him, deciding I've got nothing to lose from opening up a little more as long as I'm sparing with the details. I take the map from him and tap my finger on the area where I used to live. "I last saw them here, but my partner managed to get away with the kids."

"Kids? More than one?"

"Two sons and a daughter. It's only Ellis I'm interested in."

"That's your little girl?"

"Yes."

"Don't be so quick to write off the other two."

I slide my finger across the map, then stop.

"I think Lizzie would have gone to her sister's house. What are these marks?"

Two circles have been drawn on the map, both centered on the main part of town. Both my apartment and Lizzie's sister's house are just outside the outermost circle. Preston explains.

"Like Ankin said, the Unchanged have withdrawn into city centers. Our information's a couple of weeks old, but we think the first circle is the extent of their occupation."

"What about the second line?"

"The outermost edge of their exclusion zone. It's a strip of empty land smack between them and everything else, pretty well defended. Makes it that much harder for us to get through unnoticed. It's not impossible, just a little more difficult."

"So how does Ankin plan to march an army through no-man's-land without being noticed?"

"He'll find a way," Preston answers. He's not filling me with confidence. I try to steer the conversation back toward Ellis.

"So that's my plan," I tell him. "Check the apartment first, then look for Ellis at Lizzie's sister's house."

"And if she's not there?"

"I haven't thought that far ahead. I don't want to."

Preston folds up the map and thinks for a moment.

"What if I said we could help you?"

"Help me? How?"

"We've got a group of people heading out that way later today, looking for more recruits. You could go with them. You'll have more chance if you go with our support."

"And what's in it for you?"

"There are just two conditions," he announces ominously. "First, if you don't find your girl, you forget about her and come back here and fight with us. Second, if you do find her, you *both* come back to us and fight."

COULD'VE HAD ALL three of them," Adam says, his voice weak and frail but somehow still filled with adrenaline-fueled enthusiasm and excitement. "I didn't need your help. I'd have been perfectly fine if you hadn't come back—"

"Sure you would," I interrupt. "You're full of shit, do you know that?"

"You're the one who's full of shit." He laughs. "You were the one hiding up a ladder!"

"I wasn't hiding—"

He coughs and laughs again, showering his bare chest with speckles of blood. There's no two ways about it, he's on his way out. His breathing is increasingly shallow and uneven. He was already severely weakened by the injuries inflicted by his dad and the subsequent untreated infections, and the brutal beating he took this morning did more than enough damage to push his broken body into total submission. He's covered in bruises and swellings. He's hardly moved in hours, and his condition is continuing to steadily worsen.

It's another swelteringly hot day. The air is dry, and the relentless heat makes the smell of thousands of badly decayed corpses even harder to stomach. The insect population is flourishing. It's hard to take a breath without sucking in a lungful of buzzing little fuckers. We're not heading into town until after dark, so there's nothing to do for the next few hours except try to relax and ready myself for the next fight.

"Need a drink," Adam gasps. I grab a half-empty plastic bottle of water and hold it up to his chapped lips. He tries to swallow, but most of it runs down his chin. He coughs again and winces with sudden pain, but he doesn't complain. Unbelievably, he's still fired up by the rush of battle. Poor bastard's completely oblivious to the fact he'll probably be dead before the morning.

"Next time," he says, every word an effort, "I'm gonna aim straight for the head, know what I'm saying?"

I nod. I don't have the heart to tell him there's not going to be a next time.

"I know," I lie.

"See," he continues, trying to prop himself up on his elbows but immediately dropping back down again, "they'll look at me and think that because my arm and leg are fucked, I'll be a pushover. But they'll be wrong . . ."

His eyelids flutter closed, and just for a second I think he's gone. I reach out to check his pulse, but he bats me away when I touch his skin and mumbles something unintelligible. He's like an animal, blissfully unaware of his own mortality, convinced he's going to go on and on and on. In a way I can't help but envy his ignorance. He fades into unconsciousness.

"He dead?" a woman asks, her voice uncomfortably loud. I stand up and try to usher her away from Adam, but she stands her ground. Her name's Julia. She's coordinating the group of us heading out, and, from what I've heard from some of the others, she's a hard bitch who doesn't stand for any bullshit. She has a strong Irish lilt to her voice, and I can't help thinking of the IRA and the Troubles when she speaks. It's wrong of me, but who cares. Equality, diversity, and political correctness are all things of the past now, condemned to history by the Hate—the great leveler. All the name-calling, insults, and discriminatory language we used to avoid using have lost their impact now.

"Not yet. He's still hanging on."

She nods, her stern face devoid of any emotion. "There's more food in the van. Make sure you eat before you leave. Don't know when you'll get the chance again."

What with the heat, the flies, and the smell, the last thing I want is more food.

"Poor bastard," I say quietly. "Just look at the state of him."

Now that I've taken a step back from Adam I can see just how bad his condition really is. He has open, weeping wounds all over his body, and his shattered bones haven't been properly looked at since his father first broke them. It makes me feel uneasy; this is a harsh and unforgiving world we're suddenly all living in. This man is going to die before the day is done, but none of his wounds are truly life-threatening. The medicine, the expertise, and the means to save him exist, but they're all out of reach. Julia seems to second-guess what I'm thinking with uncomfortable accuracy.

"Don't bother beating yourself up about it," she says. "There's no point. Face facts, he's useless to anyone like this."

"I know, but—"

"But nothing. We don't have time to waste patching up people like this who aren't going to be able to fight again. It'd take him months to recover, and even then he'll still be next to no good. And who's going to look after him? We don't have the people to spare. Right now there's no such thing as doctors and nurses and surgeons and the like. At the end of the day we're all fighters, and that's all there is to it."

I feel like I should protest, that I should try to say something in defense of my fallen friend and fight in his corner, but I know there's no point. She's right. Christ, it was only this morning that I was thinking about walking out on him anyway.

"A fighter who can't fight," she continues, preaching at me, "is just a corpse. If you want to do something to help him, then find yourself a gun and put a bullet in his head."

9

I'M AWAY FROM THE slaughterhouse and the corpses and the flies and the stench now, and the land stretches out in front of me forever. The sun-bleached, knee-high grass shifts lazily from side to side in the warm wind like waves on a gently rolling sea. The world is suddenly absolutely beautiful, calm and almost completely silent. I feel strong and relaxed, revitalized and ready for the next fight. It'll be time to leave soon.

I take a few steps forward, the blazing sun blinding me and burning my skin, my boots trampling down the long grass and leaving a flattened trail behind me. Considering how close to the cull site this place is, it's remarkably tranquil and clear. Ahead of me there's nothing, the land from here to the horizon barely even undulating, only a handful of distant, parched trees daring to stretch up from the yellow-green ground into the intense blue sky above.

Wait. What was that?

I hear something. The rustle of grass. Footsteps? I'm starting to think it was just the wind when, a few yards ahead of me, a childlike figure appears, emerging from the long grass where it had been hiding. Virtually naked and desperately thin; I can't even tell from here what sex it is. It slowly stands upright, watching me intently, swaying slowly. I don't care who or what it is. I know that I have to kill it.

I start sprinting, totally focused on catching the small figure up ahead and nothing else. He runs (I can tell from the way he moves it's a male) and makes a sudden, darting turn to the left, moving far faster than me. The gap between us increases, and I follow his trail through the flattened grass, around and around in a lazy arc until I end up back where I started. The child disappears momentarily, and as I scan the horizon I see that up ahead of me now are the ruins of my hometown. It's been weeks since I've been here, but it's almost exactly as I remember, just a little dirtier than before. The dark, ugly buildings are in stark contrast to the beauty of everything else. There's a steady haze of smoke, wisps of white climbing up between the tallest buildings and clouds of dirty gray lying at street level like a heavy fog.

I've completely lost sight of the child now, but the trail of trampled grass will lead me straight to him. I start running again. The chase is getting harder now. The air is scorched and dry, and I can feel the fierce sun burning the skin on my bare back. I force myself to keep moving forward, driven on by the thought of killing again. My mouth salivates at the prospect of tearing Unchanged flesh from bone . . .

A thin strip of brittle hedge marks the farthest edge of the grassland. I crash through, ignoring the spiteful branches and thorns that slash at my skin, then keep running along an empty street I don't recognize. There are buildings rising up on either side of me now, dilapidated and skeletal but still tall and imposing enough to finally block out the sun. It's hard to see anything in the sudden change from light to dark, and it's ice cold in the shadows. Disoriented, I start to slow down. The child I'm chasing is long gone.

I hear footsteps again—more than one person this time, and they're behind me. I turn around and see a huge crowd of people charging up the long straight street after me. There's enough of them to fill the entire width of the road, but their true numbers are masked by the worsening gloom. I start to run again, willing myself to keep moving faster. My energy levels are dropping now that I'm the one being chased, and every step takes ten times the effort it did before. My hunger has been replaced with fear, and the crowd's getting closer. Every time I look back over my shoulder they're nearer still. There's a gap in the row of buildings to my left—leading to another even straighter, even narrower road—and I take it, my heavy boots and aching feet pounding the concrete, shock waves shooting the length of my tired frame. All my strength and energy have gone. Can't keep going . . .

I stop halfway down the second street, unable to go any farther. I look back, and the crowd is still surging after me like a herd of stampeding animals, close enough that I can see their faces now. They suddenly stop, maintaining an unexpected, cautious distance. I sense they could attack at any moment, and I'm scared. For the first time in months I feel genuinely afraid. I look at the people at the front of the hunting pack, and I see that they're like me, but I sense they're going to attack. Why? Do they think I'm one of the Unchanged? I open my mouth to try to explain, to try to make them understand, but I can't force out even a single word. I feel crushed, devastated, and humiliated, wishing I were like them again. They look at me with total hatred . . .

I turn around to run and find myself facing Ellis. In disbelief I move closer toward her. She backs away from me, matching every step forward with a single step back, then stops again when I stop.

"Ellis," I start to say, my parched voice barely audible, "I thought you'd..."

She throws herself at me, leaping up with lightning speed and grabbing hold of my throat. I'm down before I know it, my face slammed hard into the ground...

10

BAD DREAM, SLEEPING BEAUTY?" the man sitting next to me asks. I nod but don't answer. I rub my head where it just thumped against the window of the van and immediately remember where I am. It's late in the day, I'm on my way back home with three other fighters, and I'm feeling travel sick. Can't remember the last time I went anywhere by road like this. Is it safe? The confidence of the rest of the people in the van makes me feel out of step with everyone else.

The cocky, sour-faced guy next to me is Paul Hewlitt, and he seems to have a far higher opinion of himself and his own abilities than anyone else does. In the front of the van are Carol and Keith, who's driving. As far as I'm aware there's nothing between them, but they bicker, fight, and argue like an old married couple. I feel like I don't belong here. I think I'd rather be doing this alone. Maybe I'm just not used to being with groups of people anymore?

"Will you put that damn thing out?" Keith moans as Carol lights up a cigarette. She blows smoke in his direction, deliberately antagonizing him.

"No," she snaps abrasively, her voice dry and harsh.

"Don't know where you keep getting them from."

"You don't want to know," Paul pipes up.

"What's that supposed to mean?"

"I saw you," he says, "checking the pockets of corpses."

"Well, they don't need them anymore," she argues. And she's got a point. But does that make her any different from the Unchanged I saw fleecing bodies earlier?

"You're disgusting," Keith sighs.

"I'm addicted," she answers back quickly, "and I don't want to quit. Cigarettes are one of my few remaining pleasures. Where else am I supposed to get them?"

"At least open the window, then. Last thing I want to do is be breathing in your secondhand smoke all night."

"Hold your breath, then," she grumbles, begrudgingly winding down her window. The cool, relatively fresh air that floods into the van is a relief, and I breathe it in deeply.

I look around at the three people I'm traveling with tonight, and I can't help but feel concerned. I haven't seen any of them in action yet, but I don't hold out much hope. Keith looks like he'd be more at home in his garden than on the battlefield. Carol appears permanently angry. She has bulging eyes and short, dark hair that obviously used to be colored (the dye's grown out, leaving a brassy red tidemark). She has long nails that probably used to be filed and painted but that now look more like talons or claws. She reminds me of a woman I used to work with—a bitter, drink-addled ex-publican. She has the ruddy complexion of a heavy drinker and looks like she'd be happiest either behind a bar or propping one up. Paul, on the other hand, at least looks like he's ready to fight. He's an arrogant fucker. Since we've been driving he's already told me several times what a great fighter he is and how he's lost count of the hundreds of kills he's made. I can see straight through him. His bragging and aggressive talk are there to hide his insecurities. He's struggling just as much as the rest of us.

So, all in all, not a great team. Still, if they help me get closer to finding Ellis, I'll put up with them.

"Give us a clue then, friend," Keith says, glancing back at me over his shoulder. I lean forward to try to get a better view of where we are. The van vibrates intensely and lurches from side to side as we move quickly down a wide, rubbish-strewn road, and it's difficult to see very much from where I'm sitting. The fact that Keith's driving without lights on doesn't help, but when the ominous black shape of a huge enemy helicopter crawls across the early evening sky just ahead of us, taillights flashing in the gloom, I'm thankful that we're hidden.

There's a road sign up ahead. Keith stops the van, and all four of us stare up at it, trying to make out the place names and directions. Much of the sign is covered in a layer of green-brown dirt and moss.

"This is Chapman Hill, isn't it?" Paul says. I look in front and behind, trying to get my bearings. He's right. I bought my last car from a garage close to here, but I didn't recognize the place. Now that I know roughly where I am, though, everything slowly comes into focus, and the streets and buildings begin to regain some semblance of familiarity. This is bizarre—everything looks basically the same, but it's all changed, too. The landmarks and structures I used to know are mostly still there, but absolutely everything seems to have been indelibly scarred by the war. A long line of once-thriving shops is now a crumbling, blackened ruin, almost completely destroyed by fire. The front part of the garage I remember has collapsed, flattening the few dust-covered cars that remained unstolen and unsold. Next to the garage an office building now stands at barely half of its prewar height, surrounded by mounds of rubble that used to be its top five floors. In the fading light it looks like every road and sidewalk for as far as I can see is covered with a layer of dust and debris. The bodies are the only shapes that are easy to distinguish among the chaos. Just ahead of us a skeletal hand is sticking up from a pile of fallen masonry as if its dead owner wants to ask us a question or hitch a ride.

"Well," Keith says impatiently, "you just here to sightsee or are you gonna tell me which way to go?"

"Sorry," I answer quickly, forcing myself to snap out of my trance. "Keep going straight for another mile or so, then it's a right. I'll tell you when we get closer."

Keith's about to pull away again when Carol stops him, leaning across and grabbing his arm.

"Wait. Something's coming . . ."

There's an intersection up ahead. She watches it intently.

"There's nothing," Keith whispers, instinctively lowering his voice. "You're just overreacting again. It's like the time—"

He immediately shuts up when a short but powerful and fast-moving convoy races across the crossroads in front of us. It's just three vehicles long: a huge, military juggernaut at the front followed by a battered single-deck civilian bus, then a heavily armed jeep bringing up the rear. They move with reckless speed—far too quick to notice us. Keith waits. He glances over at Carol, who remains perfectly still. Eventually she nods. On her signal he moves off again.

"Can we get through that way?" he asks, slowing down at the point in the road where the convoy crossed our path.

"You want to follow them?" I reply, surprised.

"They've done us a favor and cleared the road. Yes, I want to follow them."

He's right. There's a clear line through the debris where the vehicles have just been.

"It's a little farther, but yes, this'll get us to roughly the right place."

He nods and pulls away, and I can immediately see the sense in his actions. We're able to move with more speed now, and the clear channel makes it easier to follow the direction of the road. I sink back into my seat and turn to face Paul.

"Are we safe out here?"

"Truth is we're not safe anywhere," he answers quietly, "but I haven't seen much trouble here recently."

"So what was all that about?"

"Looking for survivors, I guess," he says, shrugging his shoulders.

"That's what they'd say," Carol interrupts, turning around to face us both and blowing out smoke through the corner of her mouth, "but there can't be many of them left out here now. They just come here to take potshots at us."

"Which way now?" Keith shouts, fighting to make himself heard over the noise of the engine. There's another intersection looming, but yet again I'm struggling to work out where we are. In the distance I can see occasional flashes of red from the brakelights of the three Unchanged vehicles. They're heading straight into the center of town, the last place we want to go. I glance from left to right and back; then I see a large, familiar-looking pub, and I know where I am again. The building appears intact at first, but I can see from here that the back of the structure has been almost completely destroyed, leaving the relatively undamaged frontage standing like something from the set of a movie. I went to a going-away bash for someone from work there once. Or was it a birthday party . . . ?

"Straight ahead takes us closer to them, so do we go right or left? Come on, for Christ's sake, we don't have time to screw around like this—"

"Left," I answer, biting my tongue, determined not to let my anger show. These people don't understand how hard this is for me.

We follow a familiar route, and I realize this is the way I drove to the apartment with my father-in-law the morning of the day before I killed him. Retracing the last steps I took as one of the Unchanged is unexpectedly unnerving. The road runs past the front of a row of houses before swinging up and left over a bridge that spans the highway below. Keith stops the van when we're halfway across. I press my face against the window and look down at the once-busy road below. One side of the highway is relatively clear— the debris no doubt brushed aside by heavy, but infrequent, Unchanged traffic. The other side is a single clogged mass of stationary vehicles. Some look like they've simply been abandoned, others like they've been picked up and hurled over the median strip. It looks more like a rusting scrapyard than a road.

"Busy tonight," Carol says. I look up and see that she's staring down the highway in the other direction. I follow her gaze, and for the first time I can clearly see the enemy-occupied heart of the city. Silhouetted against the last golden yellow light of the rapidly fading sun, the tall buildings in the center of town stand proud and defiant. Even from here, still several miles away, I can see that the refugee camp is filled with movement. Planes and helicopters flitter through the darkening sky like flies around a dead animal's carcass. The fact that there are lights on in some of the buildings takes me by surprise. They still have power! Keith starts driving again. I keep my eyes fixed on the buildings in the distance, watching them until they disappear from view.

"All right?" Paul asks, watching me as I crane my neck to keep looking.

"Fine," I answer quickly, hoping he doesn't pick up on my unease.

There must be tens of thousands of Unchanged here, and I know that every last one of them has to die before the war will be over. Seeing their city center stronghold makes me appreciate the enormity of the task ahead of us. It makes me realize that Chris Ankin might be right. We're going to have to work together to defeat this enemy.

11

TAKE A LEFT, THEN straight to the top of this road," I tell
Keith, my voice so quiet I have to repeat myself twice before
he hears me. We're very close now. I used to walk this way when I
came home from work at night. When we turn the corner I'll be able
to see the apartment building at the top of the hill. I brace myself,
not looking forward to going back. Keith stops the van suddenly
and waits. He's finally been forced to use the headlights and the
bright beams of light illuminate several flashes of sudden, darting
movement across the road in front of us. We watch in silence as a
pack of stray dogs streaks through the ruins in search of food. Once
probably lazy, well-fed, pampered pets, they're now nervous, thin,
and savage creatures. One of them, a mangy fawn brown mongrel
with protruding ribs and ragged fur, stops in the middle of the

road and stares defiantly at the van, ears twitching, light reflecting in its eyes. The standoff lasts for just a few seconds before something more interesting causes the hound to turn and chase frantically after the rest of the pack.

The interruption over, Keith drives on again, and in seconds I can see the outline of the house I used to share with Lizzie and the kids. In the winter I was able to see the lights on in the windows from here, and sometimes I could see the shadows of the kids as they ran from room to room, aggravating their mom and each other. I've got to forget about all of that now, but it's hard. As I get closer, each new wave of familiarity hits me like an undefended punch in the face. At the same time, I feel a nauseous disgust—shame almost—that I was ever a part of this place. I can't believe I allowed myself to stay trapped in such a pathetic, restricted, and pointless life for so long.

"Lovely spot," Paul grumbles sarcastically as he surveys the battered remains of the run-down development I used to call home. The sky's clear tonight, and the moon's severe but limited light illuminates all the details I was hoping not to see.

"It's hardly changed," I tell him, semiseriously. "It looked this bad before the fighting."

Another helicopter flies overhead, the constant chopping of its rotor blades audible even over the rattling engine of this ancient van. The others watch anxiously as it banks high above us, then turns around and flies back on itself, but I pay it hardly any attention. I'm focused on the dark apartment building we're fast approaching, wondering what the hell I'm going to find inside. I know Ellis won't be there. I just want to find a trace of her, an indication, no matter how small or how slight, of where she might have been taken.

Keith stops the van in the shadows, nestling it up against a tall wooden fence, and switches off the engine. Two more helicopters drift overhead. Are they tracking us? None of the others seem overly concerned.

"You've got five minutes," Keith says with a slight trace of urgency in his voice. "Spend too long screwing around in there and when you come back out you'll find us gone. There's a fair amount of activity around here tonight, and I don't want to get caught in any crossfire. Understand?"

"I get it."

I reach up to open the door, then stop when Keith speaks again.

"Just remember," he warns, "we're here to find other people like us, not just your kid. If she's not here or at the other house, you forget about her. Is that clear?"

Who the fuck does he think he is, talking to me like a goddamn drill sergeant? I ignore him and get out of the van before anyone can say anything else. I slam the door without thinking, and it echoes around the desolate neighborhood like a gunshot.

I stand at the end of the path that leads up to the communal front door of the apartment building, carrying only my backpack, a flashlight, and a knife. Except for the broken window and the ragged curtains whipping in and out in the wind, the apartment looks just like it always did. Seeing this place seems almost to cancel out the last three months. It feels like only yesterday that I was last here . . .

Keith angrily blasts on the horn, the uncomfortably loud sound forcing me into action. I walk down the uneven path and push the door. It sticks at first but opens when I shove it hard, making the same loud, ear-piercing creak it always did, except it sounds a thousand times louder tonight because everything else is so deathly quiet. I step inside and shine the flashlight around. The shared lobby has been trashed, and the ground beneath my feet is covered in bits of broken furniture and other rubbish. I recognize some of these things. They used to belong to me and my family. The kids used to hate being out here.

The front door of the apartment is open. It swings to and fro slightly in a gentle breeze. The wood is splintered and cracked across its width, and there are several dirty boot marks, most probably left by the soldiers who were forcing their way in as I was trying to get out when I was last here. With trepidation I push it open and go inside, and immediately I'm sucker-punched by the familiarity of everything again. I kick my youngest son's upturned stroller out of the way and move farther down the hall. The first room I reach is the kitchen. I go inside, and I can smell my father-in-law's corpse before I see it. He lies exactly where I left him, still covered in his blood-soaked duvet shroud, decay having deflated his lifeless bulk down to half its former size. Hard to believe that this rancid, shrunken, germ-filled mass is all that's left of Harry. When I think of him I still remember the man who used to look after the kids and who always gave me such a hard time, a crotchety, white-haired old bastard who did all he could to make my life difficult. In spite of everything that's happened it's hard to look at him in this state.

I look up and shine the flashlight back across the room toward the doorway, suddenly remembering the screams and the terrified faces of my family when they saw what I'd done. I remember Ellis's frightened face clearest of all, desperate for answers that I didn't yet know I could give her.

I retrace their steps, moving back along the hallway until I reach the living room, the small circle of light from the flashlight providing more than enough illumination, and step over what's left of the furniture Lizzie stacked up here to keep me out. It's cold and damp in here, the broken window having left the room open and exposed to the elements for weeks on end. There's black mold on the walls, and the paper's peeling. The apartment has been ransacked, but I don't think Lizzie did this. Our things have been trashed by scavengers looking for food, weapons, and valuables. They were wasting their time here. We never had anything worth taking.

A missile or jet roars through the air above the apartment with a piercing scream. Silence returns in seconds, but Keith blasts the horn again, and I pick up my pace. I don't bother with Edward and Josh's room. Instead I go into the bedroom Lizzie and I shared, and I look down at our bed. The thought of being so physically close to her makes my skin crawl. Surprisingly, the thought of being so far from her now makes me feel equally bad. I grab a change of clothing from the wardrobe (all of Lizzie's clothes are still here—proof that she never came back), then run through to Ellis's room. I shove some of her belongings into my backpack—a doll and a rainbow-colored sweater she used to live in—figuring that the familiarity will help when we're together again. Didn't matter what she was doing or where she was going, when we asked her to get dressed, this sweater was what she always chose. I hold it to my nose and sniff it, hoping to remember her scent. It just smells of the apartment, damp and musty.

I take one last look around, then make my way back out to the others, knowing that whatever happens, I won't be coming back here. Keith hits the horn again as I run through the lobby. I push my way back out into the open and take a deep breath as soon as I'm outside, relieved to be out of that foul-smelling, claustrophobic hellhole full of reminders of the person I used to be. I hear gunfire nearby, followed by a scream that could be either rage or pain. I throw my bag into the van, then climb in and slam the door.

"Any sign?" Paul asks.

"Nothing."

Yet another helicopter hovers nearby, this one using a search-light to illuminate the ground below.

"We're not going anywhere else for a while," Keith announces as he starts the engine and pulls away. "This place is too damn busy for my liking tonight. Anywhere close where we can hole up until it quietens down?"

All eyes are on me, and the pressure is unwelcome. The only

thing I'm sure about is that I'm not going back into the apartment. I try to think of other places nearby that might still be standing. Through a gap between two houses at the very bottom of Calder Grove I see the tall, dark outline of a high-rise that looks reasonably intact. That'll do.

"Turn left at the bottom of the road," I tell him. "I know somewhere."

12

KEITH STOPS THE VAN behind a row of overflowing garbage cans, almost directly beneath the high-rise apartments. We each grab our individual bags of weapons and supplies and head for the shelter of the building. The front doors are missing, and the entrance foyer is as trashed as everywhere else. Like an idiot I instinctively press the button to call the elevator. Old habits die hard.

"Don't think that's going to do anything, my friend," Paul whispers sarcastically. I push past him and follow Carol, who's already heading up the stairs, the glowing orange tip of another cigarette illuminating her route through the darkness. There's a woman's badly decomposed body at the very bottom of the first flight of steps, her neck snapped and her decayed face wedged against the wall. She was like us, and that immediately puts me on edge. I step over the corpse and start to climb, wondering pointlessly if she fell or if she was pushed.

For a few minutes we do nothing but climb, our footsteps echoing up and down along the entire length of this dark and otherwise silent stairwell. We move quickly, most of us climbing two steps at a time. It's hard work, but the pain is easy to ignore. It's a perverse reality of my situation: I eat scraps, survive out in the open, and live from day to day, but I'm in better shape than I've ever been. The others are the same. Carol races ahead like a woman half her age. I feel strong and powerful, my body lean, toned, and efficient. Makes me wonder how, when everything was available to me on a plate and all I had to worry about was my family and my piss-easy job, did I manage to fuck everything up so badly? The memory of who and what I used to be is embarrassing. I wish this had happened to me years ago.

"How far?" Carol shouts down from several flights up.

"Just keep going," I answer. We're more than halfway up now. The higher we go, I think, the safer we'll be.

"Wait," Keith yells. I stop climbing and turn back. He's still a floor below me. "Look at this."

"Look at what?" Paul grunts breathlessly as he pushes past and starts heading back down again. I follow him back to floor eight (of eleven or twelve, I think). This floor is different from the others. I passed it too quickly to notice, but the doors leading from the staircase to the rest of the building here have been boarded up. There's plenty of broken glass and other debris around here, but it doesn't look like the barrier has been breached.

"This has been done from the inside," Keith says, stating the blindingly obvious.

"So there might still be someone in there," Carol adds, equally pointlessly.

"Must be Unchanged," Paul says under his breath as he runs his hands over the large sheets of plywood that have been nailed to the inside of the door frame, pushing and prodding in different places, trying to find a weak spot. He finds one near the bottom right-hand corner where the door frame is rotten. He brushes away shards of broken glass with his feet, then sits down on his backside and pushes the board with his boot. When it moves slightly he beckons for me to help him. I position myself directly between him and the handrail of the staircase so he can't move backward, then brace myself as he starts to kick at the wood. The noise is massively amplified by the confines of our surroundings, but in the moments of silence between kicks, everything else remains reassuringly quiet. He's barely forced open a wide enough gap when he turns around, drops his backpack, and scrambles through. Once on the other side he pulls at the plywood and manages to yank away a piece about a yard square. I slide his bag through, then follow him.

We're standing on an empty, relatively uncluttered landing. There are three apartments on this floor, two doors on one side of the landing, one on the other. Two of them are open. I quickly check one over. Its three main rooms are empty and fairly undamaged. There's even the stale, mold-covered remains of a final untouched meal on a table in front of a lifeless TV. The owner of the apartment must have left (or been dragged out) in a hurry. Keith disappears into the other open apartment and reappears on the landing after a few seconds.

"Nothing," he says quietly, "just a corpse on a bed."

"On a bed?" Carol says, surprised.

"Someone's laid out their missus or their mother or something. Dressed her up nice and brushed her hair. Still looks fucking horrible."

"Very touching," Paul mumbles as he presses his ear against the closed door of the remaining apartment. He pushes it gently, but it doesn't move.

"Smash it?" I suggest, my axe ready in my hand. He thumps it pointlessly, then nods his head and moves to one side. I lift the axe and thump it down, the clang of metal on metal filling the air as I mis-hit and catch the Yale lock. I lift my arm again. Keith grabs my wrist before I can bring it down.

"Listen."

I do as he says, but I can't hear anything. I try to pull my hand free, but he tightens his grip and glares at me.

"I hear it," Carol whispers. Then I do, too. A quiet, muffled voice shouting at us from deep inside the apartment.

"Not my . . ." it shouts, the third word unclear.

"Not my floor?" Keith suggests.

"Not my fault?" Paul offers, shrugging his shoulders. "Get the door open, man, and let's get him killed. It's just some nutter."

I do as he asks, smashing the blade down again and again until the weak wood splinters and the lock gives. I kick it open and peer into the gloom. A well-timed explosion outside bathes everything in ice white light like a camera flash for a fraction of a second, just long enough for me to see that there's someone standing at the far end of a short hall on the other side of the door. I catch a glimpse of his motionless outline, or hers, directly ahead. The door slowly swings shut again.

"How many?" Carol asks.

"Just one that I can see," I answer. "Pass me the flashlight, Keith."

Keith switches on the flashlight, but before he can pass it to me, the door flies open and the figure throws itself at me. The force of the sudden, unexpected attack takes me by surprise. I trip over my own feet as I stagger back, and before I know what's happening, I'm lying flat on my back with a foul-smelling fucker right on top of me. He grabs the collar of my coat and lowers his face until it's just inches from mine. His breath is so bad it's making me want to puke.

"Not my fight," he shouts, peppering me with spittle. "Not my fight—"

Keith smashes the side of his head with the flashlight, sending him reeling.

"Not my problem," he sneers, trying not to laugh at his own joke. The man who attacked me rolls over and gets up and stupidly starts walking back toward Keith again.

"Not my fight," he says, blood running down his face. "Leave me alone. It's not my fight. Get out of here . . ."

Keith lunges forward again, flashlight held ready to strike, sensing the kill.

"He's one of us, Keith," Carol warns, but it's too late. He swings the flashlight around and smashes it into the man's face again. He drops to the ground, and this time he doesn't get up. Keith shines the light down. Christ, Carol's right. He was one of ours. Keith looks at him with disdain, then steps over the corpse and goes into the apartment.

The small, squalid place is like a cocoon. The door I broke down hadn't been opened for weeks. The air is musty and stale, and the rooms are filled with boxes of supplies. On closer inspection, we find that almost all of the supplies have been used up. The dead man on the landing hardly had any food left.

"He'd done well to last this long," Paul says, watching me as I check through more empty cartons.

"If you ask me," Keith says, wiping the flashlight clean on a floral curtain, then opening a door into another room and glancing around it, "people like that are as bad as the Unchanged. Not fighting with us is almost as bad as fighting against us. You don't have a choice whether or not you want to be a part of this war. There's no opt-out clause for anyone."

"That was his wife, you know," Paul says, following me out onto a small veranda that overlooks what's left of my hometown. I've been out here for a while, just getting some air.

"What?"

"The guy Keith did in, that was his missus lying on the bed next door."

"How d'you know?"

"Found a photo of the pair of them together. Lovely couple," he murmurs sarcastically.

"Was she like us?"

"Nah, one of them."

"But he couldn't let go?"

"Looks that way. Probably killed her, then regretted it. True love, eh?" he jokes. "Never runs smooth."

"You're not wrong. My other half was..."

"I know. Bad luck, man."

"What about you?"

"Good question."

"What do you mean by that?"

"I've been with my girlfriend for three years now. Then all this happened..."

"Was she Unchanged?"

"No, nothing like that. We stuck together for a while after the Change, then just drifted apart. Just didn't need each other like we used to."

I glance across at him. He's hanging his head out over the high balcony next to me, staring into the distance.

"I guess relationships and stuff like that have had to take a back-seat with all this going on."

"You're not wrong," he sighs. "You know, I was thinking the other day, I haven't had a hard-on for weeks."

"Thanks for sharing."

"I'm not complaining," he says quickly. "It just hadn't occurred to me before. I've stopped thinking about sex, stopped looking at women... hope to God this is just temporary."

I'm the same, although I don't bother telling him. It's just a question of priorities, I expect. When the fighting's over, things will get back to normal again.

I look out toward the city center in the distance, glowing like the embers of a dying fire. There's a strange beauty to the devastation tonight. This place always seemed ugly and oppressive to me before, but these days I see wonder and detail in things I used to look straight through. The Hate has opened my eyes. The area immediately around this high-rise—the place I used to call home—is dark and largely silent, just a few small fires and the odd flash of movement visible through the early evening gloom. From up here tonight the world seems vast and never-ending. There are clouds looming on the horizon, swallowing up the stars. There's rain coming.

"What're you thinking?" Paul asks after a couple of minutes have passed. "Not still thinking about my dick, I hope!"

"Just how massive the world feels tonight," I answer honestly as I watch a lone helicopter leading a distant convoy of Unchanged vehicles across their so-called exclusion zone. "First time I've been back here in months. From up here I can see where I lived and where I worked and everything in between. Can't believe I used to spend virtually all my time in the same few square miles of space. Kind of makes you feel insignificant, doesn't it?"

"The best thing about this life of ours now," he tells me, "is how open it's made everything. All the walls and barriers that used to hold us back have gone."

"I've been thinking about my apartment. It was just barely bigger than this place, and there were five of us living there. Five of us! How the hell did we ever manage to cram that many lives into such a small space?"

"That wasn't living, that was just existing."

"I can see it now, but when you're in the middle of it you just make do, don't you. You try to make the most of what you've got . . ."

Paul nudges my shoulder, and I look across at him. He gestures out over the city.

"All of this, my friend," he says, "is ours now."

_ii_

I N A SITUATION WHERE everybody was either on one side or the other and there was no in-between, ascertaining who was who was a priority. A DNA-based "test of allegiance" had been developed early on, and from it the Central System had been born. It was little more than an electronic checklist—a massive summary of names cribbed from the electoral roll, voters' roll, and births, deaths, and marriages records. The details held on each person were sparse: name, sex, date of birth, last known address, whether the person was dead or not, and, most importantly, whether he or she was Hater or Unchanged.

Many records—no one knew exactly how many—were incomplete or inaccurate. Up-to-date information was increasingly hard to find. Data gathering had been carried out at cull sites, evacuation camps, temporary mortuaries, military checkpoints, and anywhere else there was a controlled flow of civilians. Within the first two months of the crisis, however, that flow had been reduced to a trickle, then a drip. The thousands of bodies lying rotting in their homes, in overgrown fields, or on street corners remained unaccounted for, blank records returned should anyone inquire about their names.

The quality of data wasn't the only problem with the system. Administration, backups, integrity, access rights, security . . . the speed and chaotic nature of the Change meant that these and so many other aspects of development were truncated, attempted halfheartedly, skimped, skipped over, or simply abandoned altogether. Nevertheless, the ever-decreasing number of people still using the system continued to do what they could, believing that, eventually, what they were doing would prove worthwhile.

Almost thirty-six hours since he'd been back to the hotel room. He'd managed to catch a few hours' sleep in the back of one of the empty food trucks this afternoon, but Mark was still exhausted. Volunteers were becoming increasingly hard to find, and they weren't about to let him go until they had to. He continued to do it because of the promises of extra rations (which had, so far, been fulfilled) and because he felt safer being on the side of the people who had the biggest guns. The city streets were increasingly ugly and unsafe places. Better to walk them with the protection of a little body armor and a weapon, he thought, than without.

All that aside, Mark decided, *when I get back to the hotel this time, I'm not coming out again.*

Over the past few days he'd begun to sense a change in the air—a difficult situation becoming impossible, a slight risk becoming almost a certainty. Things were deteriorating, and the rate of decline was accelerating. He hadn't completely given up hope of some semblance of normality eventually being restored, but he knew things were going to get a lot worse before they got any better.

Processing. Of all the jobs they had him do, he hated processing the most. Maybe it was because, bizarrely, it reminded him of working in the call center? Perhaps it was just because it was so desperately sad. Those people who today still staggered into the military camp after months of trying to survive alone were little more than shells. Traumatized. Empty. Vegetative.

Heavy rain lashed down onto the roof of the tent, clattering against the taut canvas. A steady drip, drip, drip hit the corner of his unsteady desk, each splash just wide enough to reach the edge of his papers. Hot days and generally clear skies frequently meant cold nights, and even though it was cloudy tonight, it was still damn cold. He warmed his hands around the gas lamp while he waited. Wouldn't be long. He'd just had word that a food patrol had found another few stragglers hiding in a warehouse storeroom, drowning in their own filth. Kate had worked here when they'd both first arrived in the city. Back then there'd been a steady stream of refugees coming through here 24/7. Now there were just a handful being processed every day.

"Should have seen him, Mark," Gary Phillips said, sitting on the dry corner of the desk. "He went fucking wild when we found him."

Phillips had been out in many of the same convoys as Mark over the weeks. This afternoon he'd won the toss and had taken the last available seat, leaving Mark to fill the desk job. Now he was back telling Mark in unnecessary detail how one of the survivors they'd found had gone crazy when they'd arrived at the warehouse. Mark wasn't sure whether it was Phillips's way of coping with what he'd experienced or whether he derived some sick pleasure from watching refugees suffer. Whatever the reason, Mark didn't tell him to shut up or fuck off like he wanted to do. Instead he bit his lip and put up with Phillips's pointless drivel. Better that than to show any kind of reaction that might be misconstrued.

"It was just unbelievable, I tell you," Phillips continued, still pumped with adrenaline. "There were six of them shut in this fucking storeroom smaller than this tent. They'd used up just about every scrap of food they had, but on the other side of the door there was a warehouse still half full of stuff. Too fucking scared to put their heads out into the open."

"Gets to us all in different ways, doesn't it?" Mark said quietly, drawing lines on a piece of paper with the longest ruler he could find and writing out the questions he needed to ask. All the photocopied forms had been used up weeks ago.

"I know, but this was a bit fucking extreme by anyone's standards. Anyway, the soldiers force the door open, not knowing what they're gonna find in there, and this guy comes charging out, convinced they're Haters. Fair play, they gave him a chance, which is more than I'd have done, but the dumb bastard wasn't listening. He just kept coming at them."

"So what happened?"

"What do you think happened? Fucker didn't stand a chance. They put so many bullets in him I thought he was gonna... What's the matter?"

Mark nodded toward the entrance to the tent. Phillips stopped talking and looked around. Behind him stood an elderly couple, who, if you looked past the emaciation, and their haunted, vacant stares, could have just stepped out of their house to go out shopping together. Their surprisingly smart clothes, albeit drenched with rain and streaked with dirt, looked several sizes too big for them. Phillips jumped off the desk, feet splashing in a puddle of mud, grabbed a chair, and placed it next to the one that was already opposite Mark.

"I'll leave you to it," he said. "See you around."

With that he was gone. Mark gestured for the new arrivals to sit down. He hated doing this. It was hard. Damned hard. Too hard. He watched as the man sat his wife down, almost slipping in the greasy mud, then sat down next to her. Christ, after all they'd probably been through, he was still managing to be a bloody gentleman. He'd probably been looking after his wife for so long that he was hardwired to do it. She'd no doubt be the same, darning the holes in his clothes and checking he'd had enough to eat when both of them struggled to find any food and the world was falling apart around them. The couple huddled together for warmth, rainwater running off their clothes and dripping from the ends of their noses. The woman sobbed and shook, her shoulders jerking forward again and again. Her husband couldn't help her or console her. He tried, of course, but she wouldn't stop. He turned and faced Mark and stared at him, begging for help without saying a word, eyes filled with tears, mouth hanging open.

"Okay, what are your—?" he began to ask, stopping short when a low-flying jet tore through the air above the park, sounding like it was just yards above the roof of the tent. The gut-wrenching noise and blast of wind made the canvas walls shake and the woman wail and screw her eyes shut. Her husband took her hand in his and gripped it tight. Mark waited a few seconds for the jet to completely disappear before trying again.

"What are your names?"

Nothing.

"Do you have any identification papers with you?"

Nothing.

"Do you have any credit cards, letters . . . anything with your names on it, or an address?"

Nothing. Mark sighed and held his head in his hands, barely making any attempt to hide his frustration and fatigue. He looked up again, reached across the table, and gently shook the old man's wet right arm. The man reacted to his touch, shaking his head slightly as if he'd just been woken from a trance.

"Can you tell me your name?"

"Graeme Reynolds," he finally answered, his voice barely audible over the rain.

"Okay, Graeme," Mark continued, looking down and scribbling the name at the top of the form he'd drawn up, "is this your wife?"

He nodded. Mark waited.

"What's her name?" Mark asked finally.

Another pause, almost as if he were having to dredge his memory for the answer.

"Mary."

"Your date of birth?"

No answer. Graeme seemed to be looking past Mark now, gazing into space. *Waste of fucking time,* Mark thought to himself. *He's gone again. What's the point?*

"Wait there," he told him, although he knew the man wasn't going anywhere. He got up from his chair and walked across the dark tent to another table, where he added the couple's names to a register and entered the same names against the next available address in another file. He wrote out the details on a slip of paper and took it back, wondering if anyone was ever going to collect the files and update the Central System. When he and Kate had first started volunteering, the system had been updated religiously by a dedicated team tasked with keeping the information as accurate as was humanly possible. Now, whether it was because of a lack of functioning computers, a lack of trained operators, or any one of a hundred possible other reasons, the system seemed to be falling apart as quickly as everything else.

Mark handed the slip of paper to Graeme. He took it but didn't look at it.

"Take that to the next tent," Mark told him, unsure if there was anyone left working there tonight. "Those are your billet details. The people next door will give you ration papers. When you're finished there, they'll send you to the food store. They'll give you something to eat if there's anything left—"

He stopped speaking. Neither of them was listening. Poor bastards were barely even conscious. They didn't know where they were, who he was, what he was doing, what he was trying to tell them . . . Graeme and Mary Reynolds didn't move. He looked long and hard into their empty, vacant faces and wondered, as he now did with increasing and alarming regularity, why he was bothering. What was the point? *When the fighting's over,* he thought, *will we ever return to any kind of normality? Or have we gone too far for that? Is this as good as it's ever going to get? All trust, hope, and faith gone forever . . . nothing left but fear and hate.*

Mark stood up, took Graeme's arm, waited for his wife, and then led them to the next tent. Without even stopping to see if there was anyone there, he grabbed his coat and the heavy wrench he always carried with him for self-defense and left. He went out into the rain and walked, determined not to stop again until he was back in the hotel room with Kate and the others.

13

I WAKE UP STRETCHED out on the threadbare living room carpet
of the apartment we broke into last night. I ache like hell, but I
slept pretty well considering. Our position midway up the high-rise
has kept us out of sight, separated by height from the rest of town.
The apartment is filled with dark shadows and the dull blue-gray
light of early morning. It's raining outside, and the rain clatters
against the glass like someone's throwing stones.

Paul's asleep in an armchair in the corner of the room, looking
up at the ceiling with closed eyes, his head lolling back on his shoulders. Carol's curled up on the floor near his feet. I get up and stretch,
looking around the dull room in daylight for the first time. The de-
cor's badly dated, and the entire apartment's in a hell of a state as
a result of its owner's self-imposed incarceration, but it still feels

strangely complete and untouched—isolated to a surprising extent from everything that's happened outside. I glance at my monochrome reflection in a long-silent TV, then pick up a framed photograph that still sits on top of the set. It's a twenty- or thirty-year-old wedding day memory. The guy's just about recognizable as the man from last night. His bride is the corpse next door.

I find Keith in the kitchen with a map spread out on a small Formica-topped table.

"All right?" he asks as I trudge toward him, eyes still full of sleep.

"Fine. You?"

He nods and returns his attention to the map.

"We'll get moving in a while," he announces. "It's all quiet out there for now."

I look down at the map with him and start trying to work out the best route to Lizzie's sister's house. The same two circles representing the edge of the enemy encampment and their exclusion zone have been drawn on this map as on the one Preston showed me yesterday. Except the lines are in slightly different positions on this map. According to this, Lizzie's sister's house is just inside enemy territory. I point to roughly where the house is and look across at Keith.

"That's where we need to go."

"That's where you think you need to go," he answers quickly. "That's where we're going to try to go, but I'm not promising anything. We're out here to find recruits. If we get your kid it's a bonus."

"I know, but—"

"But nothing. We'll head in that direction and see how far we get."

"Is he still going on about that damn kid of his?" Carol says as she shuffles into the kitchen, bleary-eyed. She drags her feet across the sticky linoleum and lights up the first cigarette of the day.

"I've already told him," Keith starts to say, trying (and failing) to stop her from getting involved.

"You've got to let her go," she tells me, blowing smoke in my direction.

"No I don't—"

"Yes you do. What's the point of looking for her? What are you going to do if you find her?"

"I just want to know that she's safe. I want her fighting alongside me."

"And if you don't find her?"

"Then I guess I'll..."

"Assuming she's still alive, what'll happen if you don't find her?"

"She'll just carry on fighting wherever she is."

"Exactly. So what difference does it make?"

"She needs me. She's only five."

"I reckon you need her more than she needs you."

"Bullshit!"

"Not bullshit," she says, shaking her head and flicking ash into a sink filled with dirty plates and cups. "I doubt she needs you at all."

Stupid woman.

"Did you not hear me? She's five years old. I don't even know if she can fight—"

"Of course she can fight. We can all fight. It's instinctive."

"Okay, but what about food? What about keeping warm in the winter and dry in the rain? What if she gets hurt?"

"She'll survive."

"She'll survive?! For Christ's sake, Carol, she can't even tie her own fucking shoelaces!"

Keith folds up his map and pushes his way between us, clearly fed up with being caught in the crossfire of our conversation. I shake my head in disbelief and follow him.

"You need to wake up and start living in the real world," Carol shouts after me. There's no point arguing, so I don't.

. . .

We're back in the van and ready to move within minutes of Paul waking up. The rain has eased, but the ground is still covered with puddles of dirty black rainwater that hide the potholes and debris and make it even more difficult to follow the roads than it was in the dark last night. Keith manages to avoid most of the obstructions, but when he oversteers to avoid an overturned trash can, one of the rear wheels clips something else. We go a few more yards, and then there's a sudden bang and hiss of air as a tire blows out.

"Shit!" Keith curses, thumping the wheel in frustration.

"Got a spare?" I ask.

"No idea."

He stops in the biggest patch of dry land we can find, and I get out. Paul follows me out and opens the back. He rummages around and manages to find the jack and other tools. The spare's underneath. He starts to get it out. While I'm waiting I walk over to the other side of the road to where the contents of someone's front room have been strewn across the pavement. Their flat-screen TV lies smashed in the gutter, and an expensive-looking rain-soaked sofa hangs precariously out of the broken bay window. Before all this happened we each lived in relative privacy in individual brick-built boxes, what we did and how we did it hidden from view of the rest of the world by our walls, doors, and windows. Strange how the physical worlds of so many people are now as dilapidated and ruined as their emotional state. There's no privacy anymore, no boundaries. Everything we do is in full view and exposed. There's no longer any—

"McCoyne!" Carol shouts at me from the van. "Get out of the fucking way!"

I spin around quickly, but it's too late. Christ knows where he came from, but a powerful-looking man is running straight toward me. He's six foot tall and just as wide, and I can tell from the focus and intent in his wild, staring eyes that he's a Brute like those I saw back at the cull site. Does he not know we're on the same side?

"Wait," I try to say to him, "we're—"

His bulk belies his remarkable speed, and before I can move he's grabbed hold of my arm. He spins me around, then throws me over and slams me down onto my back. I'm already winded and gasping when he drops down onto my chest, his knees forcing the air from my lungs with a violent cough. I try to shout for help, but there's no noise coming.

"Get off him, you fucking idiot," I hear Paul say. I manage to turn my head to the side and watch as he starts hitting the Brute with part of the jack from the van. The Brute doesn't react, barely even notices that he's being hit. He bears down on me, a bizarre mix of terror and excitement on his face.

"Like you," I manage to squeak. "I'm like you."

Working together, Paul and Carol pull him away. They drag him back, drop him on his backside, then scatter like they've just lit the fuse on a stick of dynamite. I try to scramble away, moving back until I hit the wall of the house behind me. The Brute springs up with a low, guttural, warning growl and looks at each of us in turn. Then, painfully slowly, realization seems to dawn. He looks from Paul to Carol to me again. Paul moves toward him with the jack, ready to attack. Carol pulls him back.

"Don't aggravate him," she hisses. "Just drop it and walk away. He doesn't know what he's doing."

Paul does as he's told, dropping the heavy metal tool, which clatters loudly on the ground. Carol stands motionless as the Brute looks her up and down, her back pressed up against the van. Then he slowly turns and slopes away. He's barely made ten yards when something else catches his eye and he breaks into a slow, loping run.

"What the hell was that all about?" I ask as I pick myself up.

"No fucking idea," Paul answers as he returns his attention to changing the tire. I watch the Brute until he's disappeared from view. Did he think I was one of them, or was I just in the wrong place at the wrong time? Did he see me and think I was Unchanged? Are the Brutes really like us, or was he reacting to a difference between us?

14

THE HEAT AND DAMP have combined to make the world stink more than ever this morning—the relentless, choking, suffo-cating stench of decay combined with overflowing drains and Christ knows what else. Other than the noise of this tired old van, every-thing is generally quiet, but the fragile silence is frequently inter-rupted by sudden bursts of noise: the Unchanged military moving and attacking, distant fighting, a scream as someone is hunted down and killed, the smashing of glass and the crumbling of collapsed buildings, the pained howl of a starving animal searching for food . . . The constant, smothering noise of the engine is unexpectedly wel-come. It drowns out everything else.

I'm traveling in the front with Keith now, giving him directions. I'm trying to concentrate, but I'm distracted by the fact that a pub

I used to occasionally drink in has disappeared—there's now just an unexpected gap and a pile of blackened rubble on the street where it used to be—and for a second I don't realize the significance of where we are. Then it dawns on me.

"Stop!"

"What's the problem?" he says, slowing down but not stopping.

"No problem. Take a left here."

He does as I say.

Carol leans forward from the back. "Trouble?"

"The kids' school," I explain. "They used to go to the school down here. My missus worked here, too."

"So?"

"So if I was in Ellis's shoes and I couldn't go back home, school might be the next best option."

"Worth a look since we're here," Keith reluctantly agrees, "but if there's nothing here we move on quick, and so do you."

The school is tucked away behind a church and a row of stores and offices. In the morning light everything looks a little more familiar than it did yesterday, but a little more mutated and alien, too. Windows are smashed, doors hang open, and there's evidence of fighting almost everywhere I look. The road ahead is blocked by the rusting wreck of a car that has mounted the pavement and crashed into a bus shelter. Its heavily decayed Unchanged driver has been thrown—or dragged—through the shattered windshield. Looks like he was attacked as he tried to get away. His body is sprawled out over the crumpled hood of the car, his blue-tinged skin slashed and sliced by jagged shards of glass. His right shoulder is a gnarled stump of ripped flesh and protruding bone. The rest of his arm is missing. Keith mounts the curb and gently steers the van through a narrow gap, scraping against a wall with a vile, high-pitched grating noise. I look down as we drive over another, equally mutilated body. Whoever fought here was vicious. Probably more of those Brutes.

"Turn right down here. Down the alleyway next to the church."

He does as I say, driving the van slowly down the narrow track that leads into the school grounds. I glance over the low stone wall to my left and see that there are several more bodies in the church graveyard, none of them in one piece. Some are badly decayed, others relatively fresh. I hold my favored knife tight in my hand, ready to attack or defend myself if the need arises. Even though I'm certain whoever did this was on our side, the brutality and savagery of these kills is remarkable. Keith drives through the empty teachers' parking lot and stops outside the main school gate.

"Holy shit," Paul says from the back. "What happened here?"

He jumps out and walks over to the wire-mesh fence that surrounds the small rectangular playground. I follow him and immediately see that the violence so apparent out on the streets has spread closer to the school, too. The enclosed asphalt play area is completely covered with a virtual patchwork quilt of body parts. I press my face against the tall fence, which bizarrely makes the playground look like some kind of caged gladiatorial arena. I look down at the ground, and in the few clear spaces between the dead I can still see brightly painted markings: hopscotch, snakes and ladders, oversized letters and numbers . . . I look up again and remember this place as it used to be, filled with a couple of hundred kids in their identical school uniforms, laughing and playing and—

"Brutes?" Keith shouts from the van, derailing my train of thought.

"Doubt it," Paul answers quickly. "Why would they be here? More to the point, why would anyone still be here?"

"Unchanged hideout?" I suggest. "Think someone gate-crashed an evacuation?"

I crouch down to look closer at some of the nearest corpses. It's impossible to be sure because of the extreme level of mutilation and deterioration, but all the dead faces I see here seem to be Unchanged.

I push open the gate, and we start walking down toward the entrance to the school, leaving Carol and Keith guarding the van. The ground's much clearer here. In fact, it looks pretty much like it used to when we used to walk the kids down to class. Paul nudges me. I look up and see a sudden flash of frantic movement up ahead as a small figure darts along the side of the building, then jumps down off a low brick wall and disappears inside. I sprint down the path after it and shove the still swinging door open. I push my way inside, then stop suddenly, recoiling at the obnoxious stench that immediately hits me. I can smell human waste, rotting food, and other even worse odors.

I kick my way through the rubbish covering the floor of the small reception area. Directly in front of me is the door to the main assembly hall. To my left are what used to be the staff rooms and offices, and to my right a short flight of steps and a corridor that leads down to the classrooms. My eyes are slowly adjusting to the lack of light in here. What used to always be a bright place full of noise, energy, and life is now just as dark and dead as everywhere else, and it's a stark contrast to what I remember. There's a display on the wall with photographs of the teachers and kids, and I force myself not to look for Ellis's, Edward's, and Lizzie's faces.

"There," Paul whispers, pointing down toward the classrooms. There's another shadowy blur of fleeting movement as something dashes from one room to another. I race down toward a classroom and push the door open, but I'm immediately sent flying back as something hurls itself at me with unexpected force and lightning speed. I slide across the floor on my backside and struggle to fight off a fast-moving attacker that grabs hold of my neck and starts to squeeze. Can't tell if it's claws or teeth I feel digging into my flesh. I try to lift my knife and fight, but before I can even raise my arm another one of them dives on top of me and bites my hand until I drop the weapon. I feel the sharp pinprick of another blade being forced up under my chin, almost breaking skin, then feel more small but savage hands grabbing both of my feet and my other arm and holding me down and then . . . and then they stop. One by one, Paul pulls them off me. My heart pounding, I scramble back across the floor, stopping only when I reach the wall and can't go any farther back. I pick myself up and see there's a crowd of seven children of various sizes and ages standing in front of me. They stare back, immediately losing interest when they realize we're all on the same side. They slowly scatter and trudge back into the classroom. Paul and I follow them at a cautious distance.

"None of these your daughter?"

"Can't see her," I answer, still panting after the attack. I look around the room into a succession of pallid faces. Some of the children crawl away under desks, leaving only the biggest kids out in the open. They look like they've been here for some time, living in what used to be their classroom. Tables and chairs have been shoved to the sides of the room, the wood-tiled floor now covered in litter and discarded clothing. Random scraps of material have been used as bedding, and in the far corner wisps of smoke climb up from the ashes of a fire built from torn-up textbooks. The room is in a horrendous condition. It smells like a toilet and feels like a slum, but if I look past the dirt, the bruises, the blood, and the other stains and marks on the faces of these kids, they look completely fresh and alive. Their eyes are bright and full of life.

There's a boy who looks about the same age as my son Edward, squatting on top of what used to be the teacher's desk. If he came to this school they'd probably have been classmates, but I don't recognize him. He's digging into the wood with the tip of a fearsome-looking knife. I automatically go to tell him not to, but I stop myself—it doesn't matter, and he's not going to listen to me anyway.

It's already clear that these kids do what they like, when they like. That's probably how they've managed to survive.

"I'm looking for my daughter."

He shrugs but doesn't say anything.

"Are there any other children here?"

Still no answer.

"This is a waste of time," Paul whispers. "We should just get these kids into the van and get out of here."

I'm not going anywhere until I've had some answers.

"Are there any adults here?"

The big kid sitting on the desk finally looks up. "There was."

"But not now?"

He shakes his head.

"So what happened to them?" Paul asks.

"They went."

"You didn't go?"

"No point."

"What about the war? The fighting?"

"What war?"

His answer surprises me. I take a step forward and accidentally kick an outstretched leg, which is immediately pulled back out of sight. I crouch down and see a small girl curled up under a desk on a bed of soiled cushions and pillows. She doesn't react, but she watches me. She remains perfectly still, her eyes following my every move. These children, I think to myself, must have a strangely blinkered view of what's left of the world. Like all kids, they're only interested in themselves. I know they'd kill any Unchanged stupid enough to get too close, but do they feel the same compulsion to go outside and hunt them down as the rest of us do? As long as they're warm and relatively comfortable and they've got a decent supply of food, what more could they want? They're nesting here.

"I'm going to check the rest of the place out," I tell Paul, eager to keep looking for Ellis. I leave the classroom and work my way back toward the main entrance, checking the other rooms as I pass them. They're all empty.

"There's no one else here," a quiet voice says when I reach the top of the stairs. I turn around quickly, but I can't see anyone. A little girl cautiously steps out of the shadows and looks up at me with huge, saucer-shaped eyes. I try to estimate her age, but it's difficult. She appears completely innocent but at the same time strangely switched-on and knowing. She's a pitiful sight—desperately thin, pale white skin, dirty and bedraggled with long, knotted hair. She's wearing pajamas and has bare, muddy feet. Her clothing is blood-stained, and instinctively I'm about to ask her if she's hurt herself. But then I realize the blood is more than likely from someone else, someone she more than likely killed. I don't know what I'm supposed to say. We both stand there awkwardly, staring at each other in silence, until something I see just over her shoulder catches my eye. It's a line of metal coat hooks, hung on a long wooden rail about a yard and a half off the ground. The name on the peg directly behind her is Edward McCoyne. The girl suddenly becomes invisible as I reach out and lift a small cloth bag off my son's peg.

"That's just old stuff," she says. "My bag's down there. Want to see it?"

"No, it's okay..."

I open the bag and take out Edward's soccer shirt. His name's on the label inside the collar, written in pen in Lizzie's handwriting. I remember when we bought this for him. Christ, he nagged at us for months to get it because all the other kids had one like it. The team changed part of their uniform a couple of weeks later and the little shit stopped wearing it, complaining that he didn't have the right one anymore and... and what the hell am I doing? Got to stop thinking like this and get a grip. That life is gone now.

The girl brushes past me and leans against the assembly hall door. "What's in there?" I ask, glad of the distraction.

"More stuff," she answers nonchalantly, shrugging her shoulders. She pushes the door open, and I follow her inside. I stop immediately, rooted to the spot. The entire floor of the large, rectangular school hall is covered with bodies. Some of them are piled up, almost as if they're being stored here. There are bloody handprints on the walls, some of them too big to have been made by kids. The girl tiptoes through the carnage without a care and disappears out through a gaping hole in the outside wall where a fire exit used to be. I follow at a distance, stepping over dismembered cadavers and swatting away buzzing flies. I'm distracted by an Unchanged woman's half-naked corpse at my feet, only a few days dead. She's facedown with her arms stretched out and fingers clawing the ground as if she died trying to get away. There are chunks missing out of the back of her naked thighs. Are those bite marks?

The overpowering stench in here is unbearable, and it's making me gag. I follow the girl outside, desperate to get some fresher air. I find her at the edge of a murky, weed-filled pool. I don't know whether it's a deliberately dug pond or the crater left by a small explosion or other impact. Whatever, she's lying on her belly in the mud, thirstily lapping up the dirty green water.

It's a struggle to get the children rounded up and into the van. There were eight of them, but three managed to get away. Generally it's the older kids who understand what we're trying to do and why we want them to leave here. The promise of fighting and food is enough to persuade them to go.

"Good result," Keith says. "Job done. We'll get this bunch back to the others. Preston can't complain about a catch like this."

I knew that was coming. For the last half hour they've been

making noises about getting back to the people we left at the slaughterhouse. As far as they're concerned, it's mission accomplished. I know I should go with them, but I can't. Ellis is still out there somewhere . . .

"I'm not going."

"You soft bastard," Carol snaps angrily. "Don't be so goddamn stupid."

"We've got a van full of kids," Keith argues.

"Yes, but we haven't got *my* kid."

"We don't need your kid."

"I do."

"You don't. All you need is—"

"I'll find her and bring her back to the rest of you," I shout over my shoulder as I start to walk away. "I won't be far behind. Few hours at the most."

I can hear them arguing, but it makes no difference.

"McCoyne, wait," Paul shouts. I take a few more steps before, against my better judgment, stopping again and turning around. "He's right," I hear him say to Carol and Keith. "We've been told to find as many people to fight with us as we can, haven't we? It makes sense to split up. You deliver this bunch, we'll keep looking for more. Okay?"

Keith thinks for a minute and eventually nods his head. "Fair enough. Makes no difference to me."

I start walking again, my backpack on my back and my axe held ready in my hand.

"I'll go with him," I hear Paul say. "Julia told me to keep an eye on him."

I speed up, more determined than ever to find Ellis. Seeing the kids in the school has made me feel more confident that she's survived, but at what cost? What condition is she in? If I don't find her and look after her, will she end up like the children we've found here?

"Hold on," Paul shouts, but I just keep walking. I don't need him. I don't need any of them.

15

IT SEEMS THAT EVERY couple of minutes, something I see catches me off guard. This time it's a gas station, an innocuous, desolate shell of a building that I normally wouldn't have given a second glance. I stop in the middle of the road and stare at it. Lights hang down from its high canopy. The tall and once brightly lit welcome sign lies on its side, blocking the way to the now lifeless fuel pumps. Metal grilles pointlessly protect long-since-smashed plate glass windows. Inside, the shelves and displays have been stripped of everything of value—

"Problem?" Paul asks.

"Nothing," I lie. "Just thought I saw something."

I take a couple of steps closer, wishing I were alone. There's nothing here, and he knows it. I just wanted to stop for a second and look and remember. It feels like five minutes, but it was probably about five months since I was last here. Lizzie took her dad to the hospital, and I was left with the kids. I took them to see a film. We drove halfway across town and used half a tank of gas to get to the cheapest theater. They argued about what they wanted to see. Ed and I wanted to watch one thing, Ellis wanted to watch something else. Edward and I won the argument. Josh slept through the film, and Ellis whined all the way through it. We stopped here on the way back home to fill up the car, and I bought Ellis some candy just to shut her up. Then that started the other two moaning . . . If I half-close my eyes I can still see her in there. She took forever to choose her candy, dragging it out and trying to get as much out of me as she could.

It's the contrast that's taken me by surprise today. Everything was so trivial and unimportant back then. I walked into this shop with Ellis and I was just like any other dad, trying to pacify his whining kid. Now look at me. A killer. A soldier (apparently, although I don't feel like one). Virtually unrecognizable as the man I used to be. Living from day to day and hour to hour . . . and if the war's had this much of an effect on me, what might it have done to Ellis? I wonder what the little girl who, on that day five months ago, had nothing more important to worry about other than what candy bar she wanted, is doing now?

"Any time today would be fine," Paul moans. "Stop fucking daydreaming. It's dangerous out here, you know."

"I wasn't daydreaming."

"You were. For fuck's sake, get a grip."

"I'm fine," I say as I march past him.

"You were away with the goddamn fairies again. You need to clear your head, man. Get some focus."

This guy never gives up. He's like a dog with a bone.

"I am focused," I snap back at him.

"Focused on what? A fucking gas station? Face it, McCoyne, you're drifting. You don't even have a proper plan."

"Yes I do."

"What, walk halfway across an enemy-occupied city to get to a house where you think your kid *might* have been? You're making it up as you go along, man. Just give up and move on. You've got to start putting the fight first and everything else second."

"If it's such a bad idea, why did you come with me?"

"Like I said, to find more volunteers. Besides, I wasn't crazy about being shut in the back of that van with a load of feral kids."

"Volunteers—is that what you're calling them now?"

"Well, what would you call them?"

"Conscripts . . . lemmings . . ."

"So are you not bothered about this war anymore, then? Are you happy just to let the Unchanged carry on attacking us? You saw the gas chambers—you know what we're up against."

"Nothing's changed, Paul. I still want to kill just as much as you do."

"Start showing it, then. Listen, man," he sighs, "I'm just trying to help you out. I understand what you're going through."

"Understand! How the hell can you understand? My five-year-old daughter is out there on her own somewhere!"

For the first time in an age he's quiet.

"Do you really think you're the only one who's had it hard?" he finally says, his voice suddenly full of tension and previously suppressed emotion. "Think you're the only one who's been dealt a shitty hand by all of this?"

"No, I—"

"Because I'll tell you, sunshine, you're not. We've all had it hard. What's happened has fucked everything up for every last one of us, and all we're trying to do is put things straight."

"I'm not saying that I—"

"You've never once asked me about my family, have you? About what happened to me? What brought me here? And do you know why? I'll tell you, it's because you don't care, and you're right not to. It doesn't matter. It's not important, none of it is. What's done is done, and all that matters now is what we do from here on in."

"I understand that, but if I can find Ellis, then I . . ."

I stop speaking because he's stopped walking again. I carry on for a few more paces, then turn back to face him.

"It was a Wednesday night, about a quarter to ten, when it happened to me," he says. "It was all so damn ordinary. I'd been watching soccer on TV. My girlfriend had just gone to bed, and I was on my own downstairs. I was just sitting there, staring at the walls, when everything clicked into place and started to make sense. It was like someone had switched a fucking light on, you know? Like I could suddenly see everything clearly for the first time in years."

"What are you talking about?"

"So I sat there for a while," he continues, ignoring me and wiping something away from the corner of his eye. "Then I went out to the garage and got myself a mallet and a saw, best things I could find. Then I went back inside, went upstairs, and killed Sharon. After I'd finished with her, I did the same to Dylan. He was awake in his crib when I went into his room. He was standing there, bouncing up and down on his mattress, grinning at me, but I did it just the same. I had to."

"I'm sorry," I mumble quietly, feeling like a total shit and not knowing what else to say. He shakes his head and walks on, trying unsuccessfully to hide his anger.

"Thing is, since I heard the things Preston's been saying, I can't help wondering what would've happened if I'd left him. Could I have made him like us?"

"Do you believe all that?"

"I don't know what I believe. All I know is that you've got no fucking right to question whether I understand what you're going through. You've got a kid who's probably still out there fighting somewhere, and these days that's as much as anyone can hope for. Now shut up, wise up, and get a fucking grip. Forget about her."

16

WE WORK OUR WAY along the outermost edge of the Unchanged exclusion zone, either just inside or just outside the boundary depending on whose map you're looking at. It's been uncomfortably quiet out here, and we've seen only a handful of other fighters since splitting from the others back at the school. Here, though, things suddenly feel different. Paul and I make our way quickly through the ruins of a sprawling college campus, moving away from the collapsing, battle-damaged buildings, then climbing up a number of terraced soccer fields, stacked like hugely oversized steps. From the farthest edge of the uppermost playing field we're able to look out over a huge swathe of the exclusion zone. In the distance I can just about make out the area of town where Lizzie's sister lived, and I can see all the way across the wide stretch of no-man's-land to the heart of the enemy refugee camp, too. But it's what's directly below us that is of more immediate interest. We're overlooking what's left of St. James's Hospital, and it's crawling with activity. Our fighters are all over it like ants over forgotten food.

"What do you reckon?"

Paul shrugs his shoulders. "Got to be a reason for them being here," he answers, and before I can speak again, he crawls through a hole in a section of chain-link fence and starts running down a steep, grassy slope toward the hospital.

I try to resist for a second and force myself to concentrate on finding Ellis, but then I think about the fact that there must be Unchanged close by, and the temptation becomes too strong to suppress. My mouth begins to water as I sprint down the hill after Paul, desperate to get down to the hospital and start killing. I hear gunfire as I start to run, a sure sign that the enemy is close. Suddenly all I can think about is satisfying my hunger and ending Unchanged lives.

The main hospital entrance has been partially demolished, the automatic doors stuck midway through opening, their metal frames buckled. As I catch up with Paul he's looking for a way around what's left of this part of the site. It sounds like most of the heavy fighting is concentrated around the parking lots and the other buildings at the far end of the complex.

"Cut straight through," I suggest as I squeeze through the gap in the doors. He follows me as we head down a long corridor that has somehow remained surprisingly white and clean and that even now still has the faintest tang of antiseptic in the air. The building feels vast and empty, and our footsteps echo as we run along the hard marble floor toward the battle. A huge, dark, zigzagging crack in one of the walls makes me question my decision to come this way momentarily, but it's too late now and it's worth the risk. We're nearing the fighting. We're closing in on the enemy.

I burst through a set of swinging double doors, then stop at a staircase. Instinct tells me to head down, but the way through is blocked by fallen rubble from a collapsed wall. Paul doesn't wait, deciding quickly to head up and work his way around whatever damage he finds up there. I follow him through more doors, then along another, much shorter corridor, which ends with a sharp right-hand turn. We instinctively slow down when we enter a ward filled with corpses. I start to wonder whether these well-decayed people were just abandoned and forgotten when the war began, but a closer look at their injuries quickly tells me that wasn't the case. A skeletal woman has been skewered with the metal support that once held her intravenous drip, the stained and tattered threads of her flapping nightgown still wrapped around her shoulders. Sitting on the floor to my left, the withered husk of an old man is slumped with his legs apart. There's a vertical scar in the middle of his badly discolored chest, running in almost a straight line down from just below the level of his sagging nipples. At the bottom of the scar, right where his navel would have been, the wound has been forced open and his innards pulled out. This guy's been disemboweled by someone with their bare hands. The ingenuity and brutality of whoever did this is breathtaking. These bodies are old, though. Why are people still fighting here today?

A huge hole in the ceiling and a corresponding hole in the floor farther down the ward force me to concentrate again. I follow Paul as he edges cautiously around the narrow ledge that remains around the dark chasm. I glance down and see a mass of rubble, beds, and bodies directly below, then look up. There are more holes in each floor above us all the way up to what's left of the roof.

At the end of the ward we reach another staircase. I look down through a large safety-glass window over a vast crowd of people battling outside. Our fighters are swarming around a collection of outbuildings right out on the farthest edge of the site. Standing separate from the main hospital campus, they look like they might have been storerooms or boiler rooms. There are enemy soldiers in every visible window and doorway and more on the roof, all of them now firing relentlessly and indiscriminately into the surging crowd. On the other side of the wrought-iron railings that surround the hospital grounds are their vehicles, ready for them to beat a hasty retreat if we get too close.

Paul's halfway down the stairs, but I stay standing at the window. Something's not right here.

"Come on!" he shouts.

"Wait . . ."

I watch as another surge comes from deep within the crowd of fighters. People are jostling for position, trying to get closer to the enemy, using each other as human shields by default. A pair of Brutes almost get close enough to strike before they're driven back and brought down by another hail of bullets. Other fighters immediately clamor to take their places, trampling their fallen bodies. Apart from those few brave attempts, the enemy seems to be managing to keep the bulk of the crowd at bay.

"You fucking idiot!" Paul yells at me. "They'll all be dead by the time you get down there."

He disappears, but I don't move. On the face of it this looks like any one of a hundred battles I've witnessed or been a part of before, but there's a subtle difference, and alarm bells are ringing. I sprint after Paul to try to stop him.

"Paul," I yell, just managing to catch sight of the back of his head before he disappears out through an open door. "Wait!"

"We'll tear them apart," he shouts, glancing back at me. "They're sitting ducks."

"No they're not."

"What?"

"They could get out of here at any time. I saw it from up there.

They're tight up against the perimeter, and they've got vehicles on the other side waiting to take them out. They're playing us."

"What?" he shouts again.

"It's a fucking setup! Think about it . . . Their secure area's just a mile or so from here, there's no way they've been cut off from the others, and they don't look like they're out here for supplies . . ."

"I don't care," he says, thinking more about the kill than anything else, acting like a drug-starved junkie who's desperate for a hit.

"They're not waiting here to be evacuated," I tell him. "They're here to draw us out into the open."

Paul shakes his head, then turns and runs, charging deep into the sprawling, ever-growing crowd of fighters, which now almost completely fills the entire space between the main part of the hospital and the Unchanged-occupied buildings. Bullets shatter windows in the wall high above, and jagged daggers of glass rain down around me. Forced to move, I follow him outside but stay right at the very back of the crowd, using the mass of surging figures as cover and trying to squirm around the edge of the building and head back in the direction from which we just came. Paul's already disappeared—just another face in the swollen crowd of bloodthirsty fighters, all of them desperate to kill. I don't know what's more terrifying, the fact that I think we're being set up or how singularly focused this huge mass of people has become. It's like nothing else matters; the scent of blood is in the air, and they're all behaving like Brutes, prepared to sacrifice anything for the thrill and satisfaction of the kill. The closeness of the enemy and their constant gunfire just seems to rile the hordes and make them even more aggressive. Maybe that's what they want?

I feel like I'm fighting against everyone else here now, and a moment of indecision and distraction costs me dear. Too busy watching what the bulk of the crowd is doing, I don't realize another group of fighters is approaching from behind until it's too late. They push past me, shoving me out of the way and to the side, slamming me against a wall. Before I know what's happening I'm on the ground, desperately trying to cover my head and scramble out of the way as people stampede all around me. The noise of the chaotic battle is muffled and distorted down here, increasing my disorientation. I try to follow the wall I just smacked into, still moving against the tide of people and hoping I'm heading in the right direction. I'm finally able to pull myself back up onto my feet, using a drainpipe for support. I haul myself up onto the top of a metal and glass smokers' shelter outside a blocked entrance door and look back over the heads of the crowd. Almost all of the shooting has suddenly stopped, and I see that our fighters have finally reached the small buildings. They're pouring inside, steamrolling anyone who gets in their way. I stand on the shelter and curse myself for overreacting. Maybe Paul was right. Did these stupid Unchanged bastards really just screw up and get themselves stranded out here?

I'm about to jump down when I hear something. The noise makes me stop and stare again. Then I see it—a line of armored trucks and jeeps heading away from the back of the buildings. A handful of fighters manage to make it over to the other side of the perimeter fence, but, judging by the number of vehicles now racing across this part of the exclusion zone at speed, it looks like most if not all of the Unchanged soldiers have got away. More people scramble through the buildings and chase after the Unchanged, but they give up quickly and slow down and watch the enemy escape through clouds of dust.

Wait.

The sound of engines is getting louder.

The vehicles are almost of out sight, but the noise is continuing to increase in volume. It becomes vague and directionless and seems to wash and fade before becoming stronger, louder, and more definite again. Then I realize that these engines are above us. I know what's coming next. The enemy's tactics are becoming all too easy to read.

I jump down off the shelter, going over on my ankle and accidentally taking out another couple of fighters in the process. There's an uncomfortable malaise about this place now, with only a few people on the frayed edges of the crowd making any serious attempt to get away. Most of them just stand there, some with their faces pressed against the railings, still watching the Unchanged flee. I'd do something about it if I could be bothered, but all I'm interested in now is getting myself out of here before it's too late.

I start running, pushing my way through crisscrossing bodies and trying to ignore the sharp, jabbing pain in my ankle. Above the roof of the hospital I catch a glimpse of a massive low-flying, slow-moving plane with an enormous wingspan, and I will myself to keep moving faster and faster as I hear the high-pitched whistle of the first bombs beginning to fall. I'm away from the bulk of the crowd but still nowhere near far enough to be safe. I keep trying to force my legs to work harder, but my muscles are burning with effort, and I think my ankle's going to give way at any second. Can't keep moving. I lean against a wall and half hop, half drag myself along, knowing that the building I'm holding on to is about to be obliterated. I can almost see the grassy hill Paul and I ran down now, but it's still too far. I'll never get there. The piercing whine of the fast-falling munitions keeps increasing in volume until it's all I can hear. Then it stops.

Nothing.

A split second later and the air is filled with more noise than I can believe, the power of the blast forcing the air from my lungs. I drop down and cover my head, ready for the world around me to explode. The ground shakes violently, and I curl myself up into the smallest shape possible, waiting for the remains of the hospital building to start to crumble and fall. My guts churn with fear, and I brace myself for what's coming next, knowing that the worst is yet to come . . .

The noise starts to fade.

Everything sounds muffled. Debris starts falling. In the distance people are yelling for help and screaming with pain.

Was that it?

I tell myself I'll count to thirty, and if nothing's happened I'll try to move. I only get to seven when I feel people starting to get up around me. Did all the bombs explode? Did the Unchanged pilot fuck up?

I cautiously stand up and turn around, not knowing what I'm going to see behind me. The air is filled with spewing clouds of dust, like a thick, dirty, grainy fog that quickly settles and coats everything with gray. As it fades I realize I can still see the far end of the hospital building intact. The outbuildings that were the focus of the fighting have gone, but the main campus is in much the same condition as it was before the attack. The only other thing that's missing is the crowd of fighters, and I realize that they were the target today, nothing else. Those Unchanged bastards have managed to wipe hundreds of us out and still leave their infrastructure relatively undamaged. I don't know whether it's the sight of the unscathed hospital building or the empty space where the crowds of fighters were standing that makes me hate them most.

As the haze settles, everything takes on a bizarrely calm, almost dreamlike state. Those who've escaped the full force of the blast begin to stagger past me, some soaked with blood, others looking like white-faced ghosts, covered in powder-fine debris. Behind those who can walk I see others who've suffered much worse injures. A woman, I think she may have been a Brute, tries to drag herself along the ground. Both of her legs have been blown off below the knee, and she leaves an uneven snail trail of glistening blood behind her. She manages to travel a couple of yards farther before she dies. I shake my head clear and try to force myself into action as a man stumbles closer, walking like a drunk, carrying the lower part of his left arm in his right hand. He's asking me for help, I think, but I can't hear him. Is there something wrong with his voice? I try to answer, but I can't hear my own voice properly either. Everything sounds muffled and low, and I realize the problem's with my ears. I nervously look from side to side, suddenly aware that if I can't hear properly, I'm wide open to attack. I need to get away from here and find somewhere safe so I can get my head together, then get on with what I came back out here for. For half a second I wonder whether I should stop and look for Paul. It's a stupid, pointless idea. He's probably nothing more than a pile of blackened bone and ash at the bottom of the bomb crater now. He was no help anyway. Stupid fucker didn't listen to a word I said.

Pull yourself together, I tell myself again as the shock and disorientation slowly start to fade and some clarity returns. I need to forget this place and get back on track and keep moving toward Lizzie's sister's house—and, I decide as I start to hobble away, my ankle still weak, I need to do it on my own. I have to keep away from everybody else because when we're together we become an easy target for the Unchanged to pick out from the sky. Cowardly bastards. Face-to-face they know they don't stand a chance. Long-distance battles are the only ones they can win.

I start to run, slowly at first until the pain in my ankle becomes slightly more bearable. I head back toward the entrance to the hospital I first came through, desperate to put some distance between me and everyone else. I reach the bottom of the grassy slope below the college playing fields, and this time I take a right, moving toward the ruins of a housing project, hoping that the closely packed row houses on either side of the road will provide me with some temporary cover. I tuck in tight against the buildings on my right, hiding in their shadows. As I move past a succession of grim, crumbling facades, I start to think I should maybe stay here for a while. The enemy has already hit this place; what would they gain from striking here again? And now that I've made the decision to only travel alone, would it be better to wait until dark? But then I think about Ellis and the kids at the school, and I know I have to keep moving.

Shit, there's someone in the road up ahead. I crouch down behind a low stone wall in the front yard of one of the houses and watch. Don't think he's seen me, but he's coming this way. He must be Unchanged, I can tell by the way he moves, from his slow, cautious movements and lack of confidence. So why the hell am I cowering like this? *Stay calm and consider the options*, I tell myself. He's alone, and if he is one of them, I'll just kill him. I must still be shook up from the bombing, because my heart's pounding and I'm suddenly sweating like a pig. I need to face this fucker head-on, whoever and whatever he is. I try to focus on the euphoria I know I'll feel when I end his miserable life.

I grab my axe, then stand up and run at him. When he sees me he immediately reaches for his belt, and I curse my stupidity, certain that he's about to draw a gun and fire—but he doesn't. He backs away, running from me faster than I'm moving toward him, screaming into a handheld radio. Now I'm sure he's Unchanged, and I know I can't let him live. He accelerates, moving with a frantic speed that I can't match. It's a struggle for me even to keep up, but I can't let him go. Have to kill him . . .

He turns a blind corner. I follow, then stop dead in my tracks. There are three more of them racing down the road ahead toward me, one on a motorbike in full leathers. It's four against one, and I'm fucked. But I can't let it end like this. Do I go out fighting or . . . ? The bike rider lifts what looks like a riot baton and accelerates, and my decision's made. Like a fucking coward I turn and run, not even bothering to attack, the screaming sound of the bike's engine ringing in my ears.

I run through the open door of the nearest house and slam it shut behind me. That should slow the bastards down. Rather than risk heading upstairs in this ruin I instead stay down, running through a ransacked living room and jumping over the outstretched legs of the corpse of a woman that's leaning up against an empty fireplace, looking like she's praying. The kitchen of the house is filled with rubble. There's a gaping hole where a window used to be. I scramble up onto an unsteady counter and jump out through the gap, landing in a concrete yard on my injured ankle. I bite my lip hard, refusing to shout out, and breathe through the pain. In the brief moment of quiet I listen to the echoing sound of the motorbike as it fades and swirls and seems to move away. Then I hear the Unchanged enter the front of the house, and I force myself forward again. I run down a narrow path in the middle of a wild, overgrown lawn, heading toward a tall brick wall at the back of the garden. There's a half-empty water barrel in the corner. I use it to climb up onto the top of the wall, then kick it over to stop anyone from following. Down the other side and I find myself standing in space in the middle of a block of six lockup garages, a row of three on either side. I can either hide here and wait to be found or make a break for it. Apart from going back over the wall there's only one way out. I sprint forward but then stop when the bastard on the bike appears from nowhere and cuts me off, swerving the bike around so that it blocks the road. I manage to weave around his back tire and get past, but I've only taken a few steps farther when I hear him accelerate again. I look back over my shoulder as he rears up, riot baton held ready. I try to change direction again, try to wrong-foot him, but my ankle gives way and I stumble, barely managing to keep upright and keep moving. I feel sudden, searing pain as the baton cracks against the back of my legs, and I hit the asphalt hard and roll over in agony.

More of them are coming, their Unchanged faces hidden by motorcycle helmets, face masks, visors, and scarves. I try to stand up, but one of them slams me back down, pinning my arms to the ground. Another one holds my legs. I struggle, but they're too strong. There are too many of them.

"Just do it," I yell at them. "Fucking do it! Kill me now and get it over with."

Yet another one appears, looming over me. I can see this one's face. He looks me up and down, then pulls the plastic stopper off the tip of a hypodermic needle with his teeth and spits it out. I try to arch my back and get away, but I can't do anything to stop the fucker from thumping the needle hard into my chest.

WITHIN WEEKS THE MECHANISM for the ongoing distribution of food and medical aid to the population of the refugee camp had begun to falter and fail. In retrospect it had seemed a large-scale but reasonably straightforward undertaking, but, as what had originally been envisaged as a short-term operation dragged into its fourth month and with no end in sight, the situation continued to rapidly deteriorate.

The initial ground rules and hastily cobbled-together official procedures had been simple. Under military control, all resources were to be coordinated via the City Arena—a vast, cavernous, ten-thousand-seat concert venue. Its huge, soccer-field-sized concrete floor had been cleared, and all rations, supplies, emergency aid, and "collected" foodstuffs were held there under armed guard. Trucks full of provisions were shipped out to ten nominated distribution centers within the huge camp on a daily basis—a movie complex, the town hall, two sports centers, and various other similar-sized public buildings. From these centers food was distributed to the city's population, who carried ration books with their identification papers.

By the beginning of the second month, supplies had already dwindled to dangerously low levels, the authorities having severely underestimated both the number of refugees requiring rations and the duration of their enforced incarceration. Similarly, they'd overestimated their ability to source and replenish food stocks. Officially acquired (looted) food continued to enter the city on a daily basis as a result of frequent military excursions, but it was nowhere near enough. More importantly, no more food was being produced. No crops were being grown and harvested, no factories were operating, every transportation and distribution system had been rendered unusable . . .

By midway through the second month, supplies had fallen to such a low level that the daily restocking of the ten distribution centers was reduced to every other day. By the beginning of the third month, deliveries were only being made weekly.

A black market emerged on the streets, and for a short while it thrived and flourished. Also in month two, a militia faction known colloquially as "the Milkmen" because of the herd of stolen cows they kept penned in on the heavily guarded field of a local soccer team, assumed control of two of the distribution centers. The irony of small-time criminals dealing in milk and occasionally beef alongside the usual staples of drugs and weapons was not lost on either the military, who tolerated their activities (it took some of the pressure off them), or the poor bastards forced to trade with them. Business boomed temporarily until the basic economic principle of supply and demand could no longer be applied. Food, water, and medicines became both the commodities and the currency. The demand was inexhaustible, the supply nonexistent. Trade stopped. The militia groups closed their doors, emerging only to attack and raid other distribution centers to continue to feed and water themselves. When even the black marketeers could no longer source enough food and water for their own needs, infighting took hold, and their previously untouchable operations imploded.

As the end of month three approached, the City Arena was all but empty, and eight of the distribution centers (including those previously run by the militia) had ceased to function. Of the three remaining sites, the Arena was now being run by the military, purely for the benefit of the military. One of the distribution centers housed in an old warehouse continued to be maintained by a rapidly dwindling group of do-gooders who were stupid enough to still believe in helping other people and who dutifully handed out almost microscopic portions to the ever-growing crowds continuing to line up outside the building twenty-four hours a day, seven days a week. Truth was, the only reason they were still in business was because they drip-fed provisions, literally a mouthful at a time. Perversely, the sheer mass of desperate refugees both protected the distribution center from the threat of militia attack and isolated it from the military authorities and supply routes.

This morning, the last remaining functioning distribution center—housed in a long-empty factory building—collapsed. The food supplies had finally run dry, and the news predictably caused a riot. The military commander responsible, overseeing the center from a safe distance, wasted no time in locking the site down and ordering the execution of the three hundred or so rioting civilians trapped inside. The public had to be controlled, whatever the cost. Disorder like that couldn't be allowed to spread. The implications were unthinkable.

· · ·

Three-quarters of an hour ago, Mark had left the cramped hotel room for the first time since returning from his final shift as a volunteer. Kate had pleaded with him not to go, but what choice had he had? He had a duty to provide for her and his unborn child, not to mention the other family members they'd found themselves unwillingly imprisoned alongside.

Walking the streets was a bizarre and frankly terrifying experience, and he quickly realized how much he missed the security of traveling with the military. Even being outside the exclusion zone with the army, surrounded by Haters, felt safer than this. He desperately tried to keep himself to himself, looking at the ground whenever he passed anyone else or looking over the heads of the crowds he walked through. He didn't know where he was going or what he was hoping to achieve, but he had to keep trying. He couldn't just sit there with the rest of them and wait for something to happen. They were starving, cold, and frightened, and he begrudgingly felt responsible for all of them.

Mark made his way in the general direction of the factory building where he, Kate, and the others had collected their rations in the past. He walked via Leftbank Place, an area of waste ground that had been planned for redevelopment for years. That was never going to happen now. He struggled to see through the never-ending mass of temporary shelters that blanketed the ground, making it look more like a third-world slum than anything else. The remains of entire families sat huddled together under polyethylene sheets, desperately clinging to their last few belongings and each other. For a while it made him almost feel grateful for the relative comfort and security of the hotel room where he and the others had been billeted.

It was obvious as soon as he got near the distribution center that it had closed down. Where he'd expected to find uneasy, virtually silent lines of people he now saw only an empty space. Any space was at a premium now, so the fact that people were completely avoiding the site was a bad sign in itself. He'd already decided to turn around and head back to the hotel before he saw bodies being dragged away. A drifting plume of hazy gray smoke drifted up from behind the large, boxlike building. He knew that was the smoke from a funeral pyre—a typical military cleanup operation. They burned all dead bodies now to stop, or rather slow, the spread of disease.

He changed direction gradually, so self-conscious and afraid of everyone else that he didn't dare make any sudden alterations to his route, paranoid that people were watching him. He found himself at the base of the McIver Tower—the building where he used to work—and he allowed himself to look up just for a moment and remember. Up there, on the seventh floor, was where he'd spent endless hours before all of this had happened. Up there, alongside around one hundred and fifty co-workers, all sitting in front of identical computers, wearing identical headsets and working toward identical targets, he'd sold insurance and dealt with people's claims. Those were the days, he thought, almost daring to smile, when a burst pipe or a broken window was considered an emergency . . . It all seemed so trivial and unimportant now, but it had mattered then. Not just to him, but to everyone. He'd struggled with the monotony of the job at times, but he'd have given anything to return to the boredom and routine of his former life now. He stopped by a telephone booth to look a little longer and tried not to look suspicious, avoiding making eye contact with the man who was sitting on the floor inside it, his back pressed against the door to prevent anyone else from getting in. Mark counted up to floor seven of the office building, then worked his way along to the window nearest to where he used to sit. There were people living up there now. Even from down here he could see them, hundreds of them packed in together, desperate for space. Around the base of the building, in a low-walled, rectangular area that had once been an exclusive parking lot reserved for company executives and senior managers, was an enormous pile of redundant computer equipment—hundreds of unneeded screens, keyboards, and tower units thrown out as the floors above had been emptied to make room.

Mark looked down at the man in the phone booth again. He hadn't moved. Was he just sleeping? He casually tapped the glass with his knuckles, but the man didn't react, so he did it again. Then, moving slowly, he shook the door. Still no reaction. Was he dead? Whatever it was that was wrong with him, Mark saw that he had a plastic grocery bag tucked inside his filthy raincoat. It had to be food. Other than weapons and drugs, food was the only thing worth hiding now. He kicked the glass again, this time cringing inwardly as a couple of other people either turned around or glanced up before remembering themselves and looking away again.

The appearance of a small boy walking along the wall around the base of his old work building distracted him. The poor kid looked hopelessly lost and exhausted, all life and energy drained out of him. It said something about this crisis that even the kids were affected to such an extent. He'd seen film of children playing resiliently around the ruins of their homes in World War II bombsites before now, and other footage of kids laughing and running through disease-ridden subcontinent slums, but this . . . this was different. Even the most innocent and naive members of society knew how dire this situation was becoming. The boy shouldn't have been on his own. Who was he with? Was he lost? Abandoned? Orphaned? He'd adopted the same safe, emotionless, and almost vacant gaze as everyone else, trying to separate himself from the rest of the world but unable to escape its close confines. Mark had no way of knowing if this kid was okay or if he was sick or . . . He forced himself to stop. He had to look away and block him out. He couldn't afford to care.

This morning, before he'd left the hotel, Mark had argued with Kate. Neither of them had meant for it to happen, but once they'd started shouting, weeks of pent-up frustrations meant neither of them could stop. Kate was becoming increasingly claustrophobic in the hotel room, and the lack of privacy was driving her insane.

"What am I supposed to do?" he'd said to her. "Until things change, this is all we've got. There are no hospitals or clinics or—"

"So what happens when the baby comes?"

"We deal with it."

"How?"

"I don't know ... we get some towels and water like they said and—"

"What towels? Where's the water going to come from? Christ, Mark, I won't even be able to wash the kid. We don't have enough water to drink, let alone—"

"Calm down, Katie. You're just—"

"Calm down! Jesus Christ, why should I? I'm fucking terrified, and you're expecting me to give birth to our baby on the floor of a hotel room in front of my parents."

"It's months away yet. Four months. Think how much might change in another four months—"

"Think how much worse it might get."

"Now you're just being stupid."

"I'm scared."

"We're all scared."

"I'm scared about the baby."

"Millions of women give birth every year, don't they? And they used to manage before hospitals and—"

"It's not that—"

"What, then?"

"I'm scared about what our baby might be. What if it's not like us? What if it's one of them and it ... ?"

"Don't be stupid. I'm normal and you're normal. Our baby will be normal, too."

"But what if it isn't? You don't know that for sure, do you? No one knows why we're like we are and why they're different . . ."

She was right, of course, but he kept on trying to persuade her that everything would be okay, doing his best to keep up the bull-shit and pretense because it was all he could do.

A sudden noise nearby diverted Mark's attention back to the present. There was a disturbance deep in a crowd of people on the other side of the road. He couldn't clearly see what was happening. It looked like a fight—someone had probably cracked under the strain of the impossible situation that they, and everyone else, found themselves in. The sudden, unexpected outpouring of long-suppressed emotions provoked a range of reactions from the other refugees nearby. Some ran. Some did all that they could do pretend it wasn't happening. Others forgot where they were and all that they'd been through and responded with the most basic, natural of reactions and fought.

Mark didn't give a damn what was happening or why. Taking full advantage of the situation and the distraction it caused, he shoved the door of the phone booth hard. When the lifeless man on the ground still didn't react, he pushed the door again until there was a wide enough gap for him to squeeze his arm through. He grabbed the man's grocery bag, shoved it inside his coat, and walked back toward the hotel.

17

JESUS, MY HEAD HURTS.

Where the hell am I? It's dark, pitch black almost. I'm lying flat on my back on a narrow bed, naked but for a T-shirt and shorts. I try to move, but my ankles and wrists have been chained to the four corners of the metal bed frame. There's no slack, and I can't even lift my hands up off the mattress. The harder I try, the tighter the chains seem to get. I try to move my head, but there's some kind of strap right across my forehead, keeping me down. When they come back I'll kill the fucker that's done this.

My eyes are getting used to the lack of light in here, but there's not a lot to see. It's a narrow, rectangular room with this bed against one wall and a chair opposite. There's nothing on the walls except for a lopsided crucifix just to the side of the solid wooden door.

I stretch my neck back as far as I can. There's a small, boarded-up window behind me, the faintest crack of light showing around the edges.

How long have I been here? Have I just woken up, or have I been out cold for days? I feel myself starting to panic, and I make myself breathe slowly and work my way back through what I remember . . . the children at the school, traveling with Paul, the fighting at the hospital, the Unchanged in the streets who chased me down and drugged me . . . We were set up, and the bastards who did it must be the ones who brought me here. I pull on my chains again, but I still can't move. I don't understand this. It doesn't make sense. If they really were Unchanged, why didn't they just kill me? Why bring me here, wherever here is?

Someone screams. Can't tell where the noise is coming from. Don't know if they're screaming for help or crying with pain. Is this a torture chamber? A place where sick, perverted Unchanged fuckers tie us up and make us suffer? Bastards could come in here any second and start on me and there'd be nothing I could do. Maybe they're experimenting? Trying to find out what makes us better and stronger than them by cutting us up? How many others before they get to me? Is it my turn next?

Concentrate.

Calm.

Focus.

I think about killing to keep me strong. I think about all the Unchanged I've massacred over the months and how I've gotten rid of each one of them. I remember all the pointless lives I've ended and how easy it was and will be again.

Ellis.

Just for a second, from out of nowhere, I think about Ellis, and everything comes crashing down again. The chains feel tighter and the darkness closes in and I can't move a fucking muscle. I've failed her. She's out there on her own somewhere while I'm locked up here like a fucking animal. Every minute she's alone out there increases the chance of her ending up like the kids in the school. I try to move again, pulling as hard as I can and thinking for a second that I can break the chains and get out of here, but nothing happens and the ties just get tighter. I feel like I'm in the line outside the cull site again, standing there and waiting to die. And there's nothing I can do about it.

My arms hurt. They feel heavy and numb. Shoulders are burning with pain. Got an itch on the side of my right leg, just above the knee, and all I want to do is scratch it. I try to ignore it, but it won't go. Now it's all I can think about, and the more I think about it, the worse it gets. Now it's like someone's dragging the point of a needle up and down across my skin, and it's driving me fucking crazy.

Good.

Focus.

Concentrate on the pain and block everything else out.

18

HAVE I BEEN ASLEEP? I can't see the window when I tilt my head back and look behind me. Is it dark outside? Was it even an outside window? Am I in the same room, or did they move me while I was asleep, if I was asleep? Maybe I've been awake all the time. I could have been lying here for hours. Might be longer. Might have been here for days.

Everything's quiet. Just a slow drip in the corner of the room. Sounds like a leaking pipe. Steady. Constant. I count to eight between drips.

Throat's dry. Need water. Want to call out, but I can't. Don't know who's listening. Won't lower myself to speak to Unchanged even if...

"How are you feeling?"

The voice from the darkness scares the shit out of me. I can only move my eyes, and all I see is nothing whichever way I look. Did I imagine it? My heart's thumping in my chest like I've run ten miles. I try to move, but I'm still held tight. Someone's next to me. I can hear their footsteps and their breathing. Can't see them, but I know they're close. I feel them brush against my hand, and my whole body stiffens. The door opens inward a fraction, just enough to let a narrow wedge of dull yellow light trickle into the room.

"Didn't mean to startle you," the deep male voice continues in an African-sounding accent. "I've been watching you for a while. Just wanted to make sure you were all right."

The man stops speaking and stands over me. I can see his short but broad frame outlined by the light from outside. Is he waiting for a response? He'll be waiting a long time 'cause I'm not speaking to anyone until I know who and what they are and why I'm here.

What's he doing now? He crouches down, and I can hear him messing with something on the floor beside the bed.

"You might want to close your eyes. I've got a lamp here."

I try to keep my eyes wide open, but they shut involuntarily when he strikes a match and lights a bright gas lamp. I force myself to open them again, ignoring the pain, desperate to see as much of my surroundings as possible after what feels like hours and hours of darkness. The brilliant bright light burns my eyes, and all I can see is the mantle of the lamp, glowing white-hot. The roar of the burning gas jet fills the room, incredibly loud after so much silence.

The intense glare of the light begins to fade as my eyes get used to the brightness. The man puts the lamp on a chair opposite the bed. He turns back around, and I get my first proper look at his face. The bastard is Unchanged. Can't help but react. I try to lunge forward, the chains still holding me down. I arch my back and try to break free, but I can hardly move. He shuffles back into the corner of the room, too scared to get too close. Need to kill him.

Need to get rid of him, but I can't. Losing control. All I can do is spit. The spittle hits the wall and starts to drip down. Mouth's too dry to make any more . . .

"Finished?" he asks. Bastard. I relax my aching muscles, feeling searing, agonizing pain in my shoulders, wrists, legs, and neck. Can't stand being this close to one of the Unchanged and not trying to kill him. My guts are in knots. Can't think straight. Can't move. Can't do anything. Need to kill him, but it's physically impossible. Bastard. Haven't even got enough strength to spit again.

The dark-skinned Unchanged man picks the lamp up off the chair again, then puts it on the floor and sits down. I manage to turn my head to the side slightly, and I stare at him. Won't take my eyes off the fucker. I'd kill him in a heartbeat if it wasn't for these chains. Five-five, five-six at the most, he's overweight—as round as he is tall. The whites of his eyes are bright and clear. I imagine them bulging as I wrap these chains around his neck and pull them tight . . .

"Take it easy," he says. "Calm yourself down."

He's unarmed. He's sitting casually in the chair, and he's grinning at me with a look in his dark, staring eyes that's cold and evil. His legs are apart, arms uncrossed, palms open and facing upward. Textbook body language. Does he think I'm stupid? Fucker's doing all he can to try to seem open and nonconfrontational, but I don't buy it. Inside he's terrified, scared shitless because he knows what I'll do to him when I get free. Can't stand being this close to him, breathing the same air . . .

"Bet you've got more than a few questions to ask," he says. He's right, I have a hundred questions ready. He knows I won't ask any, but he still waits for me to speak. Wish he was close enough to kill. If I just had one hand free I'd have wrapped these chains around his throat and garrotted him before he'd known what was happening. If I could I'd smash his head into the wall, or burn him with the lamp or break the glass and grind it into his face or . . .

"My name's Joseph Mallon," he says, his heavily accented voice sounding composed, calm, and unhurried. "I'll be working with you while you're here."

Working with me? What the hell's he talking about?

"You were lucky to get away from the hospital by all accounts," he continues. "Now that says to me you were either incredibly lucky or very smart. I'm hoping it's the latter. You look like you've lasted well out there. You're in good shape."

Does he want to kill me or fuck me?

"I'll tell you what I know about you, just to get us started."

He pauses, and in the gap between his words I almost forget myself and speak. But at the last second I remember what he is and I stay silent, feeling my body tensing up again.

"I've been through your stuff," he says. "It's all safe, by the way. I know your name's Danny McCoyne. It's funny how we still carry things like wallets around. I guess it's just habit, isn't it? Even someone like you, someone who's so desperate not to be anything like the person he was before, you still had your wallet kicking around at the bottom of your bag. Couldn't bring yourself to get rid of it, eh? You've got no use for it, but there it was, full of useless banknotes, credit cards you'll never use again, pictures of your family. Lovely-looking kids, by the way."

At the mention of my family I automatically try to move and pull against my chains again. He grins. That was exactly what he wanted. I curse myself for being so transparent.

"That touched a nerve, didn't it?!" he laughs, looking pleased with himself. "Might explain why a big, hard man like you is carrying a doll and a kid's clothing around in his bag. Were you looking for someone?"

I look away, deliberately breaking eye contact and staring up at the ceiling. Undeterred, Mallon gets up and leans over me. I arch my back again, trying to get closer and freak the fucker out, but this time he stands his ground. The light shining up from the lamp on the floor casts strange shadows over his foul face. He grins and leans closer, staying just out of reach. I can almost feel his breath on me.

"Just relax. You're going nowhere, Danny McCoyne."

There's a noise outside that distracts him, the dull, muffled thump and rumble of a distant explosion. Mallon walks to the window and pulls the board away slightly to look outside. He doesn't say anything about what he sees, but the fact that he's able to look outside and I can't reminds me again that I don't even know where I am. I don't know where this place is. Add to that the fact that I don't know how long I was unconscious for . . . Jesus, I could be anywhere.

"Questions," Mallon suddenly announces, carefully replacing the board, then sitting down again. "If you're not going to talk to me, let me see if I can hazard a guess at some of the questions you're too proud to ask. We'll start with the basics, shall we? Who am I? Where are you? What are you doing here? How come you're still alive? How long will you stay alive? What are we going to do to you? Tell me, Danny, am I on the right lines?"

He's right, and I need to know all of that and more, but I still won't answer. I can't answer. Won't even look at him. I clench my fists, tense my muscles and grind my teeth, and stare up at the ceiling, doing all I can not to give him the satisfaction of a response. He shakes his head and sucks his teeth. If I stay quiet for long enough, maybe he'll tell me anyway? Bastard seems to like the sound of his own voice.

"Not going to talk to me at all this evening?"

Don't react. He wants you to react. He's trying to antagonize you.

"You know I can keep you here as long as I like, don't you?"

Ignore him.

"I'm thinking you're uncomfortable lying there like that. If I leave you all night it's going to get pretty bloody painful."

He won't undo these chains whatever I do. More bullshit.

"And you're gonna get mighty hungry. How long's it been since you've eaten? A day? Longer? And water, too . . . your throat must be burning."

Fucker's playing mind games. Don't bite.

He waits. Watching me. Trying to outpsych me.

"Danny McCoyne," he sighs, voice full of mock disappointment, picking up the lamp and leaning closer, "you need to spend some time thinking about your predicament. You've lost all control, sunshine. What happens to you now is totally up to me."

He stares down at me for a moment longer. I meet his gaze, determined not to be the one who'll crack. After a few seconds that feel like minutes, he stands up straight and moves back toward the door.

"Well, I'm not wasting any more time on you tonight. I'm hungry. We've got good supplies here, better than most. Going to fetch myself something to drink and some food, then get some sleep. It's been good talking to you."

With that he leaves, taking the lamp with him. He pulls the door shut with a loud thud, then locks it. I hear his footsteps walking away, then silence. The quiet is deafening and is interrupted only by the fading sound of a far-off helicopter or plane and the steady drip of the water in the corner.

The room is pitch black, no light at all. The kind of dark your eyes won't ever get used to.

Who the hell is Joseph Mallon? Is he on his own here? Just a lone crackpot trying to make a stand, or is he part of something bigger?

My gut begins to rumble with hunger again, and the itch by my right knee returns. Wish I could scratch it. That's all it'd take, just a few seconds scratching, then it would go. Feels like someone's digging a nail into my flesh.

19

I HEAR A SCREAM in the darkness, but I can't tell whether it's coming from somewhere inside this building or outside. In the smothering darkness everything has lost its form and definition. I have no concept of time or how long I've been here. I tried counting the drips, but my tired brain can't keep track, and now the noise each drip makes is like a hammer blow to the head. I can't stay still, but I can't move either. Every time I pull on my chains they seem to tighten even more.

I don't know how long it's been since I last drank anything, but my bladder's been filling steadily. I won't shout out and put myself at the mercy of Joseph Mallon or any other Unchanged scum here. That's what he wants. He's trying to get me to break under pressure by starving me and keeping me chained up and in the dark. I'm better than him. I won't let him get to me. But at the same time I can't stop my body from doing what it's supposed to. I pissed myself a while back. What else could I do? It was either that or shout for Mallon. Now I'm soaked with strong-smelling urine. It was warm, but my bare legs are freezing now, and I stink. That bastard has reduced me to this, but I won't let him beat me.

My body aches. My legs and arms are numb. Never thought it could hurt so much to stay still for so long. Just wish I could get up and walk around. And God, I'm so fucking hungry. My empty stomach keeps cramping so bad it feels like it's turning itself inside out. Don't know what I'm going to do when I need to shit. Not even going to think about it until it happens. Have to try to keep myself distracted, but it's impossible when I can't see or hear anything and when I can't move and when I don't know where I am or how long I'm going to be here . . .

Stop.

Focus.

This is what he wants. He's trying to push me over the edge. It won't work. I won't let it work.

Leg's itching again. Worse than before.

Helicopter. Long way off . . .

How long before you go crazy in the dark? A kid at school—long, long time ago—said it was just hours if there's absolutely no light at all. Pointless thinking about time, because I don't know how long I've been lying here. Part of me is starting to wish Joseph Mallon would come back just to break the monotony. Never thought I'd actually look forward to seeing one of the Unchanged, but staring at that evil piece of shit's face would be better than lying here staring at nothing, just thinking. Don't like being able to think like this. Makes me question things I've known all along are right. Makes me start to doubt myself. Makes me think stupid, crazy thoughts about Ellis—how close I might have got to her and how far I am from her now. I was within a couple of miles of Lizzie's sister's house, and now I could be anywhere.

What's my little girl doing? Is she fighting? Is she already dead? Is she in another room in this building? Is she in the room next door? What if Mallon doesn't come back? What if I've fucked up and blown my chance with him? What if he leaves me here to starve to death, strapped to a piss-soaked bed?

What a fucking failure. All that noise and fighting and bullshit—four months of it—and I've let myself get beaten by an unfit, over-weight Unchanged who looks like he couldn't fight his way out of a paper bag. He can't be the only one running this place. There were at least four out on the street when they got me, and none of them were as fat and out of shape as Mallon.

Thinking about the street makes me think about the hospital and how I criticized Paul for running headfirst into a one-sided fight that I thought was a setup. At least he went out fighting. For all I know he might still be out there while I'm stuck here...

I'm starting to get scared.

The dripping noise is getting louder and faster.

Thought I felt something moving on the bed.

Thought I saw a flash of light.

Am I hallucinating now?

Am I going out of my fucking mind? Going crazy in the dark? Need to keep focused, so I try to remember Ellis's face. But the harder I concentrate, the less I see. I'm scared I'll forget what she looks like. The face I see now isn't her, it's a combination of the faces of the feral kids we found in the school this morning... or yesterday morning... or whenever the hell that was.

Leg hurts.

Just want to scratch that fucking itch.

20

THE DOOR FLIES OPEN, and Mallon barges into the room. He's carrying something with both hands and holding the light beneath it. The combination of searing light and dark shadows stops me from seeing anything. He doesn't look at me, must be focused on whatever it is he's going to do to me. He turns his back and puts something down on the chair; then he puts the lamp on the floor in the corner of the room.

What's that smell? Christ, it's beautiful. Smells like hot food . . . some kind of soup, I think. But it can't be, can it? Can you imagine a smell? Is this another trick my tired mind's playing on me? Mallon turns around and moves closer. He's left a tray on the chair. There's a bowl on it with steam snaking up, and next to it is a plastic bottle full of water. My stomach starts to growl and churn.

"You must be damn hungry," he says, his deep voice filling the room. I stop myself answering with the words on the very tip of my tongue, remembering at the last second what he is and what his kind have done to people like me. "You look hungry. You must be starving."

He leans over me, and I instinctively strain against my chains to get to him. Maybe this time I'll reach him . . .

My arms and legs hurt too much, and I quickly drop back down. Bastard doesn't even flinch. He knows I'm not going anywhere.

"You smell of piss," he says, laughing at me and shaking his head. "You're in a bad way, big man! Lost, all alone, chained up, and soaked with piss!"

I can't help trying to lunge forward again, but the pain's intense, and this time I hardly move. He looks me in the eye and raises his hand. I screw my eyes shut and tense up, ready for him to hit me— but the pain doesn't come. I feel him tugging on the wide strap across my forehead. He loosens it slightly, then steps back. I still can't lift my head up, but at least I've got some side-to-side movement now. The freedom is bliss.

Mallon picks up the tray and sits down on the chair opposite. He sniffs the soup or stew or whatever it is, then takes a spoonful and holds it up to his lips. He stops just before he eats it.

"You want some of this?"

Fucker knows how much I want it. He's playing games with me again, and I have to resist. I won't give him the satisfaction of a response. Won't lower myself to speak to him. I watch his every move as he blows steam away, then takes a mouthful. He closes his eyes and shakes his head with pleasure, deliberately overdoing it for effect.

"Oh, that's good . . . You know, Danny, it's getting harder and harder to find food like this these days. I'm betting it's been a long time since you've tasted anything as good as this soup."

He eats more. I want him to stop. *Please don't eat it all . . .*

"It's chicken, you know. It's out of a can, of course, but man, you can still taste the meat. I don't even know if it really is meat, but oh, this is damn fine soup."

He puts down the spoon and opens the bottle of water. My mouth and throat are dry. My tongue feels ten times its normal size, like it's too big for my mouth. He takes a huge swig of water, then gasps with overstated pleasure when he's done. My eyes are fixed on him, and he knows it. My stomach churns again.

He gets up and carries the tray over. I stare at the steam coming from the soup and watch it disappear into the air, trying to imagine what it tastes like. Can't remember the last time I ate hot food . . .

"You can have this," he tells me, putting the tray down on my chest. I watch it going up and down with my fast, nervous breathing. I feel the heat from the soup on my body. "You can have all this and more; you just have to do one thing. You know what that is?"

I don't react. Don't know and I don't want to know. I don't have anything this sick fucker could want. But if there is something, something I haven't thought about that matters, then I know he'll keep pushing. And the longer I act dumb, the harder he'll have to push. If I stay silent long enough, he'll have to tell me something to keep this bullshit interrogation moving along. He clears his throat to speak again. Predictable bastard.

"All you have to do, Danny," he says, leaning closer, "is talk to me. We don't even have to have a proper conversation. You can just tell me to fuck off if you like. All I want is to hear your voice. I just want you to respond to me . . ."

I won't do it. I'd rather starve. He waits, looking at me hopefully. Keep waiting, fucker.

And he does.

"Seems strange to me," he eventually whispers after he's been watching for a couple of minutes, "that someone like you who's obviously so hungry and thirsty can't bring themselves to just do one small thing to get what they need so badly. No one else is going to know about it, Danny. No one's watching..."

Stay focused. I look up at the ceiling and count the cracks.

"You really are strange, strange people. If I had the time and inclination to wait and watch, I think you really would rather lie there until you die than drop your guard. Crazy behavior..."

He leans over me until his face is all I can see. I start to tense my body again, but he gently pushes me back down with one hand, and I know there's nothing I can do. I make eye contact and refuse to break it. I'll kill him when I get out of here. I'll rip his damn body apart, smash his face into the wall...

Mallon sighs. He shakes his head with feigned disappointment, then picks up the tray and puts it back on the chair. I stare at the bottle of water, still three-quarters full, and watch the few last wisps of steam rising up from the soup. He stands in the open doorway with the lamp.

"All you have to do is talk to me. Just say something... anything..."

Another pause; then he shakes his head again and leaves. He slams and locks the door, and the room is plunged back into total darkness.

THE RAMIFICATIONS OF THE Hate were vast and incalculable. While the impact was predominantly felt by the surviving population—those remaining on both sides of the Change—its effects reached much, much further.

The very nature of the division that had unequally split the human race in two had caused irreparable damage to every area of life where two people or more were expected to work together. Basic services had faltered and collapsed within a matter of days. There then followed a frantic, barely coordinated period of reprioritization as the remaining Unchanged resources were diverted to the maintenance of vital services and defense. Within weeks, however, even the most basic of public services had either fallen apart or been brought to its knees. A government of sorts (with a civilian mouthpiece but under military control) continued to try to coordinate what remained of the country's infrastructure. City and district councils either were dissolved or collapsed. All schools were closed. The hospitals and the health service couldn't cope. What was left of the police force and fire brigade were absorbed into the military.

The concentration of huge masses of refugees in hopelessly unprepared locations also presented a constant string of enormous, virtually insurmountable, logistical and practical problems.

The lack of food, shelter, and adequate medical care aside, water, gas, and electricity supplies failed with astonishing speed as power stations, pumps, and pipelines were abandoned, destroyed, or disabled. With every single person without exception being dragged into the war, those installations and facilities that remained operational longest were frequently those that could function unmanned.

The evacuation of the Unchanged masses to city center camps simply concentrated and exacerbated the problems faced by the authorities. Extremely limited utility supplies were maintained, with all available water, gas, and power being diverted to the military as priority. Fuck the civilians, there's a war to be won.

Without adequate supplies of clean water and basic medical care, the refugee camps quickly became breeding grounds for disease. Previously easily curable ailments rapidly became killers, and small outbreaks and infestations quickly became epidemics. Most bodies were collected and burned, but scores of others inevitably remained undetected. The almost total lack of sanitation compounded the problem dramatically.

Within the cities, the closely confined masses of refugees continued to produce vast amounts of garbage, none of which was collected or treated. As well as quickly becoming a physical hazard, the huge quantities of waste that quickly gathered also contributed to the acceleration of disease. Rats and other vermin benefited from suddenly plentiful supplies of food, and those drains and sewers that had not been damaged by the fighting instead became blocked with debris.

From late May onward, an increase in temperature combined with frequent heavy downpours of rain to further accelerate the decline in conditions in the refugee camps.

Every available scrap of indoor space had been utilized to house the displaced, but inevitably the demand far outweighed what was available. As a result, huge numbers of people were left outside. Some were housed in tents, RVs, and trailers, but most made do with temporary shelters constructed from whatever materials they could find. More than 30 percent of the total population of the refugee camp was forced to live outdoors—hundreds of thousands of exhausted, vulnerable, malnourished people left to the mercy of the elements.

"Block it up!" Mark yelled as rainwater poured in through the broken top-floor hotel window. The room was dark, almost pitch black despite it normally being bright at this time in the morning. The stormy dawn sky over the city was swollen with rain. It had been falling with the force of bullets for more than fifteen minutes already and showed no signs of abating. The guttering and drainpipes serving the dilapidated old building couldn't cope with the sheer amount of water flushing through them. A blocked section of gutter had overflowed, and the water had seeped behind a rotting fascia board, then flooded through the window frame. More water seeped through a broken pane of glass.

"Block it with what?" Kate shouted, using a bucket, a wastebasket, cups, and whatever else she could find to catch the water.

"I don't know. Stay there. I'll go and find something."

"Don't go outside," she pleaded, struggling with her heavily pregnant bulk to turn around and stop him. "Please, Mark."

"Just to the end of the hall, okay?"

He didn't give her time to answer. He weaved around the bottom of the double bed, where Katie's traumatized elderly parents lay terrified, cold, and wet, then ran past the permanently locked bathroom door. He unlocked the main door, took off the security chain, and put his head outside. Just a handful of people out on the landing—a rain-soaked woman from the room next door (who obviously had problems similar to his) and the Chinese guy with his three kids who slept in the broken elevator. Mark looked up and down, then spied a wooden hatch on the wall between two of the opposite rooms. The fire hose that used to be hidden behind the small square door was missing. He pulled at the hatch, then pushed down on it from above, feeling the hinges begin to weaken. A few seconds of violent shaking and pulling and he yanked it free with an almighty splintering crack. He ran back to room 33 with it, stopping only to pull the one remaining curtain down from the side of a large gallery window overlooking the street below. Jesus Christ, things looked bad down there. Crowds of people were pressed up against the sides of buildings, desperate for whatever shelter they could find, woken without warning by an early morning deluge of ice-cold rain. The main street itself, Arley Road, a wide, relatively straight, and gently sloping strip of pavement, looked more like a river. A fast-moving, debris-carrying torrent of rainwater surged down it toward the center of town.

Back in the hotel room, Mark threw the curtain to Kate, who started mopping up the water that was still cascading down the glass, then spilling down the windowsill and soaking the carpet.

"Who's that?!" Kate's elderly, confused father yelled in panic, lifting his head off the pillow for the first time in hours. "Is it one of them?"

Next to him, her mother lay on her side, sobbing, the dirty bed-clothes pulled up tight under her chin.

"It's just Mark, Dad," Kate shouted.

"It's me, Joe," Mark said, leaning closer to the old man so he could see his face. He'd lost his glasses weeks ago. Mark didn't know whether he recognized him or not.

Mark leaned the hatch door against the window over the broken glass and used a phone directory to wedge and hold it in place.

"Save the water," he said to Kate.

"What?"

"The rainwater . . . save it!"

"Where?"

"In the bathtub."

The flow of water into the room temporarily plugged, Kate carried the half-full bucket across the room, her bare feet squelching on the damp carpet. She knocked on the bathroom door.

"Let me in."

There was a brief pause; then the latch clicked and the door opened. Another adult refugee appeared, her face drawn and haggard-looking.

"Everything okay?" she asked. Kate nodded.

"Mark said we should try to save the water in the tub."

The woman nodded and took the bucket from her. Mark passed her several water-filled cups that he'd collected from by the window.

"Makes sense to try to hoard as much as we can," he said, taking back the empty bucket. She nodded but didn't answer.

The flood stemmed temporarily, Kate walked away and sat down exhausted on a rain-splashed chair next to her parents. Her mother continued to sob, but Kate couldn't face trying to comfort her. Instead she closed her eyes and ran her hands over her swollen stomach.

Mark picked up the last pot of water and carried it to the bathroom. The rain seemed to finally be easing. The woman in the shadows took it from him and emptied it into the tub.

"Thanks, Lizzie," he said.

21

I CAN'T STAND MUCH more of this. It must be hours since Mallon left me. Can't smell the food anymore, but I know it's still there, and I want it. My guts feel like they're somersaulting one minute and being ripped open the next. The pain's unbearable, almost like my body's eating itself from the inside out. I try to put the hunger out of my mind, but frustration takes its place. The frustration turns into confusion; then the confusion turns into fear. The fear makes my aching shoulders, arms, and legs feel a thousand times worse. I try to lie still, but even the slightest movement is agony.

What the hell was that? Something's moving over me. It feels like there are insects crawling over my itching leg. Maybe there are? I haven't looked at my legs since I woke up strapped to this bed. Who's to say that itch isn't an open, untreated wound? Who's to say I haven't got some kind of infection, that there aren't maggots and worms and Christ knows what else feeding on my flesh? I can feel them wriggling and squirming inside the cut, digging deep into me, boring through my skin.

Then it stops again.

Am I just imagining things? Or was it something bigger? A mouse or a rat?

The dripping is the only distraction. It's constant now, almost like machine-gun fire, and it never fucking stops.

I could end this. All I have to do is talk, he said. Just give him that one small victory and I'll have some light and food and water. Christ, I need to drink something so badly...

I open my mouth to shout for help, then stop myself. What the hell am I thinking? Have I forgotten what Joseph Mallon is and what his people did (and are still doing) to my kind? They're the reason all of this happened. If it wasn't for them we wouldn't have had to kill and my family would still be together. We had to kill them for protection. This whole war has been fought in self-defense . . . that's the only reason. They made us do it. And to think, I was about to beg one of them for mercy . . . Christ, what kind of a person would that make me? I'd be pissing on the memory of all those who've already died in the fighting.

But why not?

Why shouldn't I talk?

No one's going to know, and what are my options? Do I lie here and starve to death or swallow my pride and cooperate?

No . . . no way . . . they almost had me then. That's exactly what they want me to think. They're trying to get me to crack under pressure and submit. Why should I? I'm stronger than all of them. I'll outsmart them and outlast them. *I'll* break *them*, not the other way around. When all of this is done, *they'll* be the ones lying broken on the ground, not me. I'll be standing over them, their blood on my hands.

Except right now I can't stand up. Right now I can't move. Right now I can't do anything without that fucker Mallon's say-so. For Christ's sake, I'm lying in a bed of my own filth, and I can hardly think straight. I don't know what time of day it is, where I am, who's holding me here . . . and none of that's going to change unless someone gives way. They've got nothing to lose. Unless Mallon gets some twisted kick out of doing this, if I die it's just one less of us for them to worry about. But what really happens if I keep refusing to cooperate and fade away to nothing in the endless darkness here? I'll never see Ellis again. Chances are I won't find her anyway, but the fact of the matter is I'll definitely never see her as long as I'm locked up in here.

And I need to eat and drink. The hunger hurts.

Going to do it.

I clear my throat, then stop myself.

More indecision.

Bottom line—what use am I to Ellis like this?

Someone has to give way.

I try to shout, but my voice is hoarse and hardly any sound comes out, just a pathetic, strangled whine. For a second I'm relieved; then I tell myself I have to do it. But now I can't even build up enough spit in my mouth to make a decent noise. Frustrated, I try again, this time a little louder. I manage something that's half a word and half a cough and immediately wish I hadn't. I feel like a traitor, colluding with the enemy. Maybe that's it? Could this place be run by Chris Ankin's people? Are they testing my loyalty?

I wait and listen hopefully. Over the dripping of water I can hear distant fighting, the occasional burst of gunfire and shelling, a jet scorching through the sky. But the rest of this building is silent, quieter than ever. Am I on my own here? For all I know this might be the last occupied room in a crumbling ruin. Joseph Mallon might be long gone . . .

One more shout, this time so loud it feels like it's ripping the inside of my throat apart.

I lie back on the bed, freezing cold, smelling of piss and feeling pathetic. Am I really stupid, naive, and desperate enough to believe that Mallon's going to come back and feed me?! I yell again, this time more in frustration than anything else, then stop. Did I just hear something? It's so quiet and faint that I convince myself I'm imagining it. No, there it is again . . . the definite sound of approaching footsteps. I feel relief and fear in equal measure.

Joseph Mallon marches into the room, carrying a flashlight. He shines the light into my face.

"Did you say something?"

I'm immediately gagged by my emotions again, too angry and full of hate to respond. He waves the light toward the food on the chair. It's cold now, but I still want it. The light makes the water look sparkling, clear, and pure. He walks up to the window behind me, looks outside for a second, then turns around and shines the flashlight back at me again.

"I thought I heard you say something?"

Still can't speak. The words are stuck in my throat, choking me. It's like the strap across my forehead has slipped down across my windpipe, stopping me from speaking. I want to, but I can't . . .

"My mistake," Mallon sighs. "Sorry to have disturbed you."

He steps back out through the door.

"Don't . . ."

My voice stops him. He turns back around to face me. The weak yellow light from the flashlight makes him look old beyond his years and tired, but slowly his expression changes from a scowl to a smile, which becomes a broad grin.

"Good man! I knew you'd do it!"

He doesn't say anything else. He doesn't try to get me to talk like I thought he would. He doesn't try more of his stupid mind games. Instead he just picks up the plastic bottle of water and squirts it into my mouth. It tastes so good . . . stale and warm but refreshing. I swallow and feel it running down the sides of my throat. Thank God . . .

The bottle empty, Mallon does the same with the cold soup, ladling several spoonfuls into my mouth. I almost gag on its cold and lumpy, gristly texture, but I force it down, knowing that every mouthful helps replace the nutrients and energy I've lost since being held here. As I finish eating he loosens the chains on my wrists slightly. They're still attached to the bed, but at least now I have some limited freedom of movement. The relief I feel when I finally move my shoulders and arms is indescribable.

"Didn't hurt, did it?" He grins before he leaves and locks the door.

22

I OPEN MY EYES again, and this time the narrow room is full of long shadows. Rain is hammering against the window, and the water in the corner is trickling constantly now, no longer just dripping. I tilt my head back as far as it will go and see that the board over the glass has been moved. Mallon must have done it when he was last here. It's only been shifted slightly, but it's enough to let dull shards of light slope across the opposite wall, stretching almost halfway from the window over to the lopsided crucifix. I must have been asleep.

Wish I'd never spoken. Feel like a traitor, like I've betrayed myself and my kind, like I'm somehow now less of a man because I spoke to Mallon. But if I hadn't done it I'd probably still be in total darkness with my ankles and wrists bound tight and my stomach still empty. I tell myself that I didn't give anything away (not that I have anything to tell) and I haven't compromised anyone but myself. It's survival of the fittest now, and if I stay stuck here like this I'll be fucked when the next fight begins. And there will be another fight . . .

I can hear something happening outside, someone moving on the other side of the door. Suddenly it's unlocked and thrown open and Mallon barges in, the loud noise startling me. I curse myself for not concentrating and realizing he was close. Can't afford to let my guard down like that. Lying here I'm vulnerable and exposed. If he decides to turn on me I'm dead.

He puts a fresh bottle of water down on the chair, then locks the door.

"How are you this morning, Danny?"

I won't answer. He leans over me and looks into my face. Instinctively I try to attack, forgetting the chains that still hold me down. My arms are yanked back down, my already aching shoulders feeling like they've been pulled out of their sockets. Mallon, standing a little farther back, is unfazed. Fucker. I want to see fear and hate on his face, but there's nothing. More games. More fucking games.

"Let's get some proper light in here so we can see each other," he says, walking over to the window. He moves the board completely, and for the first time I can properly see every corner of the small rectangular room I've been held captive in. It's grubby and well used, with dirty handprints all over the door like someone's been hammering to get out. And the walls are pink, for Christ's sake! Christ knows what this place really is. I know it's not a prison (there are no bars on the window), but this room is definitely a cell.

Watching me with caution, Mallon crouches down at the side of the bed and reaches underneath it. He's pulling on the chains, probably tightening them again. He gets up and moves away, and I find that I can now move my left hand with a little more freedom than before. He tosses me the water. I'm just barely able to catch it, open the lid with my teeth, hold it to my lips, and drain it dry. I crush the empty bottle and throw it back at him with a flick of my still-restricted wrist. Smug bastard just smiles.

Mallon moves the chair marginally closer, carefully positioning it as if there's a specific mark on the floor at the point where he's safe. He sits down and looks long and hard into my face. I hold his gaze, determined I won't be the first one to break. He makes it easy for me when he's the one who looks away.

"You've been here for almost two days now, Danny," he says, "and you haven't had any answers to those questions of yours, have you? I'm also betting that if you're anything like the rest of your people I've gone through this with, you're probably not ready to start asking yet. In fact, if I was to loosen your chains just a little bit more, I know you'd try to get off that bed and kill me."

Damn right. There's nothing I want to do more than wrap these chains around his windpipe and choke the life out of this vile, pathetic bastard. But I know it's not going to happen. Not yet, anyway.

"Now what I want this morning," he continues, his voice low and infuriatingly calm, "is just for you to lie still and listen to me. I want to tell you my story. It won't be anything you haven't heard a hundred times already. Well, maybe you won't have heard a story like this, but I'm betting you've seen plenty of similar things. Hell, I'm sure you've *done* worse things yourself than what I'm going to tell you. You see, Danny, you and your kind ripped a hole in my life. I lost everything because of you. You tore my world apart."

What the hell's he expecting from me? Pity? An apology? It makes me feel good to know that we've made him suffer, and I want to hear more. I want every detail. I want to know exactly how we hurt him and what we did.

"Picture the scene, Danny," he begins, his voice almost too calm.

"It's a Friday night, and I've just got home from work. I won't bore you with the details about where I lived and what I used to do for a living before all this because, if I'm being honest, it *was* boring. Thing is, it was *my* life and *my* routine and I was happy with it. And you and your kind took it all away from me."

He remains composed, but I sense raw emotion bubbling just under the surface. Is he going to crack? I want to see this bastard's pain, want to see him hurt. He stops speaking, closes his eyes, takes a breath, and then continues.

"It was pretty early on, I suppose. You remember what it was like in the early days when we thought there wasn't really a problem and that the streets were full of copycat vigilantes fighting just because everyone else was? Before we knew that people like you were actually changing? Back in the days before we all got too scared to even look at each other? Remember?"

He automatically looks at me for a response, but he doesn't get one.

"Anyway, like I said, it was a Friday night. We'd just finished eating, and I was watching the news on TV, hearing about how bad everything was starting to get. My wife was in the kitchen, arguing with Keisha, our seventeen-year-old, about going out. She was going through the whole protective mother routine, you know? Telling her how she didn't like her going into town on weekends anyway, but especially not then with all the trouble going on . . . you get the picture. Now I'm sitting there with my feet up, trying to block out the noise and concentrate on the TV, but it's getting louder and louder in there. Keisha's shouting at Jess, Jess is shouting at Keisha, then Keisha's shouting back again, and I'm just staring at the screen, wishing they'd both shut up . . ."

His voice trails off again, and in the sudden silence I remember all the TV and kid-oriented arguments that used to grind me down in my dead-end former life. I check myself quickly. Am I identifying with this fucker? Maybe that's what he wants? This is probably just more calculated bullshit to try to get me on his side.

"The shouting gets louder and louder," he says, "and I hear the back door swing open, then slam shut. I think that's it, that Keisha's stormed out, but then I realize I can still hear both their voices. Then I hear a crash and one of them starts screaming, then a thump and another crash. And then all the screaming stops."

He looks straight at me. There are tears rolling down his cheeks. He wipes them away with his sleeve.

"I get up and start walking toward the kitchen, and there's this guy just standing there in the middle of the room with his back to me, both my girls lying at his feet. I know they're dead as soon as I see them. He's got a baseball bat in his hand, and there's blood dripping off the end of it. I can only see Keisha's legs, but Jess is lying on her back, her head just a yard or so from where I'm standing, and her face . . . Christ, there's nothing left of it, like her whole skull's been caved in. Just a dark, bloody hole where that beautiful face used to be . . .

"Now our house was just a small, modest place—narrow, middle of the block, you know the type? I start backing away from the kitchen, praying the killer's not gonna see me. I'm halfway across the living room when he starts to move. We had a closet under the stairs with one of those slatted louver doors. I drop down to my hands and knees, crawl behind the sofa to the closet, then shut myself inside. And the worst thing is, when I get in there I've still got a clear view of everything. I see the man step over my wife's body and walk into the living room. Bastard was crying like a baby. I can't even remember what he looked like now. I just remember him wailing and sobbing like it was him that had just found his family dead. I reckon the Change had just hit him, you know? It was like he was regretting what he'd done, like he was trying to work out what he was and come to terms with it. Tell me, Danny, was it like that for you?"

I think about the nervous panic and confusion I felt immediately after killing Harry, but I don't tell him. Mallon wipes his eyes again and continues.

"Anyway, after a while he started to calm down. He sat down in my seat like he owned the place and watched my TV. Even helped himself to a couple cans of my beer from the fridge. He stayed there for hours, and I stayed shut in the closet, just like you're stuck in here now. Except you don't have to look at the battered bodies of the people you loved most in the world, do you?"

A trace of bitterness has crept into his voice, but I still don't react. I'm just wondering how long this pathetic sob story's going to go on.

"Eventually he just got up and left. Didn't even look around the rest of the house. He just upped and went, and I didn't have the balls to stop him or try and fight back. I wanted to stay there with my family, but I couldn't, not when I saw what he'd done to them both."

If they were Unchanged, they had to die. Simple as that. I'm on the verge of telling him as much when he starts speaking again.

"Like I said," he continues, a little more composed now, "it's nothing you haven't heard before. But after it happened I decided your kind wasn't going to get away with it, and I went out looking for revenge. Hard to believe when you look at me, but I went out onto the streets, looking for trouble. Wasn't long before I realized it wasn't working. Got myself mixed up in all kinds of nasty business. I never killed anyone, but I came close to dying a few times . . . You can imagine what it was like. I latched on to a group of vigilantes. A couple of times things got really bad, and you know why? Because people thought we were like you! They saw us trying to take a stand and fight back, and they thought we were the Haters! And then after a couple of weeks I stopped and took a step back from it all and I realized they were right. There was hardly any difference between us and people like you. And I thought about the man who killed my girls and how he cried, and I understood. He didn't *want* to kill them, he thought he had to do it."

Joseph gets up from his seat and crosses over to the window, making sure he stays well out of my limited reach. He stands on tiptoes and looks down.

"And that leads me to the main part of my sermon this morning." He grins. "Pay attention, Danny, you need to listen carefully to this! You see, when I stopped trying to fight, life started to get better again. That might sound like bullshit to you, but it's true. I was already resigned to the fact that things were never going to be easy again and that nothing I could do would bring Jess and Keisha back, but I realized that revenge wasn't the answer. You can't fight fire with fire, you know what I'm saying?"

He moves away from the window and paces the length of the short room.

"Then I found the people here, people who'd all reached the same conclusion as me. And I realized that it doesn't matter what made any of this happen, all that's important now is putting a stop to it before it's too late. So that's what we're doing. We're trying to end the cycle. I think of us like a firebreak, you know what I mean? When they're trying to stop a forest fire spreading, they sometimes burn a strip of land farther ahead. Then, when the fire finally reaches it, there's nothing left to burn and it dies out. We're like that. We've all done our share of fighting. Our battles have been fought. So when people like you reach us with your hate, there's nothing left to burn. We're putting the fire out. Stopping things from getting any worse."

He sits down again and stares straight at me. What's he thinking? Does he actually believe any of the crap he's just been spouting? I look back into his dark brown eyes, and all I can think is that

I want him dead like I've wanted all the rest of them dead. But there is a slight difference here. All the others I've killed looked back at me with hate in *their* eyes, but not Mallon. There *is* something different about him. Is there any truth in any of what he's just said, or is it total bullshit? Is he just preying on me? Wearing me down and fucking with my mind before he goes in for the kill? He's probably trying to catch me off guard. As soon as I lower my defenses, he'll attack.

He starts speaking again.

"Doesn't matter who you are or what side you're on, everybody is conditioned to react to the hate in the same way. It's all about self-preservation at the expense of everyone and everything else. Everybody fights. Everybody wants to survive. That's why everything fell apart so quickly—at the first sign of trouble we all turned on each other to protect ourselves. And despite all the noise and bullshit that was thrown around at the start, do you know which side was worst of all?"

Instinctively I shake my head, still held down by the wide strap.

"We were," he says, answering his own question. "And we still are. Did you see anything of the massacres we carried out? Gas chambers, for crying out loud! We spend years educating generation after generation about the Holocaust and how we can't ever let it happen again. Then, when it suits us and we're the ones facing the threat, we forget everything we've always believed in and resort to genocide. Thousands upon thousands of men, women and children slaughtered . . . I tell you, Danny, it makes me feel ashamed to be human."

Christ, could there actually be some substance to what this guy's saying? *Don't be stupid*, I tell myself, *he's Unchanged*. In the sudden silence I try to concentrate on the dripping water in the corner again, doing all I can not to let myself get suckered in by Mallon and his mind games.

"Question for you," he suddenly announces. "What's going to happen if we just let things run their course?"

He waits expectantly for an answer, knowing full well I won't give him one. More to the point, I can't. The future is something I've only dared to think about in my quietest, darkest moments. Until recently the virtually constant adrenaline rush of fight after fight after fight has been enough of a distraction. Surviving today has been more important than thinking about tomorrow.

"What happens if we don't break the cycle? Where's this all going to end? If I trusted you enough to take off your chains and let you walk outside, all you'd see would be rubble and ruin. We're not safe here—no one is anymore—but we're in a better position than most. The world's falling apart, but the people here are getting stronger. We've been sifting through the debris looking for people like you, Danny, to rehabilitate. We're going to form that firebreak and stop the pain and hate from spreading."

He gets up quickly, as if he's just remembered he's supposed to be somewhere else. He moves closer to the bed as he pushes the chair back, and his sudden proximity makes me react. I quickly reach out for him with my left hand, but the chain snaps my wrist back when it reaches full stretch. Mallon doesn't flinch, but I can see him watching me over his shoulder. He did that on purpose to see if I'd bite. I watch him intently as he moves toward the door and try to maintain my aggression. I've been forgetting myself.

"That's enough for now. I might bring you some more food and water in a while. Until then, just try to relax. Build your strength up. You'll need it later."

What the hell did he mean by that? He quickly crosses the room again and replaces the board over the window. The impenetrable blackness returns. Can't stand it like this. *Don't leave me in the dark again, please.* He stands in the doorway, looking at me, waiting for a reaction. He starts to close the door.

"Wait—" I say, surprising myself with the sound of my own voice, but it's too late. The door's shut and Mallon's gone and all I can hear is the dripping in the corner.

23

IT FEELS LIKE AN eternity has passed before he comes back again. He enters the room hurriedly and doesn't look at me or speak. Unusually, he leaves the door open. I can see two other Unchanged men waiting outside, and my pulse starts to quicken. Is this my execution party? But that goes against everything he said earlier. I don't know what to think. I've lost track of what's bullshit and what's fact.

Mallon removes the strap across my forehead, then lies on the floor and does something to the chains holding my arms and legs down. I try to lift my head and look, but I can't see anything. He's out of sight under the bed for a couple of minutes doing Christ knows what; then he scrambles back up and brushes himself down. He stands on the other side of the room and looks at me.

"There you go, you can—"

Before he's even finished his sentence I've realized the shackles have been detached from the bed frame. I swing myself around in a sudden single, painful movement and use my weight to throw myself forward and stand up. My legs and arms are cold, numb, heavy, and unresponsive, but I know this is my chance to kill him. I raise my aching arms and stretch a length of chain between them, ready to wrap it around the fucker's filthy neck and squeeze the life out of him. I lunge, but he sidesteps easily, then sticks out a foot and trips me. I fall quickly, too fast to put my hands out and stop myself. My left shoulder clips the edge of the chair, and then my head smacks against the wall. I roll over onto my back in agony, head spinning and vision blurred. Mallon stands over me. He looks down, shakes his head, and tuts.

"Do you think I'm stupid?"

He moves the chair out of the way and sighs with disappointment.

"Honestly, Danny, weren't you listening to anything I said earlier? Haven't you worked it out yet? The more you struggle and fight, the less you're going to achieve."

In the confusion of my pathetic, fumbled attempt to attack, I managed to kick the door shut. It opens again, and Mallon gestures for the two men outside to come in. One of them, a huge, evil-looking bastard, grabs the chains hanging from my wrists and hauls me up onto my unsteady feet with worrying ease. *If he'd been like us*, I think to myself, *he'd have been a Brute.* He grips my arms tight, and it feels like I'm being squeezed in a vise. There's nothing I can do about it. The other man walks toward me and puts something over my head. It's a pillowcase, I think, thin enough for me to be able to breathe but thick enough to block out the light and stop me from seeing. The chains around my ankles are padlocked together. The floor is cold and wet under my bare feet.

"Stay calm and keep your temper in check and you'll be okay," Mallon says. "Fight back and you'll regret it."

Is that a threat or just a warning to play by his rules? Whatever, the slight glimmer of hope I'd been feeling since Mallon's earlier visit has gone now and has been replaced by fear. What are they going to do to me? I'm completely at the mercy of these foul bastards, and there's nothing I can do about it. I feel like a failure, ashamed that I've been beaten by the Unchanged. Even if I did manage to fight them off, I'm still bound and chained. I'd never get away.

"Move," the huge man standing behind me grunts in my ear, his voice deep, loud, and emotionless. He shoves me square in the middle of my back, and I fly forward, barely managing to stay upright and not trip over the chains between my feet. I almost fall, but one of the men—it might even be Mallon—catches me and pulls me back up.

Head bowed, all I can see is my dirty, shackled feet. My legs feel leaden with pain and weak with nerves as I realize this could be my final walk. All that crap about not fighting fire with fire and trying to break the cycle . . . it was all lies—a cheap, pathetic ruse to keep me occupied and catch me off guard. And the worst thing of all is how easily I fell for it. I should have seen through the bullshit. They were just trying to keep me pacified to make it easier for them to kill me when they're ready. What am I walking toward? A firing squad? A stoning? The room where I'll be given my lethal injection? I try to stop—try to turn around and fight my way out of this—but the fuckers surrounding me are having none of it. They restrain me, but they don't strike back, not even allowing me the satisfaction of going down fighting. When I stop struggling again, they relax their grip and let me walk on alone. The journey to my final destination feels endless. I think about Ellis, and then about Lizzie, Josh, and Edward, and the pain and frustration is too much to stand. I start crying like a fucking baby, sobbing and shaking and pathetic.

We turn right, and I trip through another doorway, stubbing my toe on a low step. This must be it. I'm led across a wide, open space by one of the men before being stood still—exposed, prone, and vulnerable. I feel him tugging on my chains, removing the shackles from my feet; then I hear the clink of metal on metal as another chain is wrapped tight around my waist, then attached to something behind me. I wait and listen as he walks away again, heading back in the direction from which we just came. I'm left here alone, swaying slightly, wrists still bound, my heavy legs still stiff and aching after endless hours of inactivity. I lean forward until the slack is taken up and the chains become tight enough to support my weight. I look down at my bare feet and the grubby, years-old carpet, crying pathetic tears of anger and desperation that bounce and splash off the floor. What will I see when they uncover my head? Will they even bother? Maybe they'll just shoot me blind. I picture the two men standing at the other end of the room on either side of Mallon, both of them holding guns aimed in my direction. They could fire at any second. These might be my last few seconds of life. My legs feel like they're about to give way, but I'm determined to stand proud and defiant and face this like a man. But this wasn't how it was supposed to end . . .

The pillowcase is whipped off my head and dropped on the floor. I close my eyes for a split second, then open them wide again and look up. Mallon is backing away from me. He's the only other person here. I'm standing alone in a large, open room, chained to the back wall by an industrial-strength bracket. The fear starts to lessen, and uneasy, tentative relief takes its place, but I know it's not over. Just because he hasn't killed me yet doesn't mean he's not still going to. The room is bright and cold. There are windows along one wall, but they're too far away and too high to see through. I can see the very tops of distant trees and the squally, rain-filled sky, nothing else.

Mallon watches me intently, then turns and leaves. The temporary relief immediately disappears with him. What happens next? Is this another gas chamber? There's no pipework or exhaust fans that I can see, but there are red and brown splashes and stains on the grubby wall behind me—blood, shit, and Christ knows what else. There are two filthy buckets over to my right, one of them full of water. Waterboarding? Torture? But I don't have any secrets or restricted information, so what can they hope to get from me? Or is it worse than that? Is Mallon about to start playing masochistic games with me? Rape me, even? Whatever he decides, there's nothing I can do about it. But when it happens I'll fight the fucker until either he's dead or I am.

He's back, this time carrying more food and a pile of clothes. My last supper?

"Move back," he says, watching me carefully. "Right up against the wall."

I do as he says, shuffling backward but not risking turning around. Mallon edges forward to the spot where I was standing, watching me constantly. He puts down the clothes and the food, then moves back again. He sits down a safe distance away.

"Help yourself."

Stunned, I can't help speaking. "What?"

"I said help yourself. The food tastes like shit today, but it's warm and it's better than nothing. And the clothes are from a dead man, I'm afraid. But hey, they don't stink of piss like yours do!"

I don't move. He gestures for me to come closer, and I slowly start to edge forward, moving like a bear circling a bloody lump of fresh meat in the middle of a trap. Is the food I'm shoveling into my mouth poisoned? It wasn't before. I sit down cross-legged and start eating, too hungry to care. I can't tell what it is I'm eating, and he's right, it does taste like shit, but that doesn't matter—it's food. It's finished too soon, and I wash it down with another bottle of stale, lukewarm water.

"Better?" Mallon asks, stretching out on the floor and appearing surprisingly relaxed. "I'll get you some more later. There's soap and water for you to wash with in one of those buckets over there. Scrub yourself down, Danny. Get rid of the stink and try to make yourself feel human again."

I don't argue. I get up and move over to the buckets. They're just inside the reach of the chains. I take off my soiled shorts and rip off my shirt (the shackles on my wrists preventing me taking it off any other way), then start to wash. There's an inch of disinfectant at the bottom of the other bucket, and its purpose is obvious. I drag it closer to the wall, turn my back on Mallon, and squat and shit. I wipe myself clean on the torn clothes I've just discarded.

I wash myself as best I can, then dry off with a blanket that Mallon throws over to me. I pull on a pair of trousers that just about fit, then wrap the blanket around my shoulders to keep warm. I walk toward Mallon until the chains are at full stretch. Bastard just sits there and looks up at me. He knows I can't reach him.

But then—to my complete amazement and disbelief—he throws a bunch of keys and some other stuff out of reach and stands up. He waits, psyching himself up; then he walks closer, so close we're almost touching.

"All we need—" he starts to say, but I shut the fucker up. I grab his collar, spin him around, and slam him down on the floor. He tries to fight me off, but I brush him aside. He's had this coming for too long. I drag him nearer to the back wall, his stumpy, pudgy, pathetic limbs flailing, then take up the slack from the chain around my right wrist and wrap it around his neck. He splutters, showering me with foul Unchanged spittle, and his already bulging eyes grow wider still. I pull tighter, feeling his life slipping away, focusing on the image of him lying dead at my feet.

"Kill me," he says, his breath a hissing, choked whisper, "and you've lost everything."

I pull harder, feeling the chain digging into his neck, constricting his windpipe and cutting off his air supply.

Then I stop. What did he say? Is he right . . . ?

He flops over onto his front, gasping for breath, and starts to crawl away. He's barely gone a yard when I snap myself out of this stupid malaise. I reach out, grab his leg, and drag him back, feeling myself getting stronger by the second. I roll him over and form my hand into a chain-wrapped fist. I'm ready to smash it into his face when he speaks again.

"Break the cycle."

I punch him, just catching his jaw as he turns his head away. I straddle his out-of-shape body, a knee on either side to stop him moving, ready to end his miserable life. My left leg is wet. He's pissed himself with fear.

"Now who stinks of piss?"

I lift my fist again, and he raises his arms to cover his face.

"Please, Danny. Show some control. Kill me now and they'll leave you chained up here to rot."

I pull my fist back even farther. If I hit him this time I know I'll finish him.

"Think about your family. Think about what you could do if you got out of here."

Bullshit.

Is it?

He's right about one thing—I'm still chained to the wall and I can't escape this room. And I know he only mentioned my family for effect, but how can I do anything to help Ellis if I'm stuck here and left to starve? I can see the keys on the floor, well out of reach.

Against my better judgment—against everything I feel and believe—I stand up and step back. Mallon scrambles to safety, holding his mouth and spitting blood onto the floor. Is the fucker going to leave me here now? He staggers away, then stops. Still rubbing his jaw, he turns around and grins, blood covering his yellow-white teeth.

"You did it! I knew you could!"

"What?"

"You did it, Danny. More to the point, you didn't do it."

I don't understand. He sits down, exhausted, breathing heavily. I walk as far as the chains will let me.

"I gave you a chance to kill me, and you didn't take it. You almost did, but you stopped yourself. You held the Hate."

"Only because—" I start to explain. He holds up his hand to stop me talking and washes out his mouth with water from my bottle. One of us must have kicked it across the room in the fight. He spits red-tinged water out onto the dirty carpet.

"Doesn't matter why," he says, "fact is you did it. Takes a person of intelligence to do that. Someone who can look beyond all this hatred and fighting and see what's really important."

Patronizing bastard.

"I made a mistake and you got lucky."

He shakes his head. "I don't think so."

"I do."

"No," he says, his voice suddenly more serious, "you're wrong. This is what happened—I gave you an opportunity to kill me, which you instinctively tried to take. But, before you could do it, you stopped and weighed up the pros and cons. And you realized your choice was pretty stark: kill me and rot here, or let me go and survive."

Bastard. He's right.

"What's important," he continues, "is the fact that you over-ruled your instincts. Like I said, you held the Hate."

I can't argue. I want to, but I can't. I sit down opposite him. I should have killed him, but I didn't. What does that make me? I feel strangely dirty and defiled, as if I've just made the most embarrassing, basic mistake, like a teenaged boy caught jerking off by his mom. In the distance I can hear the muffled thump and bangs of explosions. Elsewhere the fighting continues. It should have continued in here, too. I should reach across, grab hold of him, and kill him now. But I don't.

"So how did it happen to you?" he asks, mouth still bleeding. "I've told you my story, Danny, what your people did to my family. Now you tell me yours."

I say nothing.

"Come on . . . what have you got to lose by talking to me? Face facts. I could have had you killed when you first arrived here, but I didn't. I could have done it myself, but instead I've fed you, watered you, I haven't tortured you . . . You don't have any information I want, no top secret plans of attack . . . There's no need for you not to speak now. You've already done the hard part; now finish the job. Break the cycle. Talk to me like the rational human being I know you really are. It's up to you."

I can see the frustration in his face. Truth is, I'm not trying to be defiant now. I'm thinking about what he said. Either he's right and I've got nothing left to lose, or it's too late and I've already lost it all. Or is my sudden pathetic weakness just a result of the physical and emotional stress of captivity? Have I just lost the ability to think straight?

"Back in your room yesterday," he continues, "you flinched when I mentioned your family. Those things I found in your bag, the doll and the clothes . . . Do you want to start there? Are they trophies or reminders?"

I try hard to hide it, but my reaction when he mentions my family is disappointingly obvious. He immediately picks up on it.

"So what happened? Were you with them when you changed? Are you carrying around some kind of guilt because you killed the people you used to love?"

Can't help myself. He's hit a nerve. "My only guilt is that I didn't kill them." My voice sounds loud and overamplified, alien and strange.

"Tell me more . . ."

"I was confused, disoriented," I tell him, my words sounding angry, strangled by emotion. "Should have killed them, but I didn't. They caught me off guard."

"Partner?"

I nod my head.

"Kids?"

"Three. One like me, two like you."

He looks confused. "One like you?"

"Ellis, my daughter."

"What happened to her?"

I'm about to tell him, but I stop myself, suddenly remembering that I'm talking to one of the Unchanged. Don't want him to know she's the reason I came back to the city.

"Her mother took her," I answer, spitting out the words. He nods slowly, trying to make it look like he understands.

"Must be hard to deal with," he says. "I mean, I thought I'd had it bad, but at least I know what happened to my family. I know they're both dead and I've had closure, but you, you don't have a clue where any of them are or even if they're still alive."

"I should have killed them," I say again.

"I can't begin to imagine what you've been through. The realization you were a killer must have been hard enough. How did they get away?"

"I was disoriented. I'd kill them in a heartbeat if they were here now."

"You didn't kill me."

"No, but I—"

"You're from around here, right?" he interrupts.

"Depends where here is."

"What about the other two kids?"

"Two boys. One older, one younger than my girl."

"Really tough," he says quietly, shaking his head and rinsing his bloody mouth out again. "So how have you coped?"

Is he mocking me now?

"I've killed as many of you fuckers as I've been able to find," I answer, feeling my body start to tense up again.

"Except me."

"There's still time . . ."

"Okay," he says quickly, leaning back and looking up at the ceiling, "but has it actually helped? Has it got you any closer to getting your daughter back? I presume that's what you were heading back to the city for?"

Christ, I have to give him his due, he's good. That one came from out of nowhere.

"I'll find her if it's the last thing I do."

"That's good."

"Is it?"

He nods his head vigorously. "Of course it is. It shows there's more to you than just wanting to fight and kill all the time. You still give a damn about your daughter, and that means you've still got a chance. Honestly, Danny, most of the people like you who come through here are complete no-hopers, only interested in killing. You, you're different. You're thinking further ahead than the next battle."

"Doesn't mean I won't fight. Doesn't mean I won't still kill you."

"Of course not, but from where I'm sitting, killing me would be the worst thing you could do. How would it help? Like I said earlier, you'd just be fighting fire with fire. Just stop for a second and work your way back, Danny. Think about everything that's happened to you to bring you to this point. The Hate has taken everything you ever had. It's stripped you of your soul and your identity. It's stopped you functioning as a human being."

"It hasn't. I know exactly—"

"You've lost everything because of it . . . your family, your home, your daughter. If it wasn't for the Hate you might still be with her now. Christ, man, it's even cost you your dignity and your freedom. You've spent the last two days lying in a bed of your own piss, tied up and caged like an animal. And at this precise moment in time, you're close to losing control of your future, too. If I wanted to I could walk out of here right now and not look back. I could leave you here alone to starve and die. You don't know where you are, how many other people are here, what's on the other side of the door to this room . . . Face it, Danny, right now all you have is me."

He stops talking and waits for me to respond, but I can't. All I can do is stare back at his barely human face. Is he right? He shuffles forward until he's just within reach. Is he taunting me? Testing me?

"People tell me I'm wasting my time with your type. They tell me you're no better than animals, that you've got dog blood running through your veins and you should be rounded up and shot."

"I don't care what they—"

"You know what I tell them? I tell them they're wrong. But you're the only one who can really decide who's right. If the boot was on the other foot and I was your prisoner, Danny, what would you do now?"

"I'd—"

"Stupid question. We'd have never got to this stage. You'd already have killed me. You could do it now if you want to, but I think you're better than that."

He moves forward again. I move to scratch the stabbing itch by my right knee, which has just returned, and he flinches. He's trembling. Is this just part of the act, or is his fear genuine?

"Cooperate with me and prove the rest of them wrong. Show me you can control your emotions and I'll help you. I can get access to records. I could try to find out what happened to your daughter."

That doesn't ring true at all. It smacks of desperation, and he knows it.

"Bullshit."

He shrugs his shoulders. "It might be, but what have I got to gain? More to the point, what have you got to lose?"

Head's spinning. Can't take all this in. Can't think straight. My heart says kill, but something's telling me to wait because he's right, fighting has got me nowhere. And if there's even the slightest chance he'll be able to help me, should I take it? He leans back and picks up the keys. He takes one of the keys off the ring and throws it over to me.

"For the chains around your wrists," he says. "Take them off and finish getting dressed."

I do as he says, stretching my arms and flexing my muscles. The freedom feels good after endless hours of being wrapped in chains. I walk back across the room to the pile of clothes. All the time, Joseph stays seated on the floor. He's within the reach of the chains around my waist. We both know I could kill him if I wanted to. He's terrified, I can see it in his eyes, and that gives me strength to hold my nerve. I hold the Hate.

Maybe I'll give him a chance. If he lets me down, I'll kill him.

THE TORRENTIAL RAINS WERE unexpected, weather forecasts a long-forgotten luxury. The flash floods wreaked unprecedented destruction on the city center refugee camp and its densely packed population. Those living out on the streets bore the brunt of the pain as almost a month's worth of rain fell in less than two hours, literally washing away scores of people and their few remaining belongings. Blocked and broken drains stopped the water from draining away, transforming many streets and pavements into stagnant lakes. The basements and ground floors of countless buildings flooded. Almost half of the military base in the municipal park was washed away, with a huge number of refugee-occupied tents being lost. Then, to add insult to injury, as quickly as the rains came, they disappeared. Thankfully the sun remained hidden behind a layer of heavy cloud for most of the day, but the summer heat and a few sharp bursts of sunlight were enough to dry out and bake the bedraggled world below. Every outdoor surface was caked in a layer of foul-smelling mud, a grubby tidemark on building walls a grim reminder of how high the floodwaters had climbed. Huge mountains of rain-soaked garbage and waste began to ferment, the insect population feeding on them seeming to multiply by the hour.

Constant helicopter patrols continued to police the border and the exclusion zone. All scheduled missions outside the city were temporarily abandoned as, for once, the already severely depleted military forces turned their attention to the thousands of people supposedly in their care. Their orders were simple: Get as many people off the streets as possible (living or dead), then clear the major routes through town.

Ahead of the motley collection of vehicles that crawled slowly along Arley Road, groups of soldiers on foot moved from building to building through the early evening darkness. One of the snowplow-fitted trucks was used to clear a route through, pushing tons of sodden waste toward the gutter and leaving a noxious, three-foot-high drift of garbage in its wake. Hazmat-suited soldiers followed it along the freshly scraped pavement, pulling corpses from the mire and loading them into the backs of the yellow refuse and recycling trucks that had been recently commandeered from the now-dissolved city council.

A group of three soldiers emerged from a building that had once been a large house but in more recent years had been converted into office space. By flashlight, one of them spray-painted a simple message onto the brick wall beside the door, a message for those who followed.

37 INSIDE

6 DEAD

20 MORE

Ignoring the countless frightened questions and the grabbing hands of the refugees who surrounded them, the soldiers moved on to the next building. Thirty-seven survivors, six bodies to remove, space for twenty more inside.

There was a sudden loud thump on the door of room 33. Mark jumped up from the space on the damp floor where he'd been trying to sleep and ran to the door, tripping over Kate's father's leg, which hung out of the bed. He pressed his eye against the spyhole.

"Who is it?" Kate asked, standing close behind him.

"Soldiers."

"Don't let them in."

"I have to."

The lead soldier thumped the door again and yelled for them to open up.

"Don't," Kate pleaded.

"If I don't open it they'll batter the damn thing down."

Before she could protest he pulled the door open. Three soldiers barged through, pushing him to the side. They stood in the middle of the room, each of them shining a flashlight around, exposing every corner of the small, cramped space.

"What's going on?" Mark asked, positioning himself directly in one of the beams of light.

"Assessing space," the soldier replied, looking around, his voice devoid of interest or emotion. "How many you got here?"

"Five of us. And five's more than enough. There's barely enough room as it is. We can't fit anyone else in—"

"Who?"

"What?"

"Who's here?"

"Me, my girlfriend, her parents, and my cousin's wife. And my girlfriend's pregnant. Like I said, there's no room for anyone else."

One of the other soldiers made a note on a clipboard. The others continued to look around. Kate forced her way between them, stopping one of them from getting around the side of the double bed. She stood in front of him, thrusting out her pregnant belly for maximum effect.

"He told you. There's no more space here."

The soldier ignored her, moving her out of the way, then ducking down and glancing under the bed. He shined his flashlight onto the bed's occupants, the two wizened, starving, elderly refugees shaking in fear under the sheets like characters from a Roald Dahl story.

"Your parents?"

She nodded. He spun around. Lizzie sat on a chair in front of the bathroom door, her legs drawn up beneath her, nervously chewing on her nails. She kept her eyes down, refusing to look up. Mark tried diplomatically to coax the soldiers back out.

"My cousin's partner," he explained, keeping his voice low so she couldn't hear him. "He was, you know . . . one of them? She lost her kids, and it's really fucked her up. Honestly, man, it's not a good idea to put anyone else in here with us. What with the baby coming and—"

"Not my decision, pal," the soldier said.

"But I've been a volunteer," he protested. "I've been outside the city with you. I've been—"

"Not my decision," he said again. With that the soldiers left the room. Mark slammed the door shut and leaned against it, staying there until he was sure he'd heard the door to the next room opening. He started to walk back to the others, but Kate stopped him.

"We can't go on like this," she whispered. "We should find somewhere else for her. It's not safe here."

"And where exactly *is* safe these days?" He sighed, leaning back against the door again.

"But she's—"

"She's family. They all are. Your family, my family . . . our family. We stick together, and that's all there is to it."

"But Mark—"

"Would I ask you to throw your parents out?"

"That's different—"

"Is it? I'm not talking about this again, Kate. It's a pointless conversation. She's family and she stays. No one's going anywhere."

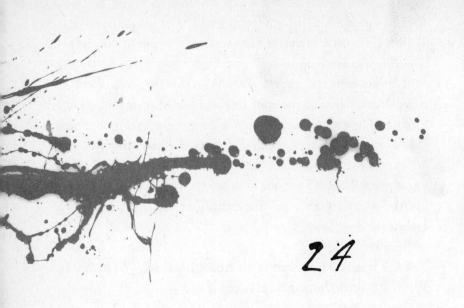

24

BACK IN THE CELL. I cooperated and let them bring me back here. Thought the silence and darkness would help me work things out. My head was covered along the short walk back.

The longer I've been left, the more uncertain I've become again. Don't know who or what I believe anymore. I can't understand why I didn't kill Mallon when I had the chance, but at the same time I know that while I'm here, he really is my best and only hope. He hasn't screwed me over so far. But if he does, now he thinks I trust him, I'll kill him before he even realizes I've turned.

I'm still chained to the bed, but now the shackles are only loosely anchored to the metal bed frame, and I'm able to move around. I've been able to move the board and look outside for the first time, but the view is disappointingly limited. All I can see from this window are the redbrick walls of other parts of this building and the gray slate roof of another section below. I can see a few other windows, and I've been watching them, hoping to catch sight of other people like me. I haven't seen anyone else yet. It's dark now. Maybe I'll see more tomorrow.

My head is spinning. Still can't think straight and work this out. The lines between what I feel and what I know are blurring to the point where I can't make sense of anything anymore. I keep swinging between feeling anger and frustration that I didn't kill Mallon, then wanting him to come back again so we can talk some more. I want him to tell me what he knows about Ellis, but at the same time I know he won't have found anything out. I don't even think he has the means to find out, but I can't rule out the fact that he might. Maybe I'll just kill him when he next comes into this room and put an end to all this pointless screwing around.

I sit back on the bed (I've turned the mattress, but it's still damp) and look up at the ceiling, tracing the familiar patterns in the yellowed paint again. If I killed Mallon (and I know I could), what would it achieve? I still don't know where I am. For all I know I could be surrounded by hundreds of Unchanged, all of them armed to the teeth. I could be dead before Mallon's body is cold. No, as hard as it is to swallow, right now he's all I've got.

But what does he really want from me? Ignoring all the bullshit, why is he doing this? He's already made it clear I don't have anything he wants, so is he still playing mind games just for the hell of it, or does he think he can house-train me like a pet? When you consider all the options, other than looking for a "cure" or resorting to extermination, trying to learn how to tame or control us is probably the only viable option the Unchanged think they have left.

So what do I do?

I'm daydreaming now, imagining walking around this place unchained, mixing freely with the Unchanged. I picture myself in a crowded room, surrounded by them but not yet killing, forcing myself to swallow down the fear and hold the Hate. I look into their faces, their stupid, evil, ignorant faces, and none of them knows who or what I am. They need their DNA tests and records and the strength of our reactions to be able to see what we are. But we, on the other hand, simply *sense* them. We know what they are without a word being spoken . . .

Fuck. The penny drops.

The enormity of today suddenly hits me like a hammer blow. Does Mallon even realize what he's done?

Today I resisted the temptation to kill. Regardless of the reasons why, I stayed in control and didn't fight. And if I truly can hold the Hate, then in time I could do exactly what I've just been imagining. I could walk among the Unchanged undetected. Imagine the power and advantage that would give me . . . I could stand shoulder to shoulder with the enemy unseen. I could go anywhere, do anything, kill anyone . . .

But can I do it? Can I really chose to hold the Hate at will? Or did Mallon just catch me at my weakest ebb?

I think back to that moment earlier today when I could have killed him but didn't. I wanted to do it, but I stopped myself. And it wasn't Mallon's words that stopped me . . . *I stopped myself.* I could do it again, I know I could.

It doesn't matter what I believe, whether or not I subscribe to Mallon's bullshit theories of breaking the cycle and not fighting fire with fire; the fact is he's handed control back to me, and I have to take advantage of it.

25

FOOD," **MALLON ANNOUNCES AS** he barges into the room, waking me up. It's late, and he's carrying his lamp. The familiar urge to kill fills me as soon as I see his face, but I force myself not to attack. I swallow it down like unspewed vomit, the nauseous unease sitting heavy in my gut. I get up and stand opposite him, and although he tries to hide it, I can see the nervousness in his eyes. The longer we remain facing each other, the more confident he slowly begins to become. But I can still feel his fear. I can almost taste it.

"You, my man," he says as I take the tray from him and sit back down on the bed and start to eat, "have done incredibly well."

"Thanks," I mumble, my mouth full. Truth is, I don't give a shit what he thinks. I'm just relieved, excited almost, that I managed not to attack. It's hard, almost too hard, but I force myself to keep control. I try to concentrate on the food to distract myself, but the urge to kill him refuses to fade. I struggle to keep it in check, almost dropping the tray and lunging at him when he moves. I manage to regain my focus at the last second. This is almost impossible. It's a constant fight, almost like I'm having to remember to breathe.

"I'm really pleased," Mallon continues, even the sound of his voice making my guts twist with agitation. "You've really understood what we're trying to do here. You know, most people take a few more days to get to this stage, but you, you've got brains. You've worked it out in no time."

"Not a lot to work out really, is there?" I say, trying to keep up the illusion. "It's like you said, the more you fight, the less you get."

"Exactly."

He watches me a while longer as I polish off the rest of the tasteless food. I glance up and see he's looking at me like a proud parent, and it dawns on me that he really does believe all the bullshit he's been spinning. I feel vastly superior to this idiot. He thinks he's the one in the driver's seat, but I'm in control. The mental advantage I have now makes it easier to cope.

"So what next?" I ask, feeling calmer and more assured. I decide to hedge my bets and see how far I can push him.

"What do you mean?"

"What's your plan? Do you just want to keep me locked up here forever? Is this some kind of rehabilitation program you've started? Or are you going to start experimenting on me and cutting me up into little pieces?"

Smug bastard starts laughing.

"You're good! No, to tell you the truth, Danny, what happens next isn't up to me."

"So who decides?"

"Two people."

"Who?"

"You, for one."

"And . . . ?"

"And Sahota."

"Sahota? Who the hell's Sahota?"

"You'll find out tomorrow."

He starts moving toward the door. Suddenly this is a conversation he doesn't want to have.

"You can't just walk out now. Who is Sahota?"

I stand up again and move toward him, but all that does is make him move faster. He stops midway out of the door—just beyond the reach of my chains—and turns back to face me.

"Boss man," he says simply. Now he's definitely playing games again, feeding me just enough detail to keep my interest, then clamming up and leaving me dangling. It's all he's got left. Other than these physical chains, information is the only advantage remaining. If he was any closer I'd rip his fucking throat out. He pulls the door shut, but then stops and opens it again. "Wait. There's something I forgot to tell you."

"What?"

"Your daughter . . ."

"You found her?!"

I can't hide my sudden interest and emotion. Please tell me something . . .

"No," he says, shaking his head. "You've got to understand, Danny, information's hard to come by these days. You learn more from what you're not told than from what you're told. The Central System is creaking under the weight of what's happened and—"

"Tell me!"

He sighs and takes a deep breath, drawing it out as long as he can.

"There's good and bad news."

"Give me both."

"The bad news is there are no records of her anywhere."

"So how can there be any good news?"

"Can't you see, that *is* the good news. It means she might not be dead."

"She might not be dead . . . that's all you can tell me?"

"Be thankful for small mercies, Danny. As far as I know, my daughter's still lying on the kitchen floor with a bloody hole where her face used to be. I could have been standing here telling you the date your girl died and where they burned her body. As it is, you've still got some hope. What you do with it is up to you."

He slams the door shut and locks it.

SIX A.M. **SANDWICHED BETWEEN** two heavily armed military jeeps and chaperoned by columns of soldiers and militia fighters, several hundred displaced refugees were led out along Arley Road. With no regard for personal preferences, friendships, partners, or relatives, specified numbers of individuals were filtered off toward each building. No one resisted or complained. They were too tired and too scared to show any defiance or opposition to what they were being told to do. Their choices were stark: put up with it or fuck off and take your chances on your own. And anyone who dared show any resistance to the military would be on the street with a bullet in the head. Public order *had* to be maintained.

. . .

"But there's no more room in here," Mark protested, blocking the door of room 33. "I told them last night—"

Uninterested, the soldier shoved him out of the way and forced his way in.

"What's the problem?" Kate asked, getting up from the end of the bed and standing in his way, instinctively wrapping her arms around her pregnant belly, cradling and protecting her unborn child.

"There's no problem," he answered quickly, his tired, gruff voice muffled by his face mask. "New roommate for you, that's all."

"But that's crazy! We don't have enough space as it is. How are we supposed to—"

The soldier put his hands on her shoulders and pushed her back down onto the bed, then turned and walked back toward the door again, pausing only to sidestep Mark. Mark knew there was no point trying to argue; at best he'd just be ignored, at worst he could be accused of being a Hater and "removed." Kate chased after the officer, far less concerned about the potential repercussions of her outburst. Behind her, her parents sat up to try to see what was happening. Her father, weakened by age, fear, and malnutrition, simply lay back again when he couldn't see anything, too tired to care. Her mother, once an intelligent, demure, and gentle woman, balanced on the end of the bed half naked, screaming like a banshee.

"There's enough of them in here already. We don't want more. You take them and find somewhere else for them to go. You can't . . ."

Kate ran back to silence her, leaving Mark at the door to placate the soldier.

"Gurmit Singh," the trooper announced as he shoved an elderly Asian man into the room. Singh protested with a high-volume, high-speed torrent of Punjabi, which was neither understood nor acknowledged by anyone. A battered leather carryall was thrown into the room after him, containing the sum total of his worldly possessions. He tripped over the bag, almost losing his light-orange-colored turban in the process, then turned around and continued his vociferous tirade. When the soldier pulled the door shut in his face, he simply turned again without pausing for breath and continued unloading at Mark, who shook his head.

"Don't understand," he said, desperate to shut the man up. "Speak English."

"No English," he snapped back, then continued his rant in Punjabi.

"He can't stay here," Kate's mother screamed from the bed. "We can't have his type here . . ."

Singh pointed at her, or was it at the bed? He rubbed the small of his back, then thumped his hand on the mattress and raised his voice to an ever louder, even more uncomfortable volume. Mark tried reasoning with him, desperate for him to be quiet. Singh ignored him, then picked up his bag and angrily sat down in the armchair in the corner of the room, still yelling furiously and pointing at the bed.

Kate stood by the hotel room door, her hands over her ears, desperately trying to block out the endless, directionless noises coming from both her mother and Gurmit Singh. Mark tried to hold her, but she pulled away from him, almost recoiling from his touch.

"I can't stand this," she sobbed. "Either they go or I go."

"None of us can go anywhere. For Christ's sake, Katie, that's the problem, there's nowhere else to go."

"I don't care. Kick them out. Throw them out on the street if you have to."

"Who are you talking about now?"

"You know exactly who I mean. It's too dangerous. We've got to think about ourselves and the baby and just screw the rest of them—"

"I can't. You know I can't—"

"Then I will. I mean it, Mark, if you don't get rid of them, I'll leave."

"Katie, there's nowhere for them to go. Please, sweetheart, just calm down and—"

"Don't patronize me. Don't tell me to calm down. How can I calm down when—"

"Shh," he begged, putting his hand up to her mouth. "Please don't shout, Katie, they'll hear us. Don't do anything that'll give them any reason to come back in here. You know what'll happen if they do."

"Maybe I should," she said, pushing him away. "Maybe that's exactly what I should do. Maybe if they knew what was going on here they'd help. They'd come up here and get rid of—"

"Shut up!" he hissed angrily, covering her mouth again.

Gurmit Singh, who had just started to quiet down, suddenly exploded into life again, startled by the appearance of Lizzie, who emerged from the bathroom.

"Who the hell's this?"

"Mr. Singh," Mark answered. "He's just been delivered."

"But we don't have any space—"

"We can't have his kind here," Kate's mother yelled, reaching out and grabbing hold of Lizzie's arm and pulling her closer. Lizzie shrugged her off.

"Too many here," Singh yelled back, suddenly switching to English. "Back bad. Need bed."

"Oh, you can do the language when it suits you, then," Kate sneered at him.

"What's going on, Mark?" Lizzie asked.

"Nothing we can do about it," he began. "We don't have any say—"

"We can't go on like this," Kate interrupted, desperate tears welling up in her eyes.

"We have to—" Mark started to say.

"Tell me what I'm supposed to do, then, Kate," Lizzie snapped angrily. "I heard what you were saying. I know what you want—"

"Then do something about it!"

"Where else am I supposed to go? What do you want me to do?"

Another outburst from Singh interrupted the argument. He got up from his seat and pushed between them, still gesturing toward the bed. Furious, Lizzie shoved him back down again.

"Back off!" she spat before turning to face Kate again. "Put yourself in my shoes, Katie. What would you do?"

"She can't stay here. It's not safe. You're putting all of us at risk."

"Look around, we're already at risk. Everyone who's left alive is at risk, for Christ's sake."

"Calm down, both of you," Mark whispered, trying unsuccessfully to separate the two women, worried that their noise would bring the soldiers back.

"I'm not going to calm down," Kate yelled, throwing open the bathroom door and pointing inside. "That thing in there is evil."

"That thing in there is my daughter."

"She killed your sons!"

"I know, but she's still my daughter."

Lizzie knelt down in the doorway. Curled up on the floor in front of her, chained to the sink pedestal, gagged and bound and heavily sedated, lay Ellis. Lizzie stroked her hair and ran her hand gently down the side of her tranquilized face.

"She could kill you, Lizzie. She could kill all of us."

"I know, but I can't let her go. Try to understand . . ."

"There's nothing to understand."

"Yes there is. What if your baby turns out to be like this? Will things be different then? Could you imagine giving your baby up?"

"No, I—"

"She's my daughter, Katie, and no matter what she is, what she's done or what she might still do, she's my responsibility. I'll protect her and fight for her until the bitter end."

"If we go on like this," Kate warned, "that will be sooner than you think."

26

THE MORNING I THOUGHT would never come is finally here. I lay on the bed for hours, but I couldn't sleep. It reminded me of being back in the apartment with Ellis, when we shut ourselves off from the others and slept on Edward's top bunk. I kept thinking about her wide, innocent eyes. Oblivious to all that was happening around her, she curled up alongside me, full of love and complete, unspoken trust.

Barefoot and cold, I've spent most of the last few hours looking out of the small window, watching the darkness turn to gray as the sun rose over the roof of this bizarre prison.

I've stood here for hours trying to work out who this Sahota might be and what he wants from me. I've taken some reassurance from the fact that I'm sure Joseph Mallon's naive trusting of me is genuine—he put his life on the line several times yesterday, and all that any of the Unchanged have left now is their lives. He's either supremely confident and brave, stupidly optimistic, or, and this seems most likely, he genuinely believes all the crap he's been peddling. So will Sahota be the same? I've been trying to work out my tactics, deciding how I should play my showdown with Boss Man. But how can I prepare for a meeting in a place I don't know with a person I've never met?

It's all irrelevant.

The only thing that matters now is getting out and looking for Ellis. The war . . . us and them . . . taking sides—all of that has to take second place from now on. I'll play along with Mallon and his hippie/pacifist/conscientious objector bullshit for as long as it takes until I get out of here. Unless, of course, they don't intend to let me out. Then I'll resort to my backup plan—my Plan B, which used to be Plan A: start fighting and don't stop until every last one of the fuckers is lying dead at my feet.

The door finally opens, and Mallon strides in. About time. There's no tray of food and no small talk or niceties either this morning. It's like he's just got a job to do. Is he abandoning me and moving on to a new pet? Or is he just unable to look me in the eye because he knows what's coming next? I want to attack him, but I don't, forcing myself to swallow the Hate back down like poisonous bile.

"What's going to happen?" I ask, instantly regretting having spoken. Christ, how far I've fallen. It's bad enough that I'm being held captive by the Unchanged; now I'm begging them for information, too. Pathetic.

"I told you last night. You're going to see Sahota."

"Yes, but—"

Mallon stands up straight and looks at me, still on guard but allowing himself to relax slightly. He puts a hand on my shoulder, and I resist the temptation to shrug it off.

"Have faith, Danny. Sahota is a good man. The kind of man who could bring an end to this war."

That doesn't make me feel any better.

"But who is he? What does he want to see me for?"

My questions obviously sound as desperate as I suddenly feel. Mallon manages half a smile.

"You'll find out."

He bends down and takes the shackles off my feet. Now the only chains left are those that bind my hands together. I could kill him now, but that would be a mistake. If I'm going to kill anyone this morning, it should be the main man, not one of his minions.

Mallon leads me out into a wide corridor. There's no security this time, no bag over my head, and I get my first proper look at the building I'm being held in. It's an odd-looking place, nothing like the prison I'd imagined. The walls are bare, their light yellow paint faded and peeling, and the air is cold. There are traces of religious paraphernalia lying around like the crucifix in my room—a painting of some serene-looking woman at the top of a staircase, some unfathomable ancient slogan scrawled across another wall, enough crucifixes to ward off a whole army of vampires.

We reach a T-intersection at the end of the long corridor, walking under an unrepaired hole in the roof where rainwater has poured in and soaked the carpet. To my left the corridor continues toward another long staircase. To my right there's a short, narrow landing, then three steps leading up to an ominous-looking door. Is this my Room 101? Is this the very end of my journey? All the fears and uncertainties I'd managed to dismiss suddenly manifest themselves again. My pulse is racing and my throat's dry. My body tenses. I stop and turn toward Mallon. The urge to kill him is strong, almost too strong...

"Don't, Danny," he pleads pathetically, my intent obviously clear, "please don't. You're so close now..."

He moves past me quickly, climbs the steps, and opens the door. He pushes it wide open, and I edge a little closer to try to look past him and see inside. It looks bizarrely like a doctor's waiting room, more like another short corridor than a room—clean, a door at either end, light flooding in through a skylight, a low table and a row of three chairs against one wall. I take a step closer, my curiosity and nerves getting the better of me. Mallon stands there, blocking my way, and it's like he's somehow taunting me. Can't stand this. This bullshit has gone on for too long. I don't think there's anyone else in this damn building. I'll kill him, then fight my way out of here.

I run at the fucker, but he sidesteps, then pushes me into the other room. I spin around as he slams the door in my face.

"Don't blow it," he shouts as it shuts. I hear a bolt slide across, then hear his muffled voice still talking to me. "Keep the faith, Danny, you're almost there. Remember everything you've learned."

I hammer on the door, but it's no use—it's locked, and he's gone. How could I have been so fucking dumb, to walk into a simple trap like this?

I'll wait for Sahota to show his face now.

I'm ready to fight. Bastard won't know what's hit him.

27

SILENCE. **ABSOLUTE, TOTAL FUCKING** silence. I stand and watch the other door, waiting for it to open, ready to attack. No one's coming. Is this another setup? More stupid games? Making me wait and trying to get me to panic and crack? Too late for that now.

Both doors are locked, but the skylight above is open slightly. I climb up onto one of the chairs, my hands still bound together, and try to haul myself up. The rattling chains are heavy around my wrists, and the frame of the skylight doesn't feel strong enough to support my weight. I'll pull it down before I—

"Going somewhere?"

I drop, spin around, and throw myself at the figure standing in the other door. I swing my chain-wrapped hands at his head, hard enough to decapitate him. He manages to somehow duck out of the way, then shoves me in the gut. I trip over the chair I was just standing on, falling back and cracking my head hard against the floor. I roll over and try to get up, but this bastard's fast. He pushes me back down and plants a boot right between my shoulder blades, stopping me from moving. I brace myself for his next strike, but it doesn't come, and he lifts his foot off. I look back and watch him walk away. Confused, I drag myself up, using another chair for support, suck in a deep breath of air, and turn around to face him.

What? How can he . . . ?

"You must be Danny McCoyne," he says, but I can't answer. "I'm Sahota."

Standing in front of me, wearing a smart, if a little crumpled, pin-striped suit and a remarkably clean white shirt, is one of our people. He's not Unchanged. I do a double take, but I know I'm right. This man is a friend and an ally, and I immediately know we're on the same side. He's short and his build is slight, but he stands tall with confidence and composure. The surprise and confusion he obviously sees on my face are clearly not unexpected.

"Apologies for all the subterfuge and bullshit over the last few days," he says, gesturing for me to follow him through into the next room. He stops just inside the room as if he's remembered something important. He checks his trouser pockets, then pulls out a key and undoes the chains around my wrists. He throws them out into the waiting area and closes the door behind us.

All I can do is stand and stare at Sahota. I don't know what I was expecting, but he isn't it in any way, shape, or form. He's a good foot and a half shorter than me, dark-skinned, with close-cropped dark hair, graying at the temples. He has a neatly trimmed mustache and wears a pair of wire-framed glasses. For the first time in months I'm suddenly conscious of my shabby appearance—dead man's trousers and shirt, no shoes, hair long and shaggy, face covered in stubble and bristle.

"Come in and sit down," he says, ushering me farther into the room. It's a wide, spacious, and relatively clean and uncluttered office-cum-living-area. In one corner is a metal-framed bed, similar to the one in my cell but with clean bedding folded back with military precision. Along one wall are several huge, mostly intact windows (only one pane of glass has been boarded up), and in front of me is a large wooden desk with a single chair on either side. Sahota locks the door, then sits down at the desk with his back to the window. He beckons for me to sit opposite.

"Where do you want to start?" he asks in a clipped, well-educated accent as he pours me a drink and slides it across the table.

"Don't know," I mumble pathetically between thirsty gulps of water. Truth is, I've got so many questions to ask I'm struggling to make sense of any of them.

"Don't worry." He grins. "It's not unusual. You've been through a lot."

"I don't know what I've been through."

He grins again. "We wouldn't have done it this way if there'd been any alternative."

"So what exactly have you done?"

"Which one of them looked after you? Selena, Joseph, or Simon?"

"Looked after me?! That's not how I'd put it."

"Which one?"

"Joseph."

"And what did he tell you?"

"Lots of bullshit about breaking the cycle, not fighting fire with fire, holding the Hate . . . He said the more I fought, the harder it would get."

"Did you believe any of it?"

I shrug my shoulders. Truth be told, I'm still not sure what I believe.

"Bits of it made sense."

"Well, some of what he said must have had an effect on you, because you're here and he's still alive. You'd have killed him otherwise."

"He said I was only locked up here because of the Hate. He said the more we fight, the less we get."

"And what do you think about that, Danny?"

"I'm not sure what I think."

"But you must have some kind of opinion. You can't tell me an intelligent man like you lay there alone in the darkness for hours and didn't think about what he'd been told."

"I think he was right when he said we were stuck in a vicious circle and that things are only going to get worse . . ."

"Go on."

"But I don't understand what difference that makes. What else are we supposed to do? We can't live with the Unchanged, we have to kill them."

"You're absolutely right."

"So how do we win a war without fighting?"

Sahota stands up, picks up his drink, and walks over to the window. He looks out, choosing his next words with care and consideration.

"There is an alternative."

"Is there? I can't see one."

"That's because you're looking in the wrong place. You need to change your perspective, Danny, and that's what this place is all about. That's why we're here. Tell me, before we brought you here, did you ever hear anything of Chris Ankin and his plans?"

"I heard his messages when the war started, and I was with a group for a couple of days. They said they were trying to build an army."

He turns back to face me. "And what did you think of that?"

"Gut reaction?"

"Yes."

"As soon as we start grouping together in large numbers, the enemy will blow the shit out of us."

"Exactly right. We're still outnumbered, and they still have a structured military with a just about operational chain of command. We'd only be able to take the fight to them on limited fronts, and yes, they'd probably blow us out of the water. While we're concentrating on one of their cities, the others would still be standing strong. They've already shown they're willing to sacrifice thousands of their own to try to wipe us out. You've only got to look at how they lost London—"

"What *did* happen to London?"

"You didn't hear?"

"Not really, only a few details."

"It was early on, before these refugee camps were set up. It wasn't something we planned; rather it was something they couldn't prevent. The capital was too big for them to defend, too sprawling . . . London showed us what we could achieve. The fighting on the streets must have been incredible. I almost wish I could have been there. There were hardly any of us in comparison to them, but the panic we caused was beyond anything we could have hoped for. They reached critical mass . . ."

"Critical mass? I don't understand."

"The point of no return . . . the point where it was impossible for them to regain any order, where the number of individual battles was so high and the fighting so intense that they could no longer separate them from us. They didn't know who was who anymore. The only option left to them was to destroy everything."

"They destroyed London?"

"The whole city and everyone in it. Wiped out thousands of our people, but they took hundreds of thousands of their own with them."

We're digressing, and I'm confused.

"I still don't understand. What's that got to do with you holding me here?"

"In the end it was their confusion and panic that destroyed London, simple as that. But like I said, if we'd attacked with an army, they'd have seen us coming and wiped us out before we'd even got close."

"You said I was looking in the wrong place . . ."

"That's right, and so were they."

"Still don't get you. Look, I'm sorry, you've spent days fucking with my brain, and I'm tired. Stop talking in riddles and just explain."

"Have you ever heard of a text called *The Art of War*?"

"I've heard the title. Don't know anything about it, though. Never read it."

"It's a Chinese guide to warfare, written by Sun Tzu more than two thousand years ago."

"And? What did he know about us and the Unchanged?"

"Nothing at all! But even though this war is unique, some of Sun Tzu's tactics for fighting remain as valid today as they were in ancient China. He said that all warfare is based on deception. We have to fool our enemy—make them believe we're weak when we're strong, make them think we're miles away when we're next to them. 'Hold out baits to entice the enemy. Feign disorder, and crush him.'"

Sahota recites the script perfectly from memory. He waits for a reaction from me, but my head's still spinning, and I can't make sense of anything. He senses my confusion and explains.

"They're expecting us to fight head-on. As far as they can see, our only tactic is to fight and keep fighting until we're the only ones left standing. When you get deeper into the city you'll see how that stops them from interacting and—"

"Wait a second," I interrupt. "What do you mean, when I get deeper into the city?"

Sahota grins and pours me another glass of water.

"They're expecting us to run straight at them with fists flying, screaming in their faces. What they're not expecting is for us to be standing beside them and alongside them. We're going to go deep into their cities to stir up trouble and cause them to panic. Then, when they're too busy tearing themselves apart to notice, Ankin's army will come into play. We're going to make them destroy themselves from the inside out."

"But how are we supposed to do that? Get within a few yards of any of them and all we'll be able to do is fight."

"Is that right? Didn't you learn anything from your time with Joseph?"

It finally makes sense. That's what this place is about.

"Holding the Hate . . ."

"That's exactly it," he says, sitting down again and leaning toward me. "Thing is, this is the only way to teach someone how to do it. If you're not held or restricted in some way, you'll kill them before you realize what you're doing."

"But Joseph . . . ?"

"Joseph and the others are just puppets. They have no idea. They genuinely believe what they tell you, but it's all just bullshit in the end. Joseph's the best—or the worst, depending how you look at it. Some days all I want to do is kill him myself."

"Incredible . . ."

Sahota's eyes are wide with excitement. "Think of the advantage this gives us, Danny. We know who they are, but they can't tell us apart until we start fighting. They won't even know we're there until it's too late."

"Jesus Christ."

"We're having to move fast. For various reasons things are

deteriorating rapidly in the city. Normally we'd have given you a few more days here to make sure you understand, but time's a luxury we no longer have. This is the perfect time for us to do this. Think you're up to it?"

Talk about being put on the spot. I fumble for an answer for a second, before realizing that there's only one thing I can say.

"Yes."

"Good man! That's the spirit! As soon as they told me about you I knew you'd be a good candidate."

"What do you mean by that? Who told you . . . ?"

"We send people out looking for battles. They wait on the outskirts of the fighting, watching out for people like you who manage to demonstrate some degree of control and don't just attack. Let's face it, we'd be wasting our time trying to teach this stuff to Brutes, wouldn't we?! No, we need people like you who are able to take a step back and consider the options before committing to an attack. People who use the Hate and control it rather than letting it control them."

He looks me straight in the eye. "Tell me, do you remember when you first stood next to Joseph and didn't attack?"

"I remember."

"And what were you thinking at the time, Danny? Were you thinking what he was saying was right, or were you just toeing the line to get the best out of a bad situation?"

The memory of the last few days is filled with confusion and uncertainty, the distinction between "us" and "them" suddenly unclear. But now that I'm away from my cell and Sahota has put his question so simply, the answer's clear and unequivocal. Everything has been brought back into sharp focus.

"I was playing with him. Stringing him along. Doing what he wanted me to do just to get food and freedom . . ."

"Exactly! A perfect answer! From the moment you decided not to kill him, you were in control."

This is too much to take in. Sahota watches me intently, and I'm uncomfortable under his constant gaze. I try to look anywhere but back at him. The sun breaks through the heavy gray cloud cover momentarily and streams in through the dirty office window. Christ, I've been so preoccupied with this bizarre conversation that I'd forgotten my newfound freedom—in the back of my mind I still think I'm chained to the spot. I get up and walk around the side of the desk.

"You local?" Sahota asks.

"Don't know yet," I answer. "That depends where local is. Where exactly are we?"

"Not far from the hospital where we picked you up. A couple of miles maybe."

"A couple of miles in which direction? Farther away from the city center or . . . ?"

My words trail away to nothing as soon as I look out of the window. I know this place. Sahota's office overlooks a narrow parking lot. Beyond that, the long, overgrown back gardens of a row of once well appointed but now derelict houses stretch away. Beyond the houses is a small, sloping, oddly shaped patch of parkland, the brightly painted swings and slides of a children's play area looking strangely at odds with the chaos of everything else I can see. A narrow track between two of the houses connects the parking lot to the road, and a huge wrought-iron gate prevents anyone unwanted from either getting in or getting out.

"Is this—" I start to ask.

"Holy Sisters of the Poor, to give it its original title," he explains, standing beside me and looking down. "Strange place, this was."

"Strange?"

"Part convent, part nursing home. Ideal for us."

He's not wrong. The huge, strong, brick-built complex is like a fortress. Built in the middle of what used to be a fairly affluent area, and hidden from view by houses on all sides, it's set back off the road and surrounded by enough tall fences, gates, and walls to keep even the most determined intruder out. Most people wouldn't even have known it was here at all. From what I remember, this used to be a convent, which became a church-run, community-funded rest home. I'm sure Lizzie's dad, Harry, had a friend living here for a while . . .

"This is Highwell, isn't it?"

"We're on the border between Highwell and Steply, to be precise."

"But that's . . ."

"About two miles from the center of town."

"Yes, so we're . . ."

"Already in the city. Right on the innermost edge of their exclusion zone."

"Christ . . . How many people like us are here?"

"Not many, just me and a couple of others at any one time. Apart from me this place is almost exclusively staffed by my team of idiot Unchanged pacifists who think they're saving the world. As soon as people like you have learned how to control their emotions I send them out into the city. Like I said, the situation's deteriorating rapidly out there. We don't have a lot of time to waste."

For a moment all I can do is stand in silence and stare out of the window. Beyond the parking lot and the houses, everything appears completely lifeless and still. There are the usual telltale signs of battle, and everything appears even more overgrown and wild than I remember, but the world otherwise just seems abandoned and empty. The longer I look, though, the more I see. In the distance a single helicopter flies toward the city center, visible only in the gaps between the tops of trees. There's a pile of corpses in the park, dumped in a flower bed. Closer, in the shadows of the parking lot directly below, several Unchanged carry bags of supplies between one building and another, constantly looking over their shoulders for fear of attack. Along the road to my far right, a battered car is slowly approaching. It enters the complex through another gate and narrow passageway, then stops in the shadows of the tall perimeter wall. I watch as two Unchanged deliver another fighter like me, his arms and legs already tightly bound. It strikes me that the irony of what's happening here is beautiful; these fools think they're working toward some kind of salvation, but all they're doing is training their own assassins.

"I've set up a number of sleeper cells right in the heart of the city," Sahota says. "I want you to join one of them."

"Okay," I answer quickly and without thinking through any implications. It'll get me out of here, and right now that's the most important thing.

"I'll get your stuff brought up, and I'll give you directions, contact information, and some supplies. Get out there, get used to being neck deep in the enemy, then find your cell."

"And then?"

"And then you sit and wait for the signal."

"The signal?"

"When the time's right, all the cells will be instructed to take up positions deep in the heart of the city. Then, when we're ready, each cell will start fighting, causing as much panic as possible. Just imagine it, Danny . . . sudden swells of violence, loads of them in random locations, and all happening at the same time for no apparent reason. The enemy won't know what's going on. They won't even see us there. They'll look straight through us and turn on each other, and it'll be beautiful, like dropping a match into the gas tank of a car. Before you know it, the whole city will be tearing itself apart. Think of it . . . we'll be less like terrorist cells, more like cancer cells."

It sounds magnificent. All too easy.

"So all we have to do—"

"All *you* have to do," he interrupts, correcting me, "is get in there, wait until we're ready, then cause as much mayhem and carnage as you can."

I stare out of the window again, trying to fully appreciate the importance and danger of what I'm being asked to do.

"This is an honor, Danny. You've shown incredible strength and self-belief to get this far. What you're going into the city to do will never be forgotten."

28

A **COUPLE OF HOURS** ago I thought I was a dead man. And now here I am, a backpack full of weapons, supplies, and Ellis's things on my back, walking through the dead ruins of the city I used to call home, ready to help bring the enemy down. This new world order is fickle and unpredictable; one minute you're down, the next you're on top again.

The roads around Sahota's building were reassuringly quiet and empty, and I felt confident and strong. But the moment I saw the first of the Unchanged I began to doubt myself again. There were three of them, huddled together in the doorway of a partially collapsed building, barely visible from the street, just eyes staring out from the darkness. Even after all I've been through, my instinct was still to kill. No one would have been any the wiser, and with my knives and axe hanging from my belt again, I was sure I could have got rid of all three of them without even breaking sweat. But I was scared—scared that if I started killing out here I wouldn't be able to stop again. I forced myself to relax, to overcome the temptation and keep moving. The foul fuckers watched me like hawks as I passed them, but two thoughts kept me moving forward. First, I knew that if I made it into the city there'd be a chance, albeit a slight one, that I might be able to find out more information about what happened to Ellis. Second, I knew that the longer I lasted without killing and the deeper I managed to get into town, the more casualties there'd be when the fighting finally started again. It was easier letting those three live (if you could call that living) knowing that it might bring me closer to killing thousands of their kind.

Unexpectedly, the more Unchanged I've subsequently seen, the easier being around them has become. I still have to fight to control myself each time I see one of them, but their vast numbers act as a constant reminder that to start killing now would be suicidal. Or maybe it's just that seeing them like this, crammed together and on their knees in such desperate, miserable, appalling conditions, reinforces my comparative strength and superiority. These people are nothing.

Christ, I'm cold. I run my hand over my freshly shaved head and chin as I catch a glimpse of my reflection in a grubby shop window. I look like a new man, like I've been reborn on my escape from the mindfuck of the last few days. It was something Sahota said I should do, something I'd never even considered. He told me to try to blend in with the Unchanged masses. While I've been content to wear the same fighting clothes day after day until they're too worn out to be any good, some of the Unchanged, incredibly, still seem to think about their appearance. Sure, standards have slipped, and there are no downtown stores selling the latest fashions anymore, but, to a surprising number of them, how they look still seems to matter. It's all about being accepted, he told me, blending in and being part of the crowd. I saw a woman a minute ago who was still wearing makeup. Why? What's the point? Stupid bitch. It doesn't matter what you look like when you die.

Concentrate on breathing, that's my technique. I force myself to keep my breathing low and level, to move slowly and keep to a steady, deliberate pace. If I start thinking about killing and fighting, I try distracting myself with trivialities, counting lampposts, avoiding cracks in the pavement, trying to remember the names and the faces of people I used to know . . . It's the weirdest sensation— I imagine this is how a recovering alcoholic must feel. As long as I'm not killing, I'm fine. But if I were to attack just one of them, like the alcoholic falling off the wagon and having his first drink, I know I wouldn't be able to stop. I remember Mallon's catchphrase: The more you fight, the less you get. He was right. If I cause any trouble out here on my own I'll be completely screwed. Stay calm and I still have a chance.

My surroundings are bizarre, not at all what I expected. The streets and buildings on the inside of the enemy cordon look different from all the others I've so far seen. Out beyond the city limits, outside their exclusion zone, everything has been pounded into ruin by weeks and weeks of fighting. Over the weeks and months the Unchanged military attacked us with relentless ferocity and unchallenged explosive force, reducing much of the outside world to a ruined wasteland. Some villages and small towns I've seen were hit so badly that they've simply ceased to exist—just mounds of overgrown rubble are all that's left where they used to be. Here, though, the basic structures of streets and buildings are still largely intact, but they look like they're slowly decaying. Everything is covered in a thick layer of detritus and grime. Ahead of me is a slag heap of uncollected waste, some of it in ripped black sacks, most of it lying loose in the gutter. Rats and other vermin scavenge through the mountain of garbage in broad daylight, suddenly cocksure and confident, no longer afraid of man. Birds peck at bodies, and there's a steady trickle of stagnant, foul-smelling water running away from the huge decaying mound. It pools in the gutter and spreads out into the road, the street drains blocked. It's become a black lake, the gentle breeze making its surface ripple, floating bits of rubbish bumping around like odd-shaped boats.

The address Sahota gave me is a place not far west of here, on the inner border of the exclusion zone. He warned me to stick to main routes and to stay out in the open, no matter how strong the temptation was to try to disappear. I can already see the logic in his advice. The population here seems to be in a bizarre, almost trancelike state of "false calm." For the most part people line the sides of the streets, cramming themselves into the shadows, each of them trying to squeeze themselves into as small a space as possible, almost as if they want to disappear. Some hide in the dark gaps between buildings; others sit behind the wheels of useless, abandoned cars that are never going anywhere again. I glance up at the windows of the places I pass. There are pale faces pressed against the glass, not a single scrap of space left unclaimed. Around me is an apparently never-ending succession of lost, haunted individuals. Alone or in twos and threes, most of them look down at the ground, too afraid to even make eye contact with anyone other than their few remaining trusted friends or relatives. The instinctive urge to kill them is undiminished, but these people aren't even worth the effort. They are empty, vapid shells. As good as dead already.

There are other people moving along the road, many of them going in the same direction as me, some walking aimlessly the other way. None of them seem to have any purpose. They're just drifting, and I do my best to match their slow, purposeless gait. It's hard, like being forced to hold your hand in a bowl of boiling water. I want to run to get through this part of town, but I don't dare do anything that's going to draw attention to me or mark me out as different. There's an unspoken tension and fear here, bubbling just under the surface. Everyone, me included, is being forced to keep their emotions suppressed, terrified by the prospect of what might happen if they let their true feelings show. As much as the thought of comparing myself to the enemy is abhorrent, I realize that everyone here, me included, is doing exactly the same thing. We're all pretending to be something we're not.

Apart from the odd military vehicle, the constant buzz of helicopters scurrying through the air above me, and the occasional rumble of distant, directionless fighting, everywhere else remains unnaturally quiet. I walk along a road that runs parallel with the side of the City Arena, a huge, soulless concert venue I could never afford to go to. There are blockades around the perimeter of the vast building for as far as I can see, and a heavy military presence around the doors and exits. There are scores of empty trucks parked in its various lots. Was this some kind of feeding center? Whatever it was, it looks like it's been decommissioned now, but there are still huge numbers of civilians camped around its outskirts, waiting silently for supplies that will probably never come. In another fenced-off area nearby is a still-smoking mound of corpses. Must be hundreds of bodies there . . .

I'm distracted by the grim sights all around me, so much so that I collide head-on with someone coming the other way who's obviously paying as little attention to the human traffic on the road as me. The unexpected impact catches me off guard. In a sudden, uncontrollable blind panic, I spring forward and grab the disheveled-looking man by his lapels. I spin him around and slam him down onto the pavement and reach for my knife before . . . before I remember where I am and who I am. I let him go immediately and walk on, terrified that I've been seen and that my sudden violent overreaction will give me away. I look back and see him scramble away, getting up quickly and sprinting a few yards until there's a decent distance between us. He puts his head down and keeps walking, trying not to panic, frequently looking back over his shoulder. I glance from side to side. There are plenty of people watching me, but thankfully they're all too scared to get involved.

Fucking idiot. Can't afford to make mistakes like that.

I know exactly where I am now. Around the next corner is the PFP—the Parking Fines Processing center, where I used to work. When I see the building I'm immediately filled with a mass of conflicting emotions—disgust that I wasted so much of my miserable former life here, relief that those days are long gone, and, catching me off guard, a painful nostalgia when I remember all that I've lost and left behind. It all seems forever ago, like the memories belong to someone else. Being here again and remembering this place and all that happened here is like watching a TV movie of someone else's life. Christ, there are people living in the building now. I can see them in the windows I used to spend hours staring out from. Could there be a worse existence than that?

Without realizing it, I've stopped right outside the PFP. I'm standing in the middle of the street like a dumb sightseer, suddenly oblivious to everything else around me. The noise of a fast-approaching engine snaps me out of my dangerous stupor. I turn around and see that there's a jeep driving up the middle of the road toward me, flanked by several heavily armed soldiers on either side, their impenetrable face masks hiding their intent. Are they looking for me? The jeep moves forward quickly, the driver making no attempt to dodge or weave through the masses of drifting refugees that litter the street. They jump for cover, staying well back until the troops have passed by. Preoccupied by my irrational fear and not knowing whether I should do nothing or fight, I'm slow to react. A soldier shoves me to one side, and it's all I can do not to kill him. I stand firm and square up to him, stupidly defiant, my face reflected back at me in his visor.

"Problem?" he yells, his wretched face just inches from mine. I can feel bile rising in my throat, a noxious, nauseous terror building up inside me, and I don't know if I can keep it down. Can I stand to let him live? When all I want to do is kill, doing nothing is almost impossible. But I force myself to remember being back in the cell with Joseph Mallon, and remembering the fact that I was so easily able to fool him gives me much needed strength. *Act dumb*, I plead with myself. *Let this one go. You'll kill thousands more when it's time* . . .

"No problem," I answer, and I back down and slope away, trying to mimic the reaction of the countless other cowards milling around me. I feel his eyes burning into me, but I don't allow myself to look back. I keep walking . . .

Ten seconds and nothing's happened.

Don't look back.

Another ten seconds. Have they moved on?

I turn the corner and I know I'm safe.

Millennium Square.

Last time I was here I got caught in the crossfire between groups of armed police officers who had suddenly found themselves on opposing sides. I ran for cover along with hundreds of other people, each person as scared and confused as the next. That was the day, I recall, when everything really changed. That was the day the Hate took over. Strange how what was such a terrifying experience now seems, with hindsight, like nothing out of the ordinary. I'm harder now, stronger. Back then I was just one of the crowd, trying to blend in with the masses and not be noticed. Today I'm here to kill them.

This vast public square is no longer the empty, underused space it always used to be. For as far as I can see the ground is covered with a sea of temporary shelters of endless different colors, shapes, and sizes. I can't help looking into a few of those that I pass, and inside each of them I see more refugees desperately hoping that their flimsy cardboard, wood, and polyethylene structures will keep them safe inside and everyone else out. The occupants of one shelter are both dead. The green-tinged corpses of a middle-aged couple are lying together motionless, entwined and unnoticed. The stale air inside the small space is thick with flies.

Squatters have taken over the public toilets and moved in. They used to get vandalized every other week and were used more as a pickup point for gay men than anything else. A man and woman sit on chairs in the dark doorway, like a king and queen surveying their particularly grim kingdom. A fierce-looking, half-starved dog tied up with rope keeps everyone else at bay.

There's a patch of land up ahead that's unexpectedly empty. As I get closer I see that the road there is covered with streaks and puddles of drying mud, making it look like a dried-up riverbed. Flash-flood water seems to have washed away huge numbers of improvised tents, leaving an expanse of muddy block paving slabs visible. Weeds are sprouting in the gaps between the slabs. The council used to spend a fucking fortune on this place—I remember hearing someone from another department bitching about it—now it's just as godforsaken as everywhere else. Incredibly, though, a street clock I walk past is still working. It says it's coming up to 3:00 P.M. and it's a Thursday, for a fraction of a second I feel an instinctive swell of relief because the weekend's coming. Christ, how stupid is that? It makes me realize that no matter how much everything has changed, the effects of years of conditioning are going to take more than a few months to disappear. Has the clock been maintained purposely for precisely that reason? Does it help the Unchanged masses cope if they know where they are in relation to their old routines?

Something on the far side of the square has caught my eye. Covering virtually the full width of two adjacent buildings from ground level to a height of about six feet are what looks like hundreds of posters. As I get closer, I see that it's a huge collage of photographs of people that have been pinned, nailed, and stapled to massive sheets of plywood used to board up the buildings. I move nearer, figuring it's safe to do so because there are other Unchanged milling around here, too. It looks like nothing out of the ordinary. I've seen similar displays in films and on TV before, shattered populations coming together to share their grief and build an improvised shrine to remember the friends and family they've lost. Maybe Lizzie's picture is here somewhere? I start to look along the rain-blurred and sun-bleached pictures.

I stop and stare at a random face, one of hundreds, no more or less remarkable than any of those above, below, or around it. It's a man in his late forties with a mop of curly dark hair, a short beard, and dark, angular-framed glasses. There's writing in the space below his face. It says, "James Jenkins. Killed his wife Louise and daughter Claire." There's a similar scrawled message on the next picture: "Marie Yates. Murdered everyone that mattered to me." These aren't the faces of victims, I realize, these are their killers. Christ, is my face up here somewhere? I panic and start quickly scanning the display, suddenly self-conscious, hoping I'll find my picture before anyone else does. Wish I hadn't shaved my head like Sahota said. I should have stayed hidden beneath that layer of stubble and shaggy hair. Then, bizarrely, I find myself making a sudden U-turn, hoping that I actually do manage to find my photograph because that, I tell myself, would be proof positive that Lizzie's been here.

It won't make any difference.

I force myself to move on, knowing that I can't afford to waste time. Somewhere in this stinking, unhygienic, overcrowded wreck of a city, the woman I used to share my life with might still be hiding. And if I can track her down, she'll be able to tell me what happened to my daughter.

29

I MUST BE GETTING close now. I thought I knew the address Sahota gave me, but around here it looks so very different from how I remember. I'm back out on the farthest edge of the refugee camp, heading for the border with the exclusion zone. The number of Unchanged around me has quickly diminished as I've moved out from the center of the city again. It's a relief not to be surrounded by them and not to have to constantly struggle to keep myself under control. The buildings here are more empty than occupied. There are one or two Unchanged almost always in sight, but they make every effort to ignore me and slide back into the shadows when I approach.

I stop outside a fortified house, metal grilles and bars covering its windows and doors. The houses on either side have been destroyed, but this one looks like it's managed to escape much of the fighting undamaged. Curious, I walk down a dark, narrow passageway between the house and the rubble of its nearest neighbor. The badly decomposed body of an Unchanged man lies facedown in the middle of an overgrown lawn, military fatigues flapping in the wind around his skeletal limbs. He's been dead for several weeks at least. Was he the owner of this place? The back door's been pried off its hinges, and I go inside. Most of the furniture has been used to blockade each room, leaving just a chair, a small table, and a bed in an upstairs bedroom. The remains of boxes and boxes of supplies cover the floors, and the walls have been daubed with pointless, empty slogans. DEATH TO THE HATERS is one, KILL THEM BEFORE THEY KILL YOU another. There's nothing of value left here. I leave the house, shaking my head and laughing to myself at the pathetic Unchanged who clearly spent so long trying to defend and protect what was his. Total waste of effort. He'd have been better off taking his chances in the center of town with the rest of them.

The wreck of a truck blocks the road ahead. It's over on its side like a beached whale, the contents of the overturned Dumpster it was carrying now scattered across the entire width of the road. I clamber through the clutter and continue down a sloping ramp toward what was once a busy local shopping area. My footsteps echo around the small, drab, square plaza. Half of the open space is submerged under a shallow pool of black, germ-filled water. At its deepest point a dead soldier's booted foot sticks up above the rippling surface like a shark's fin.

Around me are a succession of abandoned and looted stores—a bookmaker's with signs in the window advertising odds on an international soccer match that never took place, a fish-and-chip shop, a takeout pizza joint, a hairdresser's, a general store . . . I don't waste time looking in any of them. If there was ever anything useful in there, it would have been taken or destroyed by now.

I cross the plaza diagonally, feeling increasingly uncomfortable and exposed as I walk around the edge of the lapping lake of dirty rainwater, a Hater deep in Unchanged territory. Are they watching me? Eager to get under cover, I quicken my pace and head out between another two deserted buildings. Then I finally see the place Sahota sent me to find. The Risemore Conservative Members Club is as ugly as everything else around here, a squat, square, redbrick social club that looks like it might actually have benefited from having a bomb dropped on it. I used to do all I could to avoid places like this in the days before the war. When I was little, before he walked out on us, my dad used to drag me out to his drinking club some weekends. I'd sit there with him, bored out of my mind, having to make one can of Coke last for hours while he got drunk, smoked, read the paper, argued with his equally drunk cronies or sat and watched piss-poor comics, singers, and variety acts that, by rights should have been banned from performing in public. As I edge closer to the club I automatically build up a mental image of what it's going to be like inside: loud, stale, musty, a heavy fug of cigarette smoke hanging in the air, grubby, sticky carpets, uncomfortable plastic-covered seating with the stuffing hanging out . . .

I can't get in through the front entrance; an impassable mound of fallen masonry blocks the door. I go around to the back to look for another way in, cursing my naïveté. I was never supposed to get in through the front. You don't want just anyone to be able to stroll up and knock on your front door if you're trying to coordinate a terrorist cell, do you? Is that what I am now, a terrorist? A suicide bomber without the bomb? Or am *I* the bomb?

A narrow, brick-walled passageway runs from the front of the building straight through to the back, opening out into an enclosed but largely empty parking lot. Can't see anyone around here, or even any evidence that anyone's been here for a while. There's a fire exit, a strong, metal-clad doorway. I hammer on it with my fist and wait for an answer, starting to doubt whether I'm at the right place. A mangy tabby cat darts out from under a hedge behind me, racing across the parking lot and scurrying for cover under an over-flowing Dumpster. Instinctively I whistle for him. I used to like cats.

The fire door opens, catching me off guard. I spin around and find myself face-to-face with a tall, powerful, nasty-looking bastard covered in tattoos. Thank God we're on the same side.

"I'm looking for Chapman," I tell him, remembering the name Sahota told me to ask for.

"Who is?"

"I am," I answer without thinking.

"And who are you, you fucking idiot?" he sighs, taking a step forward and forcing me away from the building, into the middle of the parking lot. He rests his hand on the hilt of a monstrous knife with a vicious serrated blade.

"My name's Danny McCoyne," I answer quickly, trying to sound confident and disguise my nerves. "Sahota sent me here."

At the mention of Sahota's name the thug visibly relaxes. He looks me up and down again, then stands to one side and ushers me into the building. I do as he says and wait for him to follow as he pulls the door shut again and secures it with a heavy wooden cross-beam. He leads me through the ground floor of the building. My eyes are slow to adjust to the darkness indoors, and I trip down off a slightly elevated wooden stage area. He looks back at me and shakes his head.

Inside, the club is as dilapidated as everywhere else, nothing like the stupid, outdated image I'd had in my head. The floor is littered with the broken remains of off-white polystyrene ceiling tiles. Makes me wonder—if the ceiling's this bad, how strong is the rest of the building? Disappointingly (but not unexpectedly), the bar has been completely stripped. There's a row of spaces on the mirrored wall where the liquor dispensers would have been. Christ, I could do with a drink just to calm my nerves. I feel more anxious in here than I did back in the center of town when I was up to my neck in Unchanged.

My chaperone doesn't want to talk. He leads me along a wide corridor, through another, much smaller second bar, then up a long staircase. There are four doors leading off a square landing. Three of them are open, and I can see at least one or two people in every room. He opens the remaining door, and I follow him into a large function room, which is almost as big as the main bar area we walked through on the floor below. It's sparsely furnished but largely undamaged. There are several wooden crates of supplies stacked up against one wall. A guy is sitting by himself at a table in the far corner using a laptop, and there's another asleep on a mattress under a window. As soon as I enter the room a woman gets up from where she's been lying on a threadbare sofa. She's hidden by shadows, but something about her is familiar. I'm sure I've seen her before. Is she Chapman?

"Who's this?" she asks. Her voice has a trace of a gentle Irish accent, which is beaten into submission by the abrasiveness of her tone.

"Says he's looking for you. Says Sahota sent him."

My unwilling guide disappears, his job done. The woman walks toward me, stepping into the light. I immediately recognize her, but I can't remember where from. Was it this life? My old life?

"The slaughterhouse," she says.

"What?"

"The slaughterhouse, few days back. You're trying to remember where you saw me before. You were there with the guy with the smashed-up hand and foot, and I—"

"You were the one telling me not to bother with him 'cause

231

he'd be dead soon," I interrupt, suddenly remembering where we met.

"That's right. And he was. I'm Julia Chapman."

"You're a happy soul, aren't you?" I say sarcastically as I shake her hand, recalling how blunt and matter-of-fact she was when we spoke before. She nearly crushes me with her viselike grip. She's just trying to let me know who's in charge.

"I'm a realist," she answers, "and I'm focused. And so should you be. I tell you, when this war's finished, I'll be the first one up dancing at the fucking party and the last one to sit down. Until then, though, all I'm interested in is fighting."

"Bit of a coincidence, though, finding you here."

"You reckon?"

"I thought you were busy recruiting for Ankin's army."

"I still am."

"So why are you here?"

"To make sure Sahota gets the right people, too."

"What? Are you trying to tell me you followed me into the city?"

"I'm not trying to tell you anything, but yep, something like that. There were a few more people involved, and it wasn't just you we were watching."

"Don't believe you."

"Believe what you like, pal, it really doesn't bother me. Thing is, we are where we are, and where we are is here. It's what we do next that matters most."

"If you say so."

I wonder if she always talks this much bullshit or if she's trying to impress me and exert her authority. She looks me straight in the eye, and for a second I think she might be about to throw a punch. She bites her lip and turns away.

"Come here. I want to show you something."

I follow her out of the room and across the landing. We walk through another part of the building, where two more fighters are resting in the shadows. They glance up at me as I pass them, but they don't move. We go out onto a narrow veranda, then use an unsteady stepladder to climb up onto a debris-strewn flat rooftop. There are large puddles of water covering much of the ground. A pair of deckchairs have been left under an improvised stretched-out tarpaulin shelter. The views across what remains of the city from one direction and the exclusion zone on the other three are vast and panoramic. Looks like they've been using this place as an observation post.

Julia leads me to the edge of the roof on the side of the building that looks out over the refugee camp in the center of the city. The view is incredible, not just because of its scope, but also because of the sense of scale and perspective it gives everything. In every other direction all I can see is abandoned buildings and immense swathes of empty land. Our land. No trace of the Unchanged.

"Takes your breath away, doesn't it?"

Julia's soaking up the view, staring with palpable hate deep into the city where hundreds of thousands of refugees are cowering in squalor. Their closeness still makes me feel uneasy.

"Is this what you wanted to show me?"

"It is, but don't just look at it, think about it. Feel it, even. All across the whole country, our enemies are hiding together in places like this. Thousands of them crammed together in the space of just a few square miles at a time, stacked on top of each other, hardly able to breathe. Now turn around and look at what we've got. Out beyond the city boundary you can walk for miles and hardly see anyone."

"I went back to where I used to live," I tell her. "Couldn't believe what little space we had..."

"And you know what makes it worse?" she continues, not listening. "Those idiots still have faith in the people who are supposed to be leading them, not that they ever see them or hear anything from them. Christ, they don't even know who they are. They're just clinging desperately to the structures and organizations that used to keep their pathetic little lives ticking along, trusting in a system that was dying long before we ever appeared."

"Can you believe we used to—" I start to say before she interrupts. Her over-the-top enthusiasm for all of this is frightening.

"You know, some of those fuckers still think they're going to be protected and that everything's going to work out all right for them in the end. Thing is, you and me and everyone else knows different, don't we?"

"They'll never win," I answer quickly, standing my ground as an unexpected gust of wind threatens to blow me forward. "They can't."

"And that's why what we're going to do is going to have such an effect. We're gonna pull the carpet out from under their feet."

"How many of us are here?"

"Including you, ten."

"Is that enough?"

"We're not the only group. There are others. I know Sahota wants to get more than a hundred of us in place when the time's right."

"And you think this is going to work?"

"No question. The Unchanged can't trust each other. Christ, they can barely bring themselves to look at the person next to them anymore. I mean, there's never been any real trust between strangers, but now they've got it into their heads that anyone could turn on them at any second. So there's real fear in the air in there, a tension and uncertainty that's never going to disappear. The more of them that cram themselves inside the city walls and the longer they're in there, the more that fear increases."

"So we just walk in there . . ."

". . . and light the fuse. They're right on the edge. I give 'em a week at most, ten days if they're lucky, and that's without us getting involved. No food, no sanitation, no medicine, the floods—"

"Makes you wonder how they've lasted this long."

"Have you been in there yet?"

"Coming here just now."

"So you know what it's like?"

"I saw enough . . ."

"Thing is, they're all out for themselves, whether they'd admit it or not. Every one of them will do all that they can to survive, screw everyone else. Self-preservation means everything to them. It's all they've got left."

"So when do we do it? When do we go in?"

"It's up to Sahota. He'll know when the time's right."

"And how will we know?"

"We'll know, trust me."

"So do we just sit here and wait?"

"We do tonight, maybe tomorrow, too. Then we'll be told to get into position. Could be hours after that, might even be days. We get in, bury ourselves deep, then explode. It's a small sacrifice to make."

Sacrifice? The word makes me go cold. I'll fight alongside these people, but I don't intend to sacrifice myself. Not while there's a chance Ellis might still be out there.

"So we do enough to push them over the edge, then get out?"

"We do enough to push them over the edge, then keep pushing," she answers quickly, sounding annoyed by my obvious lack of enthusiasm. "What we do in the city is all that matters. You don't think about the future, getting out, leaving the fight . . . anything like that. If you're left standing at the end of all of this, well done. If you're not, then that's too bad. This is way bigger than any of us."

With that Julia walks away and leaves me alone on the roof. I watch her go, feeling like I've just shut myself away with a group of kamikaze cult members.

Vii

MARK HAD TO FIND more food. He didn't want to think about what would happen if he didn't. Impossible choices would have to be made. How could it have come to this? Kate had to eat, she was his obvious priority, but who next? Gurmit Singh could go to hell as far as he was concerned, but what about Kate's parents? Her dad was in his late seventies, her mom not much younger . . . could they really justify wasting precious supplies on them at their age? Christ, what was he thinking? Leaving them to starve? He himself needed to eat because he couldn't stand the thought of Katie and their child trying to survive in this nightmare world without him. Then there was Lizzie. What was her position in the pecking order? As for that thing she kept tied up in the bathroom . . . Mark cursed the day he'd agreed to let her stay with them.

The hotel room diagonally opposite 33 was empty. He'd heard noises there a while earlier and had watched through the peephole in his door as the occupants had fled. He wasn't sure exactly what had happened; someone cracking under the pressure of this impossible situation and being hunted down as a Hater, he guessed. The soldiers hadn't come to investigate (they never did anymore), and there were at least two bodies still in the room, but he didn't care. As soon as he'd seen the rest of them thunder down the stairs in panic, he'd known he'd have a couple of minutes to get in there, strip out anything of value, then get out before other refugees claimed the precious space.

Mark felt like an amateur forensics investigator trying to piece together a murder scene as he stood in the small room and stepped over the first corpse. It was a mirror image of the room where he and the others were living. A woman lay on the floor, her face pallid and gray, savage welts, bruises, and scratches covering her neck. In the opposite corner, a man who he'd assumed was either her partner or her brother sat slumped with blood pouring out of razor slashes across his throat and wrists. The cuts were still dripping. He was the one who'd snapped, Mark assumed. Looked like he'd taken his sudden aggression out on the woman, then killed himself with regret. Another pointless waste of lives.

No time for sentimentality. He began searching for food, looking in the corresponding hiding places to those he used himself in the room across the hall. There were a few scraps; nothing much, but it was better than going back empty-handed. At least he'd be able to—

A piercing scream cut through the uneasy silence. He knew immediately that it was coming from room 33. He grabbed the food and ran, tripping over the outstretched legs of the dead woman as he frantically sprinted back. He already knew what was happening. He could hear her. She was loose.

Mark reached for the door and pushed it at the exact same moment Gurmit Singh pulled it open from the other side. In a single movement he raced into the room, dragging Singh back inside and kicking the door shut behind him. He couldn't risk him getting out and telling anyone what they were keeping in here, not that they'd be able to understand him anyway.

The kid was on the bed, naked but for a dirty gray undershirt, her wrists still bound together with a plastic tie but her legs free. Her tiny hands were wrapped around Kate's father's throat, and she was repeatedly yanking his head up, then slamming him back against the wooden headboard. Kate and Lizzie both tried to pull her off the old man, but she refused to let go, her small but strong clawlike fingers digging into his skin and holding on. Mark pushed them both aside and wrapped his arms around the little Hater's waist. He backed away from the bed, dragging both the girl and the old man with him. Lizzie pried her daughter's fingers off Kate's father's scrawny neck, then shoved him back up onto the mattress. Behind her Kate's mother screamed, a constant, vile, eardrum-piercing, high-pitched wail of absolute terror and bewilderment.

"What the hell happened?" Mark asked between grunts of effort as he struggled to hold on to Ellis. He wrapped his arms tighter around her chest, restricting her movement. She leaned her head forward and bit down into his forearm; the sleeve of his thick jacket protected his skin. "Where's her fucking gag gone?"

Before anyone could answer, Ellis jerked her head back again, cracking against Mark's chin. He bit down hard on his tongue and yelped with pain. Less than half his size, she continued to move relentlessly and with incredible ferocity, refusing to give up despite the fact that, for now, he had her held tight. He knew that if her hands hadn't been tied, several—if not all—of the people in the hotel room would almost certainly have been killed.

Ellis made another desperate bid for freedom, arching her back, then relaxing, doing it again and then kicking her feet back, catching Mark full in the balls on the rebound. She managed to wedge her foot against the nearest wall and pushed, the sudden movement catching him by surprise and sending him reeling backward. The sickening thud as he slammed against the opposite wall made him lose his grip. Ellis squirmed away from him and raced back into the room toward the old people in the bed, but Kate was waiting for her. She smashed her across the face with a heavy telephone directory. Stunned, Ellis dropped to her knees.

"Don't!" Lizzie shouted, running toward her daughter as Kate stood over her, ready to strike her again. She shoved the other woman out of the way, then crouched down and thumped a hypodermic needle into Ellis's bare thigh. Ellis yelped with sudden pain. With the needle still stuck in her skin, she spun around and lashed out at her mother with her bound hands, managing to scratch her nails down her cheek, leaving three parallel bloodred lines.

Then she stopped.

Eyes glazed, she tried to stand up again. She took two steps forward, then fell and hit the grimy carpet, face first. She tried to pick herself up again but was out cold before she'd lifted her head.

The room was instantly silent. Even Kate's parents became quiet—her mother in shock and her father concussed. Gurmit Singh, who'd been cowering against the door with his hands over his head, stood up and reached for the handle. Mark also stood, the throbbing pain in his balls beginning to subside, and shouted at him.

"You open that door and go out there and you won't get back in again. Your choice."

Singh looked at him. Mark didn't know for sure whether or not he understood, but was relieved when he hesitated with his hand on the latch, then stopped and trudged slowly back to the armchair he'd claimed as his own. He stepped over Ellis's inert body and pointed down at her.

"Evil," he hissed. He jabbed his finger at the door. "Nasty bitch! Get gone! Not here!"

With Kate busy dealing with her suddenly catatonic parents, Mark held Ellis still as Lizzie lashed her legs together with a length of nylon clothesline, then gagged her again. She rubbed antiseptic cream from an almost empty tube on the countless sores and abrasions that covered Ellis's skin, caused by weeks of struggling against her bonds.

"What the hell happened?"

Lizzie shook her head, wiping away tears and trying to stay in control.

"I'm running out of pills. I've been giving her half doses. I was just trying to clean her up . . . I thought she was out cold, but she must have just been asleep or she was trying to trick me or . . ."

She stopped speaking and began to sob, stroking her daughter's lank, greasy hair. She shuffled back as Mark dragged Ellis into the bathroom and chained her to the base of the sink pedestal.

"How many of those shots have you got left?"

"That was the last one."

"And the pills?"

He backed out of the bathroom and shut the door. Lizzie didn't answer until it was fully closed and her daughter had disappeared from view.

"A week at the most."

"Jesus . . ."

"What am I going to do, Mark?"

"That thing has to go," Kate interrupted, shouting from across the room and pointing accusingly at the bathroom door. "Get it out of here, because if you two don't, I will."

He walked over to her and reached out to put his arms around her, but she pulled away. She leaned against the wall and slid down it, cradling her distended belly.

"That thing," Lizzie sobbed, "is my daughter."

"She *was* your daughter," Kate quickly replied. "Christ knows what she is now. She's more animal than human."

"I know that, but what am I supposed to do?" Lizzie asked, sitting on the floor opposite and holding her head in her hands. "You tell me what I'm supposed to do."

"Just get rid of her. She's one of them, Lizzie. She won't stop fighting until she's killed us all—"

"I know, but—"

"She killed your boys. How can you ever stand to be anywhere near her when she took your sons from you?"

"I can't," she immediately answered, pulling her knees up to her chest and bowing her head, ashamed by her own admission. "I don't want her here either, but I don't know what else I can do. I'm her mother and—"

"You could turn her over to the military."

"You know I can't. We've been through this. As soon as they've got her they'll put a bullet in her head."

"So?"

"I can't let that happen," she snapped with sudden anger evident in her increasingly desperate voice. "You're right, Katie, I should never have brought her here, but what else could I have done? If I just let her go now, she'll start killing, and they'll hunt her down. Even if I could get her out of the city she wouldn't survive. She won't be able to find food or keep warm or look after herself or—"

"Tough. We should just do it."

"How would we get her through the crowds?" Mark asked, trying hard to remain practical and focused and not let fraught emotions cloud the situation.

"Pump her full of drugs, then. Give her everything you've got left. Kill her, for Christ's sake."

"Katie—" Mark began to protest.

"I can't hurt her," Lizzie sobbed. "She's my daughter, my own flesh and blood. Regardless of what she's done or what she might do, I still have to protect her."

30

ARE YOU MCCOYNE?"

I sit up quick. Eyes blurred. Where am I? No chains. Dull gray light. I look around and try to make sense of my surroundings. It's one of the upstairs rooms in the social club. I found these cushions on a sofa downstairs and—

"Are you McCoyne?" the voice asks again from somewhere behind me. Neck's stiff. I look back over my shoulder and see a figure standing in the open doorway.

"Yeah, what's the problem?"

"No problem. Come with me."

He turns and disappears, and I've got no choice but to follow. The building is cold, and I jog across the landing to catch up with him. I recognize him now. His name's Craven. Julia introduced me to him yesterday. I think he's her right-hand man.

We enter the largest upstairs room. Julia and another man are sleeping here. Craven gestures for me to sit down next to him at a table in the corner, where he fires up a laptop. I saw him using it when I first arrived.

"Have we got power here?" I ask, noticing that there's a power cable connected to the back of the computer. Dumb question.

"Sort of," he answers, sounding as tired as I feel. "There's electricity a few streets away. We've just run a cord here to keep the laptop going."

"What, an extension cord?"

He looks at me, dumbfounded. "Yes, a fucking extension cord."

He shakes his head and turns his attention to the laptop. I watch as he logs on to some kind of central database. Is this the same system that Mallon talked about? My knowledge of this kind of thing is limited, and I don't want to piss him off any more than I already have by asking him how the hell he can connect to anything from here, or even what's left to connect to. There are all kinds of things hanging out of the back of the machine—wires running into small black boxes and the like—I guess the secret's there, somewhere. My mind wanders as I watch him working. I stop thinking about what it is he's doing, and instead I just look at the bright display and listen to the sound of the keyboard clicking as he types. I used to hear that noise all day, every day at work. It takes me back . . .

"Sorry about the early wake-up call," he mumbles, still concentrating on the screen. "Access to the system's intermittent, so we have to make the most of it when we can. They're usually running automatic maintenance at this time of day, so the security's easier to bypass . . ."

His words fade away as the screen changes and he concentrates on entering more details.

"There . . . got it."

"Got what?"

He slides the laptop over to me. "We're in. Enter your details."

"What details?"

"Your name, date of birth, last known postal code."

I start jabbing at the keyboard with two fingers. It's months since I typed anything.

"Wait," he says. "Danny short for Daniel?"

"Yes."

"Put your full name in."

I do as he says.

"What's all this about? What are we doing?" I ask.

"Killing you," he replies without a hint of sarcasm.

"Killing me?"

"Thing about this war," he says as he takes the laptop back again, "is that it's made everybody's priorities change. Everyone's worried about their physical safety, and some of the things that used to matter now get forgotten about or overlooked. This is a prime example. This is just about the only national system that's still running outside of defense, and anyone with half a brain can hack into it and make alterations."

"But what exactly is it you're doing?"

"Is that you?" he asks, angling the screen back toward me. I scan the details.

"Yes, that's me."

"Right," he continues, working his way through various menus and submenus. "Ah, good, you're dead already!"

"What?!"

"They've got you down as being dead. Tell me, did you ever have one of those neck tests or a mouth swab?"

"Yes, why?"

"Because that's where most of this information comes from. They used it as kind of a census and tried to test pretty much everyone when everything first kicked off. It's a "who's what," rather than a "who's who," if you get my meaning."

"Sort of. Anyway, I'm not dead."

"According to this you are."

He clicks a button and scans another screen.

"Hunter's Cross. Ring any bells?"

"Doesn't mean anything to me."

"It's a gas chamber. They've got you down as being killed there."

"I ended up inside one of those places, but I got out when it was attacked."

"There you go, that explains it. They probably marked you off as being dead when they sent you down. Close shave, eh?"

"Too close."

"That's it, then," he says, starting to close up the laptop. "You can go back to sleep now."

"Wait a second," I say quickly, putting my hand on the lid of the machine and stopping him from closing it. "Can I . . . ?"

He seems to immediately know what I want. He's probably done this for plenty of other people before me.

"Be quick," he whispers. "If Julia catches me letting you do this she'll have my balls."

My hands are suddenly shaking with nerves. I look down at my details on the screen, but there's nothing on there that I didn't already know (apart from the fact that, apparently, I'm dead).

"How do I . . . ?"

"Looking for family?"

"Yes, my daughter."

"Start there," he says, pointing at the bottom of the screen. I click on a button marked OTHER PEOPLE LISTED AT THIS ADDRESS. There's

247

a pause of several seconds; then a blank screen is returned. My heart sinks.

"How old was she?"

"Five."

"Either she hasn't been listed or she's listed elsewhere. Try searching on her name."

I enter Ellis's details and press SEARCH. Still nothing.

"Was she with anyone?"

"Her mother and brothers."

"Search for them, then."

I try Elizabeth McCoyne—no match. In desperation I try my son Edward. He's listed at an address I don't recognize, as is his brother. They're both marked as being dead, and, just for a second, I feel a sharp pang of pain. It quickly fades when Craven starts making noises.

"Come on," he whispers, "that's enough. Julia will have a fucking fit."

"Wait a second," I say quickly, desperate not to let go of the computer yet.

"Now!"

"Just one more . . ."

I turn my back to him and cover the keyboard as I type. I search for Elizabeth Parker, remembering that Lizzie only took on my name informally for the sake of the kids. She always used her given name on official forms. I stare at a blank screen and frantically flashing cursor. Craven looks over his shoulder. The faster I need a result, the slower this system seems to get.

"Come on," he says, sounding agitated.

It finally returns a screen full of results—eight Elizabeth Parkers are listed. I scroll down to the right date of birth and click on Lizzie's entry. She's listed at a hotel, and I quickly memorize the address. The Prince Hotel on Arley Road—I think I know it.

Pressing my luck, I click the OTHER PEOPLE LISTED AT THIS ADDRESS button once more and just manage to scan down the first part of a huge list of names before Craven wrestles the laptop away from me and slams the lid down. I think I saw one of my cousins' names, Mark Tillotsen, but no sign of Ellis.

I get up and turn around. Julia is standing behind me.

"Whoever it was," she warns, "forget them."

31

I'M **SCAVENGING DOWNSTAIRS FOR** food, hunting through deserted kitchens and bars that have already been ransacked countless times before, hoping to find an overlooked stash of supplies to supplement the crappy rations I've had since I got here. At the back of a counter, tucked away behind a lifeless cash register, I find three small packets of peanuts. I swallow the contents of the first in a single mouthful, then do the same with the second. I shove the third into my trouser pocket for later. There's precious little time to think about food these days, but when I do get to eat I realize just how much I've missed it. Maybe one day I'll get to eat a proper meal again, if I survive the next couple of days, that is.

There's a half-open door behind the bar I hadn't noticed before. I lean inside.

"Who the hell's that?"

I back out of the low-lit storeroom quickly, startled by the voice from the darkness. The door lets some light in, and I can see someone in the corner, sitting wedged between two piles of empty boxes.

"Sorry, I . . ."

The man looks up and shakes his head. I recognize him from last night. His name's Parsons.

"Doesn't matter, my friend."

I've only been awake for a couple of hours, but already the drawn-out tedium of waiting to fight is getting to me. The idea of a conversation—any distraction—is appealing.

"What are you doing in here?"

"Keeping out of the way."

"Why? You pissed Julia off or something?"

"Show me someone who hasn't."

I know what he means. Being around Julia reminds me of working for Tina Murray, my sour old bitch of a supervisor back at the PFP. Wonder what happened to her . . . ?

Parsons gestures for me to come closer. I do as he says, then slide down the wall and sit next to him. It's stiflingly hot in the social club this morning now that the sun's up, but the dark storeroom is refreshingly cool.

"So are you ready for this?" I ask. "Ready to go out there and start fighting?"

"'Course I am," he answers, almost too quickly. "Can't wait to start killing again. Can't wait to see them panic when we get given the word."

There's an awkward silence.

"You don't sound convinced."

The silence continues as he thinks about what I just said.

"I'm not. I mean, don't get me wrong, I know what's got to be done and I know this is probably the only way to make it happen. It's just that . . ."

"You don't want to die?"

"Exactly."

"Me neither," I admit. "Who does?"

"No one in their right mind. They're all talking about this battle like it's a holy war or something, and it's doing my head in. I don't want to be stuck in the middle of the city when they level the place like they did London."

"But it's got to be done. You can't deny that."

"I know . . . I'm just nervous, you know?" he admits, keeping his voice low. "I can't stand all this hanging around. You know what it's like when you know you've got to fight, you just want to get on and do it."

He's right. It's a relief to find someone else who's willing to speak candidly about how they're feeling. Most everyone else is too busy spouting propaganda and bullshit bravado to dare admit that they're apprehensive about what's coming. They talk like I imagine Brutes think—focused on the kill at all costs.

"You been here long?" I ask.

"Got here about half a day before you."

"And were you at that convent place with Sahota?"

He nods his head.

"We've all been through that. Quite the eye-opener, eh?"

Parsons stares into space, thinking hard. I sense there's more he wants to say, but he's not sure whether he can speak. Perhaps he thinks I'm testing his dedication to the cause? I study his tired face. He looks about ten years older than me, and I wonder what it is we have in common that made us both suitable fodder for Sahota's organization.

"So did you believe any of it?"

"What?"

"All that stuff the Unchanged were spouting at Sahota's place? Breaking the cycle and all that crap?"

I don't answer immediately. Can I trust this man? Now I'm wondering if he's the one testing my allegiance.

"Some of it," I answer, being deliberately vague. "What about you?"

"I agree with most of it up to a point. What Sahota said scared me more, though. I get the feeling they're just using us as—" He stops suddenly.

"Problem?"

"Listen . . ."

I quickly get up and go back out into the bar. Someone's banging on the outside of the fire exit I entered through yesterday. Apart from me and Parsons there's no one else down here, and I realize it's up to me to confront whoever's out there. I move quickly across the room, grabbing a broken pool cue to use as a weapon, then stand by the door and wait. The hammering continues. The door's solid—no way of knowing who it is without opening it up.

"Do it," Parsons hisses from across the room. *Cowardly fucker, why don't you come over here and open it?* Rather than argue, I take a deep breath, tighten my grip on my pool cue bludgeon, then open the door. There's a teenaged girl standing in front of me, looking as tense and unsure as I did when I first arrived here. She only looks about fifteen. She's one of us.

"I'm looking for Julia Chapman," she says, her voice surprisingly confident and strong.

"Who is?" I ask, remembering back to my first encounter here.

"My name's Sophie Wilson," she answers, handling the situation far better than I did, "and I've got a message for her from Sahota."

I let her in, quickly glancing around the back of the building to make sure she hasn't been followed before shutting and barring the fire exit.

I lead her through the eerily quiet building, Parsons following us at a cautious distance. I take her upstairs to where I last left Julia talking to Craven, but she's not there. He points up at the ceiling. I double back and head up to the roof, covering my eyes at the sudden brightness. The sun is huge in the clear sky high above us. Julia's sitting on one of the deckchairs under the tarpaulin, looking into the city through a pair of binoculars. She lowers them when she hears us approach.

"This is——" I start to say.

"You Julia?" Sophie asks. Julia nods. "Got a message for you from Sahota. He said to tell you that I'm the last one."

"What else?"

"He said: Town hall, south side. Six A.M. Five others."

Julia looks at her for a second, absorbing what she's been told. Then she nods her head.

"Thanks. Get some rest while you can. There might still be some food left downstairs. Ask one of the others and they'll show you."

Sophie heads back down without question, leaving me with Julia. Parsons hovers behind us nervously.

"What did her message mean?" I ask, feeling like I'm the only one who's not in the know.

"It means there's as many of us here as there's ever gonna be. It means it's time."

I look straight ahead, determined not to let her see how nervous I'm suddenly feeling.

"South side?"

"South side of the town hall is where he wants us to base ourselves," she answers, looking through the binoculars again. "It's where I thought he'd want us to be, close enough to the military to cause them problems, far enough out not to be suspicious."

"And five others? What was that all about?"

"Five other groups like ours. That's not so good. We were hoping for double that. Should still be enough, though."

"And where will they be?"

"Don't know, and I don't care. All I know and all you need to know is that we'll go where we're told to and cause fucking chaos when the time's right. Between six groups of us, their military won't know which way to turn. The panic will spread fast, and before you know it the whole city will be fighting. And if we do it right, before long there won't be a city left."

"There won't be anything left," Parsons mumbles under his breath.

I sit down on the edge of the roof and stare into the distance. The Unchanged camp looks like a massive, dirty black machine from here. Clouds of gray smoke billow up from between buildings like belching exhaust fumes. Helicopters buzz through the air like flies around a corpse. There's no point denying it, being this close to the enemy makes me want to march in there and start killing. Or it would if I didn't feel the odds were stacked against us. It's probably just me. Perhaps I'm at fault? Maybe I should have more faith? But like I keep telling myself, I don't want to die.

"Just imagine it," Julia says wistfully, looking deep into the distance. "Imagine when we start to fight and they start to run, when they panic and try to get away from us, then run straight into the next battle. Christ, it'll be beautiful. It won't take much, you know; just the minimum of coordination from us will be enough to start it off, and they'll do the rest themselves. It'll be a chain reaction. We'll be able to sit back and watch them killing each other."

I know I should keep my mouth shut, but I can't.

"Except we won't, will we?"

"Won't what?"

"Once we're in there, there's no way back out."

"Doesn't matter. All that's important is wiping out the enemy."

"But at what cost?"

"We can't coexist, end of story. The cost is irrelevant."

I'm making things worse for myself, but I can't help it.

"What good is winning if you're dead? What did they used to call that, a Pyrrhic victory?"

"A what?" Parsons asks.

"A Pyrrhic victory," Julia sighs. "It's when you win the battle, but the end result leaves you fucked, too."

"Great," he grunts.

"You're wrong," she says to me, putting down the binoculars and standing up, "and you need to stop talking like that."

"How am I wrong? Once we're in the city, there's very little chance of any of us getting out alive, is there?"

"It's a sacrifice we have to make."

"And where will your pal Sahota be when all of this is going on? Watching from his office? When we're gone, who's left? Just kids and Brutes?"

She shakes her head. "You come up with an alternative and I'll listen. Do you want the Unchanged to survive?"

"Of course not, but—"

"But what?"

"But there's got to be a better way."

"If there was, don't you think someone like Sahota would have come up with it by now? If there was any alternative, don't you think we'd have tried it? None of us wants to die."

"My point exactly."

"But if your death results in the death of hundreds of the enemy, thousands even, then it has to be worth it."

I don't bother to respond. She's bought into this completely, like a brainwashed old-school terrorist about to embark on a jihad. Even if my death were to result in tens of thousands of Unchanged being killed, I still don't want it to happen. And what about Ellis?

I'd rather fight steadily and have this war drag on for years than sacrifice myself today. I can't stand the thought of not seeing her again.

Julia's not going to let this go.

"You need to focus on what's coming," she says, a sneering, threatening tone in her voice. "Craven said you were looking up information about your family earlier. Forget them, whoever and whatever they were. Your only allegiance now is to us. Nothing else matters apart from what we do when we get back into the city."

She stares into my face, then walks away, stopping before she disappears down the stepladder.

"If you screw up when we're in there," she warns, "then so help me, I'll kill you myself. This is too important for an idiot like you to fuck up."

I watch her go, shaking my head in disbelief. Parsons quietly takes her place in the now empty deckchair. I forgot he was here.

"Thanks for the support."

"I'm with you, pal," he says, shielding his eyes from the sun, "but I've got enough sense to keep my mouth shut."

32

HEAVY CLOUD FILLED THE sky during the late afternoon and early evening. As darkness fell we were called into the main upstairs function room and weapons were handed out. I was given a gun, a few rounds of ammo, and several grenades, but I don't think I'll use them. More to the point, I don't know *how* to use them, even though Julia and one of the others tried to show us. I'll stick to my blades.

Since this war began I've fought alongside hundreds of men and women, maybe even thousands. Who they were and what they were capable of didn't seem to matter until now. But, standing in the bizarre surroundings of the run-down social club, I looked at the ten other fighters heading into town with me and tried to imagine how each of them would fight and kill. The two women—Julia and Sophie—seemed totally unfazed, ready to face anything. Most of the others were similarly focused. Only Parsons and a guy called Harvey seemed as nervous and agitated as I felt. Harvey is a huge, lumbering bulk of a man. He wears glasses with ridiculously thick lenses, and he suffers from acute asthma. He sounds like Darth Vader, and he has appalling halitosis. You can smell him and hear him long before you see him coming. Poor bastard. He comes across as being a bit backward, and I wonder how much of what's happening he truly understands. Still, he must have something between his ears if they reckon he'll be able to keep control of himself in the city surrounded by Unchanged. I'm not convinced.

We left the social club before 3:00 A.M., splitting into four pairs and one group of three, staggering our departures and each of us taking a different, prearranged route to the rendezvous point in town. I'm with Craven, the computer guy, and he reckons we've been walking for almost an hour. We follow the towpath alongside a canal that cuts through what used to be a busy residential area. This place used to be a vibrant, noisy suburb of the city. The nearby university caused the local population to swell during the school year, and the narrow streets were full of cheap shops, restaurants, cafés, bars, and pubs. Everywhere is silent now. The only resident I can see is floating facedown in the murky canal.

The towpath has taken us almost all the way into the very center of the city. We reach a steep flight of steps that lead back up to the street. As we climb them, our closeness to the heart of town becomes apparent. We emerge among lifeless crowds of terrified Unchanged who don't even look at us when we pass them. I expected this to be infinitely harder but I'm somehow able now to swallow down my emotions, hold the Hate and not start killing because I know they'll be dead before long anyway. Seeing Sahota's plan realized will result in many more deaths than I could ever cause by myself. If everything happens as predicted, the city will have fallen by this time tomorrow. Maybe I can bear to be with them because, for the first time in as long as I can remember, the Unchanged are not my only focus. I have another agenda. Since we left the social club all I've been able to think about is getting deeper into town, giving Craven the slip, and heading for the Prince Hotel. I'll search for Lizzie, and then, when I've made her tell me where she last saw Ellis, I'll use the chaos as cover and try to get away.

"Down here," Craven says, changing direction and leading me along a tight passageway filled with people. I look into their vacant faces, and I feel nothing but contempt for them. They remind me of what I used to be before the Hate—beaten, wretched, resigned. They cower in the shadows, waiting for a salvation that is never going to come. The Hate has stripped away their identities and their purpose. They are empty, just waiting for death to come along and end their misery. Standing here, ankle deep in this scum, there's a part of me that wants to stay and see Sahota's plan fully realized. I want to watch these people burn.

The road we're now following runs along the edge of a military enclosure. Everything looks so different tonight, but I'm sure this used to be a council depot. Tall railings surround the place, and there's a massive concentration of soldiers at the gates. The enclosure is comparatively well lit, thumping gas-driven generators powering floodlights. The number of refugees under our feet here is greater, too, attracted like moths to the light and noise. Craven and I weave through the milling masses with our heads held high, without a fucking care, and no one even gives us a second glance.

"I can see why Sahota picked this spot," I say quietly as we begin a slow descent down the packed, sloping main street that leads to the town hall. Even now it's still an impressive focal point of a building, a huge, mock-Grecian hall complete with ornate carvings and rows of massive white stone columns. The civic square around it is seething with people, most of them camped out on the cold, hard ground, wrapped up in coats and blankets, their misery illuminated by more well-spaced lights. There are signs that there used to be something like a soup kitchen operating from here—abandoned tables, empty gas cylinders and tins of food, plastic plates and cutlery blowing in the suddenly vicious wind.

"It's perfect," Craven agrees. "There are thousands of them here, and they're all at breaking point. They probably came here looking for food and shelter and got neither, so they just dropped where they were standing and gave up. They'll riot in a heartbeat once we start on them."

I look around as we pick our way through the sprawled masses. He's right. There's an unspoken tension in the air here, much more fractious and intense than any I've felt before. There's an uncomfortable standoff between civilians and the military, too. I don't know which side is more wary of the other. Maybe that's the real reason why the soldiers are here in such numbers?

We move past a large stone statue, and seeing its distinctive dark outline strikes a sudden chord. For a second I remember this place as it used to be. On the rare occasions I'd get a proper lunch break from work, I'd sometimes walk here to get away from the office and everyone in it. Once or twice I met Lizzie here before the kids were born.

"There's Sophie," Craven says, nudging me in the ribs with his elbow and nodding over to where she's standing on the opposite side of the square. "Go find yourself a spot."

We separate as planned. Each of us will disappear into the crowd until the time to attack comes. It'll look less suspicious if we're all spread out, not that it matters; when the fighting starts no one will care who threw the first punch or fired the first shot. I find a narrow gap midway along a low wall, between two sleeping refugees, where I stop and wait. There's a still-functioning clock on the side of the town hall, just visible from where I'm standing. It's approaching four. Just over two hours to go. The Prince Hotel is no farther than a mile from here. I'll wait for a little while before I make my move. If I go off too fast there's a chance I'll be seen and followed.

Trying not to make it too obvious, I look around for the others. Craven and Sophie I've already seen. I see Parsons way over to my right and another man whose name I don't know sitting perched on the plinth of the statue in the center of the square. Harvey is leaning up against the same wall as me, a little farther along. His size makes him easy to pick out in the crowd.

There's Julia, too, sitting right in front of me, just a handful of people between us. I catch her eye and, stupidly, almost acknowledge her. She has a dirty blanket draped over her head, all but the top half of her face hidden. Bitch is staring straight at me, watching my every move.

33

IT'S BEEN PISSING DOWN rain for the last twenty minutes. There's no shelter here, and I, like everyone else, am soaked to the skin and freezing cold. I've been crouching down beside the wall trying to keep myself covered, but the rainwater's running down across the gentle slope of the packed square now, forming deep puddles around my feet. The conditions don't bother me—I'm getting ready for what amounts to a suicide attack, surrounded by Unchanged, and a little water is the least of my problems—but when other people start to move around me I know I need to go with them to keep up the illusion. I follow two of them, stepping over the person immediately to my left, who hasn't moved in as long as I've been here. Someone grabs my arm, and I know who it is before I turn around. I can hear him breathing.

"Is this it?" Harvey asks, his voice low but still too loud. "Is it time?"

I shake my head. "Not yet, too soon. I'm just getting out of the rainwater."

I try to move, but he keeps hold of me.

"Where you going?"

"Somewhere drier."

"I'll come."

"No, it's better if we split up. If people see us together they'll get suspicious."

"Doesn't matter. Not long now."

"I know, but—"

I shut up when the deafening rumble of a sudden, booming explosion fills the air. There's a moment of silent shock in the square, everyone taken by surprise. It lasts no longer than a second; then all hell breaks loose around me. The mass of people who'd been sheltering on the ground begin to get up and scramble for cover. Is this it? Has the signal to fight been given early? I look around, but, apart from Harvey, there's no one I recognize anywhere close in the mass of refugees suddenly crisscrossing all around me. My arm is grabbed again.

"It's not time," Julia yells in my ear, shouting to make herself heard over the noise filling the square. "Don't fight. This isn't it. Get up toward the statue."

I do as she says, sensing her following my every step. I look up and see that a surprising number of the people in the crowd ahead have now stopped and are standing still, looking back in the direction from which I've just come. Other panicking refugees continue to weave around them. One of our men is already standing on the statue. He sees us coming and beckons us closer. He points out into the distance.

"Some dumb fucker's got their timings wrong."

Still being shunted from every angle, I pull myself up next to him and look back. Behind the town hall a high-rise office building is on fire. There's a necklace of fierce flame burning about two-thirds up the side of the building, and it's taking hold with incredible speed. I can see people in the windows above the flames, illuminated by what's happening below them. Some have started to jump, choosing instant death when they hit the ground over waiting for the fire and smoke to get them.

"This isn't right," I say, thinking out loud, trying to shield my face from the torrential, driving rain.

"What isn't?" the man next to me asks as he reaches into the pockets of his jacket for weapons.

"Why there? If you want to cause panic at ground level, why start fighting halfway up a high-rise?"

"It wasn't us," Craven shouts, wading through the masses to get to us.

"How do you know?"

"Helicopter. You can see it sticking out of the side of the building. Looks like it was just an accident. Guess it was only a matter of time. You can't look up in this place without seeing something in the air. Everything's so dark that buildings like that must be pretty hard to make out, and in this weather it's even worse. Idiots must have flown straight into it."

Julia plucks Harvey from the crowd and pulls the five of us closer together, no longer concerned with trying to remain invisible. The other people around us couldn't give a damn who we are or what we're doing.

"We have to keep waiting," she says. "This is only going to help us."

"We should do it now," Craven argues, "capitalize on it. Sahota wanted more groups—"

"We wait," Julia orders.

I stare at the crash for a few seconds longer, watching the flames crawling and licking up the sides of the high-rise, swallowing the tail of the helicopter. The fire moves with incredible speed, seeming to eat up the higher floors of the building in massive gulps. The destruction is beautiful, almost hypnotic. But then something happening down here at ground level tears my attention away from the building. People. They're starting to flood into the already packed square. As if a dam has burst its banks, a deluge of desperate refugees is suddenly washing toward us, forced out from their flimsy shelters and squalid refuges around the base of the burning building. Some are injured. Others are coughing, their lungs filled with acrid smoke and dust. Most, though, are just panicking—going with the flow of everyone else around them. Their fear and confusion is invigorating. To experience their terror this close makes me feel superior and strong. They're running blind from the immediately perceived danger without giving a second's thought to what they might be running toward.

Suddenly the air is filled with more thunderous noise. Another explosion. This time it's in the opposite direction, and I'm sure this has to be one of ours. A swollen balloon of flame billows up in the darkness about half a mile from here. It disappears quickly, but its aftereffects remain. Surely another surge of refugees will start moving this way and will hit the others head-on?

"That's enough," Craven says. "Come on, Julia, let's just do it. We won't gain anything from waiting."

They can do what the fuck they like. I'm going. This is my last chance to find Lizzie before all hell breaks loose, and I'm going to take it. I climb down off the statue, and then, leaving Craven and Julia arguing, I start to move back through the crowd. I glance up at the clock on the side of the town hall as I'm swallowed up by the masses. Quarter to five. If Julia has her way I've still got an hour. Or have I? Has the fuse already been lit?

The constant movement and heavy rain are disorienting, and I'm struggling to get my bearings. I push my way deeper into the hordes of Unchanged and manage to almost reach the farthest edge of the civic square before I realize I'm moving in the wrong direction, the burned-out ruin of a nightclub looming up in front of me. People are tearing along an alleyway at the side of the ruined building in both directions, none of them making any progress. I turn around and walk straight into Parsons. He stands in front of me and blocks my way, looking as desperate and lost as one of the Unchanged. He has a grenade in his hand.

"Is this it, McCoyne?"

"No," I tell him, "not yet. Julia says we should—"

"I think it's time."

"Not yet," I say again, having to shout now to make myself heard. "She's up there by the statue. Go and speak to her. See what she says before you—"

"It must be time," he shouts over the rain. "I can't stand all this waiting—"

"Parsons, don't! It was just a helicopter crash. And the other explosion—"

He doesn't say anything else. Instead he just pulls the pin from his grenade. A sudden surge from the crowd shunts him sideways. I try to move back as he manages to get his balance and stand straight again.

"Throw the fucking thing!"

Disoriented and racked with nerves, Parsons just looks at me. I shove him hard in the gut, sending him tripping down the slope, colliding with refugees and knocking them over like bowling pins. He topples back and is gone, immediately snatched from view by the hordes. I put my shoulder down and run as fast as I can in the opposite direction, forcing my way through the masses. I trip over a body on the ground and stumble forward, barely managing to stay upright. Instinctively, I reach out and grab hold of another startled refugee, using him to haul myself back up and keep moving forward. He tries to grapple me down, but I just push him out of the way, knowing that in seconds I'll be the least of his worries. This one has more spirit and fight than most. He manages to cling to the corner of my coat, and I yank it from his grip, then duck to one side when he takes a swing at me. I try to focus on getting away and not panic. I shove him down and glance back over my shoulder, praying that I won't be able to—

For a fraction of a second the world is filled with brilliant white light and a noise so loud I think my head's going to burst. I'm thrown down by the force of the explosion behind me, and for a moment all I can do lie still, sandwiched between fallen Unchanged. I pick myself up, using the bodies around me for support. I look back again, and I can see a space in the crowd and a dark, shallow pit where, just seconds ago, countless people were crammed together. Now there's nothing, just a layer of bloody, smoldering debris. I turn and run as the shock quickly fades and panic again begins to fill the air.

People are running in every direction away from the square now, and I allow myself to be carried along with them, using their bulk as camouflage. None of them know who or what I am, and none of them care. Away from Julia and the others I'm suddenly as irrelevant and unimportant as everyone else, and the anonymity is welcome and reassuring. Running shoulder to shoulder with the enemy, I realize the desperate need to kill these people I've always felt has all but disappeared. Maybe it's because these people are all dead anyway? There's less than an hour to go now until Sahota's moment of glory, but I don't think the city will last that long. A phalanx of helicopters thunders overhead. One of them breaks off and begins firing on some unseen target close to the burning high-rise, causing the crowd around me to start moving with even more panic and speed.

Above the heads of the stampeding masses I see something I

think I recognize—the distinctive angular outline of a tall, recently built apartment building. As I run toward it there's another sudden detonation and the front of the building explodes outward in a swollen bulge of fire and heat. I turn away from the immediate blast and duck down as thousands of tiny shards of glass begin raining down around me. Most of the crowd instinctively tries to turn back and run the other way. Dumb fuckers. I keep moving forward, knowing that the ground around the center of the blast will be relatively clear now with just the dead and dying to get through. I run past the burning stump of the building, zigzagging through the carnage, dodging chunks of concrete and twisted lumps of metal and flesh. I look up and see people trapped on the upper floors. A woman falls from a third-floor window and lands on the pavement just ahead of me, shoved out by the terrified crowds behind her, hitting the ground with a wet thud like rotten fruit. It's wonderful to see. Part of me wishes I could find somewhere safe around here to sit and watch the whole city burn.

I'm back to shoving my way through the enemy masses again in seconds. I thump heads with another man, and he pushes me away angrily, his eyes full of hate. Instinctively I reach for my knife but force myself to let it go, fighting against everything I believe in. The need to kill might have subsided, but the desire's still strong. I'm like a junkie who's been clean for years but who's now surrounded by an endless supply of his drug of choice. Once I start killing, will I be able to stop? If I lose control now, all hope of finding Lizzie will be gone forever, and although I don't want to have to face her again, without Lizzie there's no chance I'll ever know what happened to Ellis. This is my last chance.

There's another momentary gap in the crowd at the middle of a once-busy crossroads. This place used to be one of the busiest intersections in town with backed-up lines of traffic all day, every day. I climb up onto the roof of an abandoned MPV—the kind of car I always wanted—and look around me. The Prince Hotel is, I think, still about half a mile farther in the direction I've just been running. Apparently endless swarms of people continue to try to escape the carnage behind me, fighting with each other to make it through the madness. As more explosions suddenly light up the area around the town hall and the civic square behind me, the beauty and simplicity of Sahota's plan comes sharply into focus. Did Julia cause those last blasts, or Craven or one of the others? Has she finally given the order to attack? If it's like this now, I think to myself, how bad will it be by six o'clock?

A helicopter crawls across the sky overhead, illuminating me momentarily with its sweeping searchlight, filling the air with thumping noise. I jump back down to the road and keep running.

34

RECOGNITION AND FAMILIARITY BRING even more fear and nerves. Not far now. The hotel's almost in view, and every footstep I take brings me closer to Lizzie and to knowing what happened to my daughter. What if I'm too late? What if Ellis is lost or dead? Suddenly turning tail and heading back to the town hall to fight alongside the others seems an easier option than what I'm about to do.

I take a shortcut through an eerily empty supermarket, in through the loading bay and out toward the smashed front windows. Before going outside again I stop and stand in the darkness to take stock of the chaos unfolding all around me. The behavior of the Unchanged population is changing. In the short time since the explosions around the town hall, most of them have abandoned their need to remain isolated and distant from everyone else. Although there are some who still cling to the protection of the shadows, desperate not to be seen, most have now joined the ever-growing exodus away from the center of the city. They move virtually as a single, snaking mass now, all of them following the person in front, none of them consciously choosing the direction in which they run. Their sudden reliance on the safety of numbers again exposes the pathetic weakness and vulnerability of the Unchanged.

I run along a narrow, shadow-filled street, then pause when I reach Arley Road and look in both directions, struggling to see anything through the hordes of people now trying to escape from the center of town down this major route. Then I spot it. The Prince Hotel stands fifty yards or so farther up the road. The once-imposing building is pretty much exactly as I remember, its frontage just becoming visible in the dull first light of dawn. The rain has finally stopped, leaving the damp air smelling fresh and clean, the dirt and decay temporarily washed away.

What the hell am I doing? I suddenly feel guilty and weak. I should be back by the town hall fighting with the others, so what am I doing out here on my own? Logic says that after three months of violence and unpredictability, Lizzie could be anywhere. Christ, she's probably dead. Craven told me the Unchanged computer system was inaccurate and easily manipulated, so why have I put so much faith in what I saw on the computer screen? The reason's simple—it's because I've got nothing else. There's no alternative. This is my last chance, and I can either take it or give up on Ellis forever. I take my axe from my belt and a knife from inside the folds of my coat and hold them ready. I feel detached from everything now. There's the Unchanged on one side, my people on the other, and then, standing alone and wedged right between them, is me.

I sprint away from the side of the road and charge deep into the river of people still flooding out of town. The first few stragglers I collide with are pushed away with hardly any effort, and it's not until I'm close to the center of the road that I have to start killing to keep moving. It's the only option left now if I want to get through, but I know I'm doing it because it's the only way to keep moving, not because I want them dead. I'm carried along with the flow of barely human flesh, so deep and so strong and fast-moving that I struggle to lift my arms to fight. I manage to raise the axe and bring it thumping down between the shoulders of a man directly in front of me. I spin him around, the blade still buried in his back, then kick him down. A woman, being forced forward by the mass of people behind her, trips over the body on the ground, and I hack at her, too, wedging the axe deep in her neck. Two down now, and the piled-up corpses act like a rock in the middle of a stream, channeling the flow of refugees around me on either side. I'm braced for their reaction, but it doesn't come. These people have seen and experienced so much that what I'm doing is nothing new to them. All they're interested in is getting away, screw everyone else. Another man trips over the bodies on the road and collides with me. I swing the axe around and hit his pelvis, sending him spiraling away and clearing even more room. I'm suddenly standing in an unexpected bubble of space. One man, tall and powerfully built, much stronger than me, breaks ranks and hurls himself at me. All I do is hold out my knife, and the stupid bastard impales himself on the blade. Another one rushes me, and now they're finally beginning to realize what I am. I duck out of the way of his amateurish, aimless attack, and he collides with a teenaged girl. A bald man with wild eyes helps her up and out of the way, then turns on the other man and punches him in the gut. I continue to move backward, working my way across the road. In my wake more desperate, panicked fights break out. Whether they're trying to get away, trying to help each other, or trying to find me, it doesn't matter—their reactions are all the same. They fight.

And once they've started, they keep fighting. I force my way through the mob with relative ease, hacking and slicing at them only when I have to. All around me the Unchanged begin to turn on each other, and I'm quickly forgotten.

Breathless and bloody, I reach the front of the hotel. I cross the parking lot and climb the steps up to the door, forcing my way inside as several others force their way out. Christ, I feel weird—strangely invisible and high on a euphoric mix of adrenaline and nerves. If I am feeling any fear, it's masked by the immense satisfaction, excitement, and relief of having just killed again. But as I disappear into the vast and dark building, a sudden wave of terror hits me. Lizzie might be here. She might be standing next to me for all I know, because I can hardly see anything. What was I thinking? How am I supposed to find her in here? Did I think I was just going to be able to walk up to the reception desk and ask for her room number? As I scout around the first floor, the full implications of my shortsighted lack of planning really hit home. This was a mistake. Time is running out. The city won't last much longer, and my only remaining option is to check every damn room. For half a second I consider turning around and just wading back out into the crowds to enjoy the killing for as long as I'm able, but then I remember Ellis again, and I force myself to stay calm and stay in control. I know I don't have any choice but to keep moving.

35

THE FIRST FLOOR OF the hotel is deserted, and it's easy to see
why. The carpet is soaked with water, and there's a tidemark
on the wall about eighteen inches off the ground. Wallpaper is
hanging down in strips, and the whole place smells of rotting waste
and untreated sewage. I thought there would be more people in here.
I guess most of them were washed out with the floodwater that has
obviously flowed through the building in the last couple of days.
Others will have left when the fighting started. Am I too late? Has
Lizzie already gone? Was she ever here at all?

I head back to the front of the hotel, feet squelching on the wa-
terlogged carpet, then head upstairs. I climb the long, straight
flight of steps to the second floor, knifing a fucker in the gut as he
tries to barge past me and nearly sends me flying. I glance back and

watch as he tumbles down the stairs, rolling over and over until he lands in a bloody, groaning heap at the very bottom.

I start checking the rooms on the second floor, but they're empty. I'm halfway along the hall when a door flies open and three terrified Unchanged men come sprinting out, carrying as many bags and boxes of belongings as they can manage between them. They can't see me over everything they're carrying, and one of them knocks me to the ground. Instinctively I get up and start running after them, but it's too late and they're already gone. Doesn't matter. Have to concentrate. Have to focus. Let them go.

The next three doors are open, and the rooms are empty. They're foul, squalid places, full of the residue of the refugees who've been forced to live here together for weeks on end. The carpets are covered with a layer of waste and abandoned belongings, so deep that I don't see the curled-up body of an elderly man until I feel the fingers of his outstretched hand crack under my boot.

Back out in the hall, I force myself to slow down. Need to try to apply some logic here. The hotel's emptying, so there's no point checking any of the vacant rooms. If any of the doors aren't locked, I decide, there's no one there.

I start hacking at the lock and hinges of the next door I find that's still shut. I can already hear the bastards inside the room screaming with panic. I keep working on the door, shoulder-charging it open when I've done enough damage to loosen the latch. One of the occupants runs at me, brandishing a chair leg. I sidestep him, then shove him across the hall, sending him crashing into the wall opposite. There are three other Unchanged in the room, with a fourth trying to get out through an open window. The light's low, but I see enough to know that I don't recognize any of them and they're of no interest. I turn and head back out to the hallway, pausing only to knife the fucker who comes back at me for a second go with the chair leg.

The lock on the door of the next room is broken, but it's held on a chain. It opens just far enough for me to see inside. No sign of Lizzie. A gray-haired woman grabs hold of the door handle and pulls it shut, snatching it from my hands. Another room empties as I approach, and this time I just press myself back against the wall and let two more sobbing Unchanged stumble past.

Almost all of the third floor is empty, and Lizzie's not in any of the rooms that are still occupied. In a room near the staircase on the fourth floor I find a small girl sitting alone in an armchair that dwarfs her tiny shape. In my haste and desperation I think for a second that it might be Ellis. It's dark, the dull dawn light just beginning to seep in through the cracks between the wooden boards that have been nailed across the window. It's only when I touch the girl and she slumps out of the chair that I see it isn't Ellis, and it's only when she lies at my feet and doesn't move again that I realize she's already dead, abandoned by whoever she was with.

The door to the last room on this floor is open slightly, but it slams shut as I run toward it. I shove it open before it's locked. Three Unchanged women and a man begin shouting and screaming at me in a language I don't understand. Sounds like Polish or Russian or something . . . I turn and leave, and one of them follows me back out into the corridor, still shouting. She grabs hold of my legs, pleading with me for help. I kick her off and keep moving.

Top floor. Running out of options.

There are more locked doors up here than I've got time for. I stop outside the first. I can hear voices inside, so I start chopping at the lock with my axe, my arms beginning to feel heavy and numb with effort. The rotten wood splinters easily, and the door flies open, but Lizzie's not here, and I move on. I can feel their relief when I turn my back. The door slams shut, and I hear them shoving furniture up against it to seal themselves in.

Two doors facing each other are both shut. I jump the sprawled-out body of a Chinese man and press myself up against the first of them. I can hear a man's voice ranting in Urdu or Punjabi or similar, so I immediately turn my attention to the other and start chopping at the wood around the latch. I stop for a second when I hear another deafening explosion outside, a flash of white lighting everything up like a strobe. It's impossible to gauge the distance, but that sounded close. Too close. I can still feel the vibrations through my feet as I start chopping again. This door is more stubborn than most. It's newer than the others, probably recently replaced. I guess I'm not the first person to have to try to break into a room here. I grunt with effort as I hammer the door again and again, desperate to get through.

viii

WITH HIS FACE PRESSED hard against the spyhole in the door, Mark stared in disbelief at the man trying to bludgeon his way into the room directly opposite.

"What is it?" Kate asked, trying to pull him away. He didn't answer. He couldn't answer. How could this be? How had he found them? Was it just coincidence or the cruelest stroke of bad luck imaginable? Had he been looking for them? How could he have known they were here? He glanced back over his shoulder at Lizzie standing in the far corner, the stunned expression on his face obviously speaking volumes.

"Mark, what is it? What the hell's the matter?" Kate demanded again, her voice now frantic. He ignored her and instead continued to stare at Lizzie. She moved closer, her pace quickening as she approached. Sensing that she already knew what was outside, she tried to push Mark out of the way. He stood his ground, turned his back on her, and pressed his eye up against the tiny glass button in the door again.

He hadn't seen him for almost a year, and he was virtually unrecognizable, but it was definitely him, he was sure of it. Danny McCoyne. His cousin Danny. His mom's sister Jean's son. The kid he'd messed around with at countless boring family gatherings and parties when they were growing up. The miserable loser with the dead-end job who'd ended up saddled with too many kids in an apartment that was too small. The notorious slacker who other members of the family had frequently cited as a prime example of how not to do things. Lizzie's partner. A murderer. A Hater.

Outside on the landing, McCoyne continued to hammer against the door. Mark was overwhelmed by the anger and hatred so visible on his cousin's twisted face, shocked and appalled by what he had become. He'd always seemed awkward and gangly, uncomfortable in his own body, but that uncertainty had been replaced now with focus, ferocity, and a vicious intent. To Mark, Danny McCoyne now personified the previously faceless Hater menace, and he felt his legs weaken with nerves at the thought he might be forced to confront him.

Lizzie grabbed Mark's arm and yanked him out of the way. She pressed her eye against the spyhole briefly, then staggered away from the door, recoiling in shock at the sight of the Hater in the hallway. The room around her was filled with noise—Kate's panicked screaming, Gurmit Singh's constant unfathomable tirade— but she didn't hear any of it. How could this be? How the hell could he be here?

"Will someone tell me what's wrong?" Kate pleaded, desperate for information.

"It's Danny," Lizzie mumbled, her voice barely audible.

"What? But how could he—?"

"Keep your voice down, Katie," Mark warned.

"Let him have the kid," Kate shouted, moving forward. Mark pushed her back away from the door. "Come on, Mark, let him take her. Give her to him. Get the little bitch out of here. We'll be safer if—"

He kept pushing her away, the noise from the hallway getting louder and louder. He shoved her back toward her catatonic parents, then ran to the spyhole and peered outside again. He watched as McCoyne finally forced his way into the room opposite. He disappeared inside but was back out again just a few seconds later, and this time there was no question as to where he was heading next.

"Get back!" Mark hissed as he stumbled back toward the others, sweeping them away from the door. He grabbed a baseball bat they'd kept in the room to defend themselves, then herded Kate, Lizzie, and Singh around the foot of the double bed, gesturing for them to get down and stay out of sight.

"Is he—" Lizzie started, the sound of the first flurry of blows from the axe against the door rendering her question obsolete before it had even been fully asked. The door rattled and shook in its frame. Mark glanced back at Kate, who cowered alongside her parents, then turned and faced the door again, desperately trying to give the impression he was ready to fight when all he wanted to do was run.

The Hater in the hallway booted the badly damaged door open, sending it clattering back against the wall, splinters of wood flying in all directions. He charged into room 33, straight into Mark, who ran toward him to try to head him off, baseball bat held high. He clumsily swung the bat at his cousin's head but missed by a mile, wrong-footed by the sudden speed of events, the close confines of the cluttered room, and the utter terror that he felt in every nerve of his body. McCoyne grabbed the end of the bat on its fast upward arc, yanked it from his grip, and threw it out of reach across the room.

The Hater stopped.

He thought he recognized the man in front of him. Mark? Mark Tillotsen? Was it really him?

The unexpected appearance of a face from his old life caught him completely off guard. For a split second he stood there in numb silence and simply stared at the other man, his head suddenly filled with memories and emotions that had been suppressed and long-forgotten since he'd first tasted the Hate. He rocked back on his feet, hardly even blinking as another explosion outside shook the entire building. Then, as Mark lunged at him again and someone else screamed something unintelligible from the far corner of the room, he snapped himself out of his sudden trance and remembered Ellis and Lizzie and why he was there. He caught Mark as he leaped forward, grabbing his collar, spinning him around, and smashing him up against the wall to his left, then dropping him onto the floor in a crumpled heap. He rolled over onto his back and lay groaning at the Hater's feet.

He sensed more movement. Another one of them was attacking.

McCoyne looked up as Lizzie ran toward him. Her face was tired, old, and drawn, her cheeks and eyes sunken and hollow, but he knew immediately that it was her.

"Lizzie, I—"

She swung the baseball bat around and smashed him in the side of the head.

36

HEAR THEM TALKING, but I keep my eyes shut. My hands are bound and strapped to radiator pipes behind me, and my ankles are tied together. There's blood in my mouth, trickling down the inside of my throat. Someone trips over my feet, but I force myself not to react. I half-open one blood-caked eye and see Mark trying to drag a pregnant woman away from me. She sees that I'm awake, then squirms free from him, turns back, and boots me in the gut. Can't defend myself. I take the full force of her foot right in the middle of my stomach, and I'm suddenly doubled up with pain, gasping for air and choking on the semicoagulated blood in my nose and mouth. Christ, that bitch is wild. It takes two of them to pull her away from me and hold her down. If I didn't know better she could almost pass for one of us. Maybe she is. Maybe she's been conditioned to fight like I've learned not to.

Mark and an Asian man keep the pregnant woman away at a distance. Lizzie catches my eye, then strides across the room toward me, grabs my shoulder, and pulls me over until I'm sitting upright opposite her with my back against the radiator. She looks straight into my face, then slaps me so hard I almost fall back down.

"You killed my dad, you fucker," she spits. "I loved you and you killed my dad!"

What am I supposed to say? She's right, and I don't regret any of it. I could kill everyone in this room and not give any of them a second thought. Except Lizzie, perhaps. I can't take my eyes off her. It's suddenly like we've never been apart, and for a single brief and foolish moment the irrevocable difference between us seems trivial and unimportant. She slaps me again. I try to turn away, but she still hits me with full force. The pain's good. It wakes me up. I start trying to get my hands free of the plastic ties they're using to hold me.

"We should kill him," the pregnant woman snarls, holding her swollen belly.

"That'd make us as bad as him," Lizzie answers quickly before turning her attention back to me. She's nervous. Scared. She forces herself to talk to me. "Why are you here?"

"Looking for you," I answer quickly.

"Haven't you hurt me enough?"

"Not about you. Ellis. Need to know what happened to her."

"Why?"

"Why do you think? She's like me. She should be with me."

"What, so you can let her loose outside to kill? So you can let her run wild and . . . ?"

I shake my head and stare into her face again, still trying to get my hands free behind me.

"I want to take her with me. I want to look after her and take care of her. I don't want her out there fighting on her own."

"I don't want her fighting at all. She's just a kid . . ."

"I just want her with me, Lizzie. I want to keep her safe."

Lizzie slumps back and drops to the floor opposite me, head held in her hands. The Asian guy is still mumbling and cursing at me from the corner of the room. The pregnant woman watches my every move, not daring to look away. Mark tries to appear collected and in control, but I can sense his terror. I feed off their collective fear. It's empowering. Even together they're no match for me.

"He's here to kill us," Mark says. "Katie's right, we should have just got rid of him. This was a bad idea."

I shake my head and spit a lump of bloody phlegm onto the carpet.

"Not interested in any of you. Just Ellis. Let me know what happened to her and I'll go."

"Don't listen to him. Let him go and the fucker will kill us."

I shake my head again.

"I won't. I can control it. I'd never have got this deep into the city if I couldn't. I can hold the Hate. They taught me."

"Who did?" Lizzie asks.

"People like you."

"This is bullshit," the pregnant woman yells. "Why you?"

"Not just me. Others, too . . ."

"But why . . . ?"

"Haven't you heard what's happening outside? It's a coordinated attack," I explain, suddenly desperate for Lizzie to understand. "I came here with other fighters, but I broke away to try to find you."

"I don't understand . . ."

"I'm not interested in killing any of you. I just want to know what happened to Ellis. Tell me what happened to her and I'll go and you'll never see me again—"

"Let him take her," the pregnant woman says. "Get the evil little bitch out of here—"

"Shut up, Katie!" Mark yells.

What did she just say? I can't believe what I'm hearing. This must be bullshit. She can't really be here, can she? How could they have kept her hidden and stopped her from attacking for so long? I look from face to face in search of an explanation.

"Ellis is here?"

"In the bathroom," she shouts, trying to get up again, pointing at a door in the wall opposite me as Mark pushes her back down and tries to cover her mouth.

"Here? But how . . . ?"

Still slumped on the floor in front of me, just out of reach, Lizzie starts to sob.

"I couldn't let her go. I knew she was like you, but it didn't matter. Even when she killed the boys I couldn't bear to let her go . . ."

Her words dry up as tears take over. I keep trying to move my wrists and bend and stretch my legs to break my binds. Got to get up and get to Ellis . . .

"He can take her," says the pregnant woman. "Let him take her."

"We can't trust him," Mark snaps at her.

"Does it matter? Throw the pair of them out the door and let them take their chances—"

Another thunderous explosion interrupts her. They're getting closer and more frequent now. At this rate the city will have fallen long before 6:00 A.M.

"She's right," I tell Lizzie, begging for her to listen and understand. "I promise I won't hurt you. I'll take Ellis and you'll never see either of us again."

Mark moves forward and picks up the bloodied baseball bat.

"As soon as we let him go he'll turn on us," he says, sneering at me.

"For fuck's sake," I scream at him in frustration, "will you just listen to what I'm saying? I don't want to kill any of you—"

"Come on, Lizzie," the pregnant woman says, calmer now, lowering herself down and kneeling on the floor next to her. "You said yourself you can't help her. This is the best option for all of us."

"She's right," I agree, as if they're going to listen to anything I say. Lizzie glares at me. She's in an impossible situation—whatever choice she makes, she loses. No matter what she is and how I feel about her now, I'm surprised that it still hurts me so much to see her like this. She's shaking her head.

"I can't. I just can't let her go . . ."

"You don't have long," I tell them. "The city doesn't have long. I can get her to safety. Get her out of here before it's too late."

"You've hardly got any medication left for her, Liz. You can't hold her if she's not sedated. Have you thought about that?"

"Of course I have," she sobs, looking back and staring at the pregnant girl. "I just can't stand the thought of her being out there on her own. She's only five—"

"But she won't be on her own," I interrupt. "She'll be with me."

"Come on, Danny," she sighs, wiping her eyes. "You were hardly the world's greatest dad at the best of times. What chance has she got with you now?"

"More chance than she's got without me. Look, you're not thinking straight. Stay here and you're all dead. This is the best option for her. The only option . . ."

The hotel room is momentarily silent, the only noise coming from outside. Vibrations shake the floor and walls. Even the Asian man has finally shut up.

Lizzie holds her head in her hands.

"I just can't. You don't understand. She's not like you, remember," she says. "She's—"

Before she's finished speaking, the pregnant woman moves. She lunges toward me, catching me and everyone else completely off guard. She grabs my head and pulls me forward, then leans down behind me. I try to shake her off, but she's too heavy and I'm squashed under the bulk of her unborn child. As quickly as she attacked she's up again. She stands opposite, holding one of my knives in her hand. What has she done? Has she cut me or . . . ?

Wait.

My hands are free.

My legs still tied together, I push myself off the wall and reach out for Lizzie. She manages to scramble back out of the way, but the other woman's not as quick. I grab her right foot and pull her over. She hits the ground right in front of me. Mark tries to react, but the Unchanged are reassuringly slow, and by the time he's made a grab for her I've already got her held tight. I wrap one arm around her throat and hold the knife to her face. Stupid bitch. At least I've temporarily silenced the constant fucking noise coming out of her mouth. I lean forward and cut the ties around my ankles, then slowly stand up. Mark goes to move toward me again, but I prick the woman's cheek with the tip of the blade, and the sight of her blood and the sound of her half-choked screams is enough to stop him.

I kick the bathroom door open, and it takes a second for my eyes to adjust to the gloom. Lying bastards, it's empty. She isn't here. There's a thin mattress on the floor, some sheets, empty bottles of water, and the remains of medication, food wrappers . . . but no Ellis. I can smell her scent, but she's gone.

"Where is she?" I yell, turning back around and holding the blade up to the woman's eye.

"Safe," Lizzie answers. "Let Kate go, Danny."

In desperation Mark tries to run at me again, but, like all of his kind, he thinks too long instead of acting on instinct. I'm far faster than he is, and I see him coming a mile off. Even with the weight of this bitch in my arms he's no match for me. I kick him in the balls and send him reeling.

"Where?" I yell again.

"Let her go and I'll take you," Lizzie says. I stare straight into her face again and tighten the pressure around the other woman's neck. Is she telling the truth? Do I have any choice? I could be in touching distance of Ellis, but without Lizzie I might as well be miles away. Mark rolls around at my feet, groaning.

"Please . . ." he whimpers pathetically.

I could kill her, but I don't. Suddenly all I can think about is Joseph Mallon. I can see his face and can hear his damn voice echoing around my cell, telling me not to fight fire with fire, to break the cycle. Was he right? As the city crumbles around us, can I risk not following my instinct and letting these fuckers live? Could it really be that the more I fight today, the more I stand to lose?

I let the woman go. She falls to her knees and crawls away on all fours, gasping for air. Lizzie walks over to me, stopping only when we're almost touching.

"I just need to know that you'll look after her and get her to safety."

"Where is she?" I shout, struggling to keep control and not attack. "Just tell me where—"

"I need to hear you say it, Danny."

"I promise you, Liz. I'll get her as far away from the city as I can. I'll look after her. She's all I've got left."

"Then you've got more than I have," she sobs. She looks into my eyes, and I can't look away. "We moved her last night," she finally admits. "We couldn't risk keeping her here any longer."

"What have you done with her?"

"She's safe. Mark and I were going to try to get her out of the city. It was the lesser of two evils . . ."

Mark gets up. He reaches into his pocket and pulls out a set of keys, which he throws to Lizzie.

"Take him."

"I can't . . ." she says, beginning to cry again.

"It's the only option. Listen to what's happening outside, Liz. It's all fucked. He's right, at least she's got a chance this way."

"But what if . . . ?"

"I won't hurt you," I tell her, meaning every word but still not knowing if she believes me. "All I want is Ellis. Take me to her and you'll never see me again."

She nods her head but still doesn't move.

"Just give him the keys," the pregnant woman says. "Let him find her for himself. Stay here with us."

Lizzie shakes her head and wipes her eyes.

"No, I'll go. I just want to see her again. One last time."

37

THERE'S A FIRE ESCAPE at the rear of the hotel, a staircase running down the back of the building. Lizzie, watching me like a hawk and carrying a knife I know she won't dare use, pushes me down the landing and around a corner toward an innocuous-looking gray door. It's already been forced open. She gestures for me to go through.

"Where is she?" I ask as I step outside, shouting to make myself heard over the sounds of fighting that fill the air. We stand at the top of a zigzagging metal staircase bracketed to the back of the old, run-down building. She points in the general direction of the streets behind the hotel, but I can't see anything specific. The sun is rising, and below us the city is beginning to burn. A fleet of planes and helicopters is taking off from somewhere far over to our left.

"There's a garage," she answers breathlessly. "The front of it has collapsed, so it's difficult to get in or out. We locked her in the back of a van."

"If this is a trick, Lizzie—"

"No trick," she says quickly, and I know she's telling the truth. We're wasting precious time. Sensing Ellis is close, I start climbing down.

There's another parking lot at the back of the hotel, and a small patch of wildly overgrown garden beyond it. Lizzie leads me away from the building down a narrow path that's barely visible through the long, damp grass. The sky is still filled with heavy gray cloud, but it's slowly beginning to brighten.

"This way," she whispers, catching her breath when a series of brilliant white flashes explodes, lighting up the early morning gloom for a fraction of a second at a time. A low-flying helicopter gunship rumbles overhead, heading back toward town.

I follow her to the end of the path, where there's a tall wrought-iron gate. Lizzie bends down and shifts a broken lump of paving slab that's keeping it shut, and the gate swings open. She pauses before going through, ducking back into the shadows as a group of people runs past. I watch them as we step out into the open, three figures chasing a fourth down a narrow, cobbled passageway. They corner the lone runner, drag him to the ground, and kick the shit out of him. It's impossible to tell who's who—am I watching the Unchanged being hunted down, or is that one of my people cornered? It doesn't matter anymore.

"Move!" Lizzie hisses, shoving me forward again. There's another gate in a wooden fence on the other side of this alleyway. We go through, and I can tell immediately from the number of rusting car parts and piles of tires and mufflers that this must be the place. I follow her through a side door into a dusty office. It's dark. She stops suddenly, and I walk into the back of her, then hold on to her as she grabs my sleeve and leads me farther forward, pausing only to pick up a flashlight she obviously left here previously. We go through another door and down a single steep step into what must be the main workshop. The air's cold, and the noise we make echoes off the walls. She shines the light farther ahead, and I see that the front of the building has collapsed in on itself, sealing it off from the street.

"Over here."

We move around the back of a jacked-up car to the farthest corner of the workspace. There's a white and blue van parked with its back to the wall. Its front fender is a light matte gray color, primed and waiting to be painted by a garage employee who's never coming back. As we move toward the rear of the van, I see there's a light on inside it. Lizzie pushes me out of the way and unlocks the door. She opens it as far as she can, then slips through the gap, and I follow her.

Lying flat on her back in the middle of the van, chained to the front seats with her mouth gagged and her wrists, legs, and ankles bound together with plastic-covered clothesline, is Ellis. She's awake and alert, her beautiful brown eyes darting from Lizzie to me and back again. She looks straight at me, but I'm not sure if she remembers. Dressed only in a dirty gray undershirt and panties, her tiny body is covered in cuts, scratches, and bruises. Lizzie leans over her, and she immediately reacts, arching away from her, then trying to lunge forward and attack. The longer I look at her, the less familiar she becomes. She sobs and whines through the gag like a frightened animal.

Lizzie, Ellis, and me all together again. I never dared dream this would really happen. Suddenly the noise of the battles outside and the helicopters and explosions don't seem to matter. Everything that I have left is in the back of this van. I swing my backpack off my shoulders and open it up. I pull out Ellis's doll, and Lizzie takes it from me and holds it close, tears running down her face.

"You went back?" She whispers.

"Looking for you," I tell her.

Lizzie moves Ellis's wild, unkempt hair away from her eyes and tries to show her the doll. She recoils from her mother's touch, desperately trying to pull away. Lizzie seems unfazed. I guess she must be used to this now. Ellis's eyes show no recognition, no understanding.

"It would have been easier on everyone if she'd just stayed with you," she admits, "but how was I to know after what you did?"

"I know."

"I didn't even realize she was like you until a couple of days after you'd gone. I didn't expect it, didn't even think it could happen. One minute she was sitting there with her brothers, the next . . . I was out of the room for less than five minutes. I came back in and saw her with Edward . . ."

She starts sobbing, tears dripping down onto Ellis, who wriggles and squirms as if they're corrosive acid drops.

"Why did this have to happen, Danny?" she asks. She knows I can't give her the answers she wants.

"It wasn't because of anything you did or didn't do. None of us could control it or predict it . . ."

She smiles and wipes her eyes. "Remember how hard we used to think we had it? How frustrated we used to get with the kids . . . ?"

"How could I forget?"

"You hated your job, I couldn't stand being with the children, Dad was sick of bailing us out all the time . . ."

"I know. I remember."

"I'd do anything to have it all back how it was."

She's right. In spite of everything, sitting here with her and with Ellis lying between us, part of me knows she's right.

"I wish I could be back there," she continues, reaching down and resting her hand on Ellis's shoulder. Ellis flinches and tries to roll away, but Lizzie ignores her violent reaction. "You, me, Ellis, and the boys in the kitchen of our shitty little apartment, fighting over the TV or who'd eaten whose candy or something stupid like that . . ."

"Me, too," I say quietly, surprising myself with my admission. Another explosion reverberates around the garage, followed by the sound of dust and debris raining down on the roof of the van. This van is like a cocoon, temporarily isolating us from the chaos of the rest of the world, but I can hear the intensity of the fighting outside continuing to increase.

"We can't stay here," I tell her. "It's not safe."

"I know."

"I have to go. I have to take her with me and get her away."

Lizzie nods and wipes her eyes again. She looks down at Ellis and smiles, then crouches down next to her and picks up the knife she was carrying. Ellis tries to lunge at her, the chains still holding her back. For a split second I think Lizzie's going to attack her, but I watch her face and I know that she won't. She can't. She removes the clothesline that has been wrapped around Ellis's legs, then slides the long blade between her bare ankles and draws it up, cutting through the plastic ties that hold her tight. Ellis immediately reacts, kicking out at Lizzie with incredible, unrestrained fury and anger.

"What are you doing? Get out of here, Liz. Just go—"

"Hold her, Danny."

I lift Ellis up, her legs still thrashing, and wrap my arms around her chest as Lizzie removes the padlock and chains that have kept her anchored to the floor of the van. Her ferocity and strength are remarkable, and I struggle to keep hold of her. Lizzie removes Ellis's gag, and her head immediately lurches forward as she tries to take a bite out of her mother's face. Lizzie ducks out of the way, then lowers the blade toward the ties binding Ellis's wrists together.

"You should go," I tell her. "Get back to Mark and the others. Try to get away from here while you still can."

She shakes her head and starts to cut.

"Let her go, Danny. I just want to hold her before you take her."

I relax my grip. The plastic ties pop open, and Ellis immediately lunges forward, her incredible strength taking me by surprise. She flies at Lizzie, landing in her arms and smashing her back against the side of the van with a sickening thump. For the briefest of moments they're locked in an embrace, Lizzie burying Ellis's face in her chest, not wanting to let her go. I watch the pair of them in the low light, huddled close together. They could be anywhere—saying good-bye in the school playground, sitting on the end of Ellis's bed last thing at night, keeping her warm when she's just come in from outside . . .

Then the expression on Lizzie's face changes. Her eyes screw shut with pain, and she opens her mouth to scream but no sound comes out. Ellis pushes her away and glances back at me, blood covering the bottom part of her face. She spits out a chunk of Lizzie's flesh, then turns back and attacks again.

I shuffle back into the corner and cover my head as she rips her mother's body apart.

38

BLOOD-SOAKED AND PANTING HARD, Ellis sits in the diagonally opposite corner of the van and watches me. What has she become? Does she even remember who I am? She hasn't tried to kill me. She'd have attacked if she thought I was a threat.

"We have to go, Ellis. We have to get away from here. It's not safe. People are going to try to kill everyone here. Do you understand?"

No reaction. No time to wait for an answer. I take her rainbow-colored sweater out of my backpack and edge closer to her.

"Put this on. Keep you warm."

I reach up to put it over her head. She swipes it out of my hands. I pick it up and try again, but she's not having any of it, and I drop it. She hisses at me and pushes herself farther into the corner. Poor kid, it's hard seeing her like this. I'd naively expected her not to have changed much. Maybe I'd just been trying to convince myself she wouldn't be like the kids we found at her school. She'll be better now that we're together.

"Come on, we're going," I tell her, forcing myself to move. I grab the knife and flashlight in one hand and Ellis's wrist with the other and drag her out of the back of the van. We hit the ground, and she immediately tries to pull away from me, but I won't let go. I drop the flashlight, shove the knife into my belt, and lean back into the van again. With outstretched fingers I reach the long length of cord they'd used to tie her legs together. It's wet with Lizzie's blood. Ellis keeps pulling against me, her strength and persistence hard to control, but I manage to keep hold and pull her closer. I tie one end of the cord around my waist and the other around hers like a leash. Christ, there's hardly any meat on her at all. The chubby puppy fat I remember around her belly has gone. She's lean and sinewy now—just skin, muscle, and bone.

"In case we get separated, okay?"

Still no reaction.

"Ellis, can you hear me?"

She looks into my face but doesn't respond. Now that she's attached to me I let her go, and she immediately darts away, almost dragging me over when the cord pulls tight. I try to haul her back, but she's fighting against me constantly.

"Stop! Ellis, sweetheart, it's Daddy . . ."

I'm struggling to keep my footing. In the brief lightning flash of an explosion outside, I see that she's trying to undo the cord. I run toward her and scoop her up into my arms again. She kicks and squirms to get free.

"Calm down," I whisper, my mouth next to her ear. "Please, Ellis, just stop . . ."

My words have no effect. Got to get out of this garage. Maybe she'll respond better if she can see me clearly and if she can see what's happening around us. Disoriented, I head the wrong way and find myself trying to get through the rubble at the collapsed front of the building. I double back on myself, past the open van and Lizzie's body, trying to retrace my steps back out. Someone shines a light in my face. I can't cover my eyes, so I instinctively screw them shut. I almost drop Ellis but manage to tighten my grip before she falls.

"Let her go," an immediately familiar voice orders.

"Julia? How did you . . . ?"

"I followed you. We knew you were looking for your kid, and Craven showed me what you found on the system."

"But what about the plan? The fighting?"

"What about it? Have you seen what's happening out there? The chain reaction's started, McCoyne. They're turning on each other."

"So you've got what you wanted. The city's falling apart and—"

"I can't let you take her. Kids like this are the future. We need them more than you can imagine—"

"She's staying with me."

"You don't understand. Sahota and Preston both—"

"No, *you* don't understand. Ellis is my daughter, and I'm responsible for—"

"Your only responsibility is to this war."

"But I'll take her back to the others. I promised Preston I'd—"

"Do you think I'm stupid? If I let you go you'd disappear and we'd never see either of you again. I can't take that risk. She's coming with me, and you should be proud to let her go. We'll take her, and she'll help us hunt more of them down until the last one's dead. Your kid's already more of a fighter than you'll ever be, and you should—"

"She's my little girl. I don't want her to fight."

"You dumb bastard, do you think you have a choice? Just let her go."

I don't answer. I run forward, trying to find a way past. Julia comes at me, and I drop Ellis to defend myself. Another flash of the light blinds me for an instant, and the sudden tightening of the cord as Ellis darts away pulls me off balance. Julia swings a punch and catches me on the side of the head. I'm knocked back and sent reeling by the unexpected angle of her attack. I trip over something hard and heavy in the dark behind me and find myself on my knees in some kind of oily inspection pit. I feel the cord tighten again, and I immediately grab it and try to pull Ellis back. It gets even tighter, then goes taut, then drops down loose as Julia cuts through it.

"Ellis!" I shout as I scramble out of the pit. Julia drops her flashlight, and for a split second I catch a fleeting glimpse of her shape as she sprints through the office and back outside, barely managing to drag Ellis behind her. I chase after them, over the land at the back of the garage, through the wooden gate, then out along the cobbled passageway. It's packed with people, far more than before, all of them running to escape the carnage that is steadily consuming the center of town. Can't see Julia—she's just one among hundreds now.

I follow the stumbling crowd until we reach the end of the passageway. I look in all directions and shout for Ellis, but my calls go unanswered, most probably unheard. Too many people. I start to wade through them, unable to see anything through the waves of foul, barely human flesh that constantly crash into me. I grab the knife from my belt and start hacking into those nearest to me, not interested in killing, just wanting them out of the way. The sun's almost up now, but the light's still poor. Dirty smoke drifts everywhere like horror film fog.

Someone grabs me from behind. I spin around to defend myself, but they're not attacking, just trying to get through. I'm on my back in the gutter in a puddle of rancid rainwater before I know what's happening. My wrist cracks against a curb, and I drop the knife. I reach out for it, but it's kicked away by one of the stamped-ing crowd. Before I can get up someone plants a boot right in the center of my chest. Suddenly struggling to breathe, I roll over and manage to crawl away through the forest of legs. Other Unchanged trip and stumble over and around me, but I force myself to keep moving until I reach the side of the street where their numbers are fewer. I'm next to a badly decayed body in a deserted shop doorway when my hand rests on a length of metal tubing about a yard long. It looks like it was a fence post or part of a road sign, but it'll make a decent weapon. I use it to help me get up, then head back into the crowd again, swinging it around like a samurai sword. On a vi-cious, upward arc, the jagged end of the tube hits an Unchanged woman on the side of the head, tearing her flesh from below her ear up to the corner of her eye. I swing the tube again and more of them go down like I'm cutting down crops, scything a path through the chaos.

There's an overturned wreck of a car in the middle of the street. The crowd splits to go around either side of it, but I climb onto it. The burned-out skeleton of the car is precariously balanced on its roof, and it quivers and vibrates with my every move. Another helicopter flies overhead, and I instinctively duck and turn around to watch it disappear, looking back toward town.

Then I see her.

I'm surrounded by a sea of heads, but back in the direction from which I've just come, there's a break in the crowd—a small, unex-pected bubble of space. I struggle to see through the smoky haze and constant, uncoordinated activity, but then I glimpse a flash of remarkably fast movement. It's Ellis. Finally free and unrestricted, she's killing at an incredible rate. I can see her leaping from victim to victim with ferocious speed and intent, using nothing but her hands and teeth to kill. She wraps herself around each one of them, does enough damage to fatally wound them, then gets up and attacks her next victim before the last one's dead. Even after everything I've seen, my daughter's ruthless, savage brutality is incredible. Awe-inspiring and terrifying in equal measure.

There's Julia. I steady myself as the overturned car rocks again, then watch as she chases after Ellis. Holding on to what's left of the cord with one hand, she chops at the Unchanged around her with what looks like a meat cleaver held in the other. She's struggling. Ellis is too strong and too fast for her.

I swing the metal pipe out over the side of the car like a golf club, taking out several more refugees and almost decapitating one of them. I jump down into the space where they were standing, then hold the tube out like a lance and run forward, shoulder dropped, toward where Julia and Ellis are fighting. I follow the trail of bodies, tripping over outstretched limbs and slipping in pools of blood and gore that Ellis has left in her wake. An unusually aggressive Unchanged comes at me with a machete. The downward sweep of the blade glances off my shoulder but does little damage, and I'm gone before he can take a second swipe.

Julia's dead ahead of me now, being virtually dragged along by Ellis as she's fighting. Yet another helicopter powers overhead, this one releasing a volley of screaming missiles into the crowd nearer to the center of town. I can feel the heat of the missiles as they scorch through the air above me, the shock wave from the explosions in the distance almost knocking me off my feet. Julia lifts her cleaver and chops it down into the pelvis of a slow-moving Unchanged man before the vibrations knock her off balance, too. She steadies herself and pulls back on Ellis's leash. The momentary delay is enough for me to catch her. I grab hold of her shoulder and spin her around.

"Let her go, Julia."

Distracted, she almost lets the cord slip through her fingers. She drops her weapon, snatches back the plastic-covered line with both hands, then tries to wrap it around her wrist. Her face is bruised, her right eye swollen purple and almost completely shut. Did Ellis do that to her?

"Help me with her," she demands.

"Help you?" I yell back, using the metal pole to shove an unsteady Unchanged out of the way. "Are you serious? Let her go—"

"We have to get her out of here. Help me!"

More missiles explode, vast swollen bulges of intense orange flames rising up from the area around the Prince Hotel, far too close for comfort. What choice do I have? I drop the pole and grab the cord, taking the strain from Julia. Together we begin to reel Ellis in. I catch a glimpse of her through the swarming crowds. We're dragging her back, but she's still fighting, still grabbing as many Unchanged as she can, sinking her teeth and claws into their skin, slashing and tearing at their flesh. She's just a yard away now, still pulling against us but unable to overcome our combined strength. Julia runs around from behind me and grabs Ellis by the waist, lifting her clean off the ground. Ellis drops the body of a young Unchanged kid midkill, then manages to squirm around in Julia's grip. I try to force myself between them and take my daughter from Julia, but Ellis unintentionally elbows me in the face, her bone catching me full force between the eyes. Blood begins pouring from my nose.

Julia staggers away, trying to keep hold of Ellis and at the same time deflect the constant barrage of kicks and punches coming from her. My girl is like a child possessed, fighting with a savage strength and intensity beyond her years. They disappear into the crowd again for a few heart-stopping seconds until, as I spit out blood from my broken nose, I catch sight of the clothesline on the ground. I drop down and grab hold of it, reeling Ellis in again. I find her sitting on top of Julia, her thumbs sunk deep into the woman's bloody eye sockets, repeatedly lifting her head up and then smashing the back of her skull down onto the asphalt. Julia thrashes her arms wildly, but there's no strength left in her, only movement. Ellis squeezes again and Julia stops suddenly, limbs falling heavy. Ellis lifts Julia's head, then slams it back down once more, then looks up and springs away. The cord whips out of my hands, burning my skin.

"Ellis!"

She leaps up at another Unchanged woman who's running toward her. The woman catches her with surprise and is then slammed back down onto the road, overcome by the unexpected force of the attack. Ellis kills her, then stands up and drags another one down, then another and another, and I'm transfixed until an Unchanged man slams into me from one side. I grab his collar, flip him over, and smash the sole of my boot into his face. The exhilaration is incredible. Suddenly, now that I have Ellis with me, this is all that matters. Another one of them comes at me with a knife. I grab his hand, twist it around with such force that I hear his elbow pop and crack, then plunge the blade into his own chest. I pull the bloody weapon back out and then, without thinking, grab a handful of hair from the head of another, yank it back, and draw the knife quickly across its exposed neck, feeling it slice easily through flesh. Beside me Ellis launches herself at a kid just a little older than she is. The kid fights back, almost getting away, before Ellis forces it over to the side of the road and smashes its head through a low window.

And this, I realize as I kill again and again without resistance, is what I'd always said I'd wanted. I'm fighting freely, without restriction or fear, and Ellis is by my side, doing the same. Except she's not here. I've lost sight of her again. I shout her name, but the chaos around me now is all-consuming. The helicopter circles overhead again, and the panicking crowd pushes me back farther. I try to carve my way through them, but getting through these people is like trying to swim against the strongest current imaginable. Through a momentary gap I see Ellis racing away, moving diagonally across the street, jumping from body to body, from kill to kill, slithering through the crowd. She jumps up onto the back of one unsuspecting man, snaps his neck, then leaps over to her next victim before the first corpse has fallen. Then she's gone again. Lost in the midst of the madness.

What has she become? She's a savage, feral monster, a million miles removed from the Ellis I knew and remembered, but she's still my daughter. Seeing her like this is heartbreakingly sad, but, at the same time, there's a part of me that's incredibly proud of what she is now and how bravely and strongly she's fighting.

Got to get to her.

I'm struggling to keep going. I'm panting with effort, legs heavy and lungs empty, barely able to keep moving, and yet the tide of Unchanged refugees coming toward me is endless. I try to force my way between them, but every time I take a step forward I'm pushed several steps back. Got to keep moving. Can't stop now . . .

The roar of another missile fills the air. It hits the side of a building less than a hundred yards ahead, puncturing a hole in the wall, then exploding outward, showering the entire street with debris. When the explosion fades, everything becomes silent and still. I stand motionless as the last few refugees to have escaped the blast continue to push past me. I slowly move closer to the blast zone as the sound gradually begins to return—the screams and moans of the injured and dying, a single car alarm that's somehow still working, the crackle and pop of flames, the hiss of fractured pipes . . .

Can't see Ellis.

I stand alone at the edge of a massive expanse of rubble and fallen bodies. Around me, a few people begin to move again, crawling through the debris, slowly picking themselves up and staggering on. I walk deeper into the madness, slowly at first, then starting to run. I trip and slide over the remains of people under my feet.

Where is she?

I run faster, barely managing to stay upright in the midst of the carnage. The closer I get to the epicenter, the fewer complete bodies there are. I look down and all I can see now is dismembered limbs and other, less recognizable chunks of bloody meat. I can't move, can't think straight, the stench of smoke and burning flesh filling my bleeding nostrils. Can't focus. I can hardly breathe. Have I lost her? Against all the odds, Lizzie kept Ellis safe for weeks on end. Just minutes with me and she's gone.

Can't give up.

There are more people moving all around me now, some of them disentangling themselves from the bloody wreckage, others continuing to flood forward from the center of town, picking their way through the gruesome ruins, the explosion just delaying their escape temporarily. I slowly cross what's left of the street, trying to see through the smoke and haze and line myself up with the buildings close to where I last thought I saw her. As I get nearer I drop to my knees and start to crawl through the bloody mire, pushing away the grabbing hands that reach up at me, desperate for help. My knee sinks down into the open chest cavity of a young Unchanged man, physically forcing his last breath from his lungs. Another one of them catches hold of my coat, and I pry its surprisingly strong fingers away when I see a small, child-sized hand sticking out from under two heavy cadavers. I drag the corpses out of the way, desperate to dig Ellis out from beneath them. She's facedown on the asphalt, a pool of deep red, almost black blood spilling out around her head. I put my hands under her shoulders, pull her out, and turn her over, but it's not her. Thank God. I drop the body and keep moving.

There are Unchanged moving all around me again now. Most are injured; all are terrified. I increase my speed, determined to find Ellis, literally throwing wet chunks of human remains over my shoulder as I look for any sign of her. Then I see it—the severed end of the plastic clothesline. As more munitions explode around me, showering me with dust and dirt, I pick up the end of the cord and follow it back, terrified at the thought of what I might find at the other end. I catch sight of a bare ankle that's smaller and thinner than the rest. I haul another blood-soaked body out of the way and shove it to one side, jumping with surprise when it opens its eyes and screams in pain and grabs hold of me. Underneath another corpse I see Ellis's shock of untidy brown hair. I push and pull more bodies away until she lies there in front of me, completely uncovered. Her tiny, emaciated body doesn't move. I shake her shoulder, but there's still no response. I lean down until my ear's just a fraction of an inch from her mouth, but it's impossible to hear or feel anything. I grip her wrist in my hand and check for a pulse, but there's nothing. I turn her over and pull her up and hold her in my arms. She looks like she's sleeping, and for the first time since I found her she looks like *my* Ellis again, like the precious little kid I used to tuck into bed at night and fetch breakfast for in the morning, the noisy little brat who made my life hell but who I loved more than anything else in the world. Bruised, blood-soaked, and beautiful.

I check her neck for a pulse again, not even sure if I'm doing it right. Did I just feel something? I pry her eyelids open. Her pupils are wide, fully dilated, but she doesn't react to the light. I hold her close, her head next to mine, and for a second I think I hear something. I concentrate on Ellis, shutting out everything else, and then I hear it again. The faintest whisper of a shallow, rasping breath. She's alive. Got to get her out of here.

39

THE SKIES OVERHEAD ARE filled with movement and noise. Missiles, mortars, and rockets whip across the clouds and detonate around the city center. Helicopters buzz overhead, some observing, most of them attacking, firing into the crowds below.

The bulk of the refugees follow each other like sheep, sticking to the main roads out of town and not even bothering to consider whether those in front know any more or less about the situation than they do. They run blind, finding the illusion of safety in numbers. There are hundreds of them moving down the wide ring road, which, as many of them must know, will eventually swing around and take them straight back into the dying heart of the city.

There's another way.

Over to my left is an enormous pile of smoldering rubble where there used to be a multiplex cinema. Still carrying Ellis in my arms, I leave the road and run around the edge of the ruins, following the perimeter of a wide, tent- and RV-filled parking lot that has been almost completely abandoned. On the far side of the site is a steep embankment, along which runs one of the train lines out of the city. While thousands of those dumb bastards have stuck to the clogged and overcrowded roads, I can already see that there are just a handful of people up there following the train tracks out of town.

Ellis starts to move. Thank God for that. It was only a small flinch, but it was enough, and I sense she's going to be okay. I hold her tight as I climb up the embankment, quickly reaching the top and running along the side of the track, still instinctively watching out for trains I know will never come. My feet dig into the gravel as if it's wet sand, every step taking twice as much effort as it should.

From this relatively high and uninterrupted vantage point, I can see clearly in most directions. I look back over my shoulder at what's left of the city behind us. Massive sections of it are on fire now. The skyline has changed incredibly in an unbelievably short period of time. Huge, landmark buildings that stood tall and proud when I arrived here just a few hours ago have been destroyed and have disappeared, changing the skyline forever. Even from this distance and over the endless noise of the helicopters, missiles, and muffled explosions, I can still hear the sounds of thousands of people fighting, and the relief at having escaped with my daughter from the heart of the battle is immense.

I keep running, exhausted but forcing myself to keep going. We're probably safe at this distance, but I want to get even farther away. The train track snakes away toward the suburbs, the desolate ruins of housing projects springing up on either side of us. Even out here there are people in the streets. I see scores of terrified Unchanged refugees who've fled the city and are looking for shelter, only to be intercepted and cut off by people like me and Ellis.

Where the hell did so many of our fighters come from? Were they already in the center of town with us? The answer becomes clear as I see more and more of them approaching. These people are coming in from outside the city now, crossing the exclusion zone. Word must have reached them that the refugee camp is imploding. Or is this a planned attack? Are these the advance troops from Ankin's army?

Another helicopter flies overhead, this one so low that I instinctively drop down to my knees and bend forward to protect Ellis. She shuffles in my arms again and groans with pain. I hold her closer to my chest and look up as the helicopter flies past and away. Then another thunders over us, then another... all of them flying away from the city. I stand up as even more gunships follow the first three. I start moving again, and as the combined noise of the aircrafts' powerful engines begins to fade, I become aware of another sound, this time much closer and on the ground. Beyond the ruined houses to my right there's a large expanse of parkland. Even from this distance I can see there's a huge amount of activity there. There are battles raging in the streets around the park, and a massive convoy of vehicles is beginning to leave the grassland and move off along the surrounding roads. Another helicopter takes off from somewhere close. It climbs quickly into the early morning air, then banks hard over to the left and follows the course taken by the others before it.

Ellis starts to wake up and move. She grunts and squirms in my arms, but I just tighten my grip, determined not to let go.

"Stay still," I tell her, not knowing if she can hear me or if she understands. "Please, sweetheart..."

The train track cuts through the projects, then runs parallel with one edge of the parkland. I've never seen it from this angle, but this place used to be Sparrow Hill Park, I'm sure of it. It's unrecognizable today. The sprawling expanse of well-tended grass I remember is now a vast, cluttered mass of abandoned tents and trailers. Once obviously filled to overcapacity with refugees, much of it now is conspicuously empty. Huge swathes of the camp have been washed away, and now several stagnant lakes where floodwaters have swept relentlessly through the site are all that remain.

There are people fighting on the track up ahead. I run down the embankment and begin to weave through a dense copse of brittle-branched trees to try to get closer to the park. Already I can see movement on the other side of the trees, and I hold Ellis even tighter as she tries to get away again. Her rage seems to increase the closer we get to the Unchanged. She wants to fight, but I won't let her. It's too dangerous here.

Through the trees and I hit a wire-mesh fence. Something's different here. Can't put my finger on it, but I sense something's wrong.

As I work my way around the wire-mesh fence looking for a way through, the penny drops. The Unchanged troops are evacuating. It's their stock response when they realize they've lost control of a building, an area, or even a city—withdraw as many of their people as they can to a safe distance, then bomb the hell out of what's left. I saw it at the hospital, at that office building with Adam, and a hundred times before that. Christ, now I know exactly what happened to London. They lost control, the same way they have here. And their response then? They leveled the fucking place. More than ever, I have to get us away.

Ellis manages to free one of her hands and slashes at my face. Blood dribbles down my cheek, and when I lift up my hand to wipe it away she shoves both her fists up under my chin and pushes my head back, then knees me in the gut and breaks loose. She runs along the edge of the park, and I sprint after her toward where a section of fence has collapsed up ahead. A truck has crashed through and come to a sudden stop wrapped around the base of a tree trunk. It can only just have happened. The half-dead driver is Unchanged.

He's hanging out of the door, and when he sees us he starts groaning and begging for help. Ellis jumps up at him, the force of her sudden attack throwing him back across his cab. By the time I get up to her he's already dead, but she continues to kick, punch, and slash at his lifeless body, her aggression and instinct taking hold. I grab her hair and pull her back toward me, then manage to get a grip under one of her shoulders and drag her back out into the open.

"Off!" she yells, her voice guttural and hoarse, sounding more like a warning howl than a properly formed word.

"We have to go, Ellis. Can't stay here. Too dangerous."

I drag her behind me into the park. She's still kicking and thrashing furiously, but her short arms can't reach my hands to break my grip. I run across the boggy grass toward the chaotic activity up ahead. There's a bottleneck at the single exit, where jeeps, huge trucks, and other armored vehicles are all vying for position to get onto a track that's barely wide enough for any of them to get through. All around the vehicles, refugees and soldiers on foot try to escape from the park. People fight with each other to get away, but there are no other people like us here. This is Unchanged versus Unchanged.

A khaki-colored Land Rover pulls away and skids through the mud before coming to a sudden halt at the back of the ever-growing line of vehicles. No one pays us any attention as I run toward it. The driver tries to weave through the stationary line and push his way in, his only concern getting away from here before the inevitable carpet bombing begins. But there's no way through for anyone. A helicopter hovers overhead, broadcasting a pointless announcement that is all but inaudible over the strain of so many impatient, overrevved engines.

The driver of the Land Rover is distracted, arguing with one of the other soldiers in the back. This is our chance. I haul Ellis up close and whisper in her ear.

"Kill them, honey."

I yank open the back door of the mud-splattered vehicle and literally throw her inside. I slam it shut again and wait for several anxious seconds until the bloody face of one of the soldiers is smashed up against the window, cracking the glass. I pull the front door open, drag the driver out onto the grass, and stamp hard on his face until he stops moving. I jump into his still-warm seat and lock the doors. Behind me Ellis stands on the chest of one of the dead soldiers, ripping out his throat with her bare hands.

"Good girl," I tell her. "Now sit down and hold on."

The way ahead is still impassable, and there are more soldiers running toward us now, more interested in the vehicle than in either their fallen comrades or us. As the nearest one reaches for the door I shove the Land Rover into reverse, skidding back across the grass and knocking one of them down, clattering over his broken legs. Into first gear and I accelerate. We struggle to get traction on the wet, greasy ground for a second, but the soldier's body helps the wheels to finally get a grip, and we career away.

"Hold on," I tell Ellis again as we slip and slide through the mud. I follow the curve of the boundary fence, looking for the way we used to get in here and hoping I'll be able to squeeze around the other side of the truck and get out again. There it is. I accelerate up over the collapsed wire-mesh fence, the side of the Land Rover scraping along the side of the beached truck. I steer hard right, then hard the other way, then change direction again as we weave through the trees. Behind me Ellis is thrown from side to side, the soldiers' bloody corpses providing her with some cushioning.

"Put your belt on."

She doesn't react. I wrench the steering wheel hard over again, then grip it tight as we burst out through the trees, crash through a low picket fence, then swerve onto a narrow residential road that's swarming with people who scatter as we power toward them. Ellis slams herself up against the window, beating her hands against the glass, desperate to get outside and kill.

There's a traffic island up ahead, and the rest of the traffic that's managing to escape from the park is driving around it. I accelerate the wrong way around the island, then force my way into the line of fast-moving vehicles. We hurtle along a wide road that's virtually clear on one side, more refugees diving out of the way as we approach. The road climbs up over a high flyover supported on huge concrete struts, and now I know where we're heading. This was obviously the Unchanged military's main route in and out of their refugee camp. In less than a mile we'll reach the highway. I'm distracted as the truck in front smashes into a person trying to sprint away, sending them spinning over the crash barrier at the side of the flyover and tumbling down a sixty-foot drop. Our speed is such that I dare only look down for a fraction of a second, but I see that the area of town below us now resembles a vast battlefield. Escaping refugees have collided head-on with an army of our fighters marching into the city. They're no match for our people. I look down over a bloodbath of unprecedented scale and brutality.

The front of the Land Rover clips a lump of concrete, and I almost lose control. I try to focus again as we start to descend toward the highway, Unchanged military vehicles ahead of us and behind. Ellis starts throwing herself at the door, trying to get out, oblivious to the danger.

"Sit down," I shout at her, reaching into the back and trying to grab her arm. I manage to catch her wrist, but she won't budge. Christ, she's strong. She straightens her legs against the back of the front seats. The harder I try to pull her forward, the more she resists.

As this road widens and merges with the highway, two vehicles try to pass me at once, a truck on one side and a jeep on the other. Still struggling with Ellis, I accidentally ram the cumbersome truck.

It veers off to the right and hits the metal barrier running along the median and spins. The back of the truck jackknifes and blocks two of the three lanes behind us. I glance up into the rearview mirror and watch as more vehicles smash into the truck, filling almost the entire road with a tangled mass of crashed traffic. Other trucks and vans manage to swerve around the wreck and keep moving.

Ellis lunges at me from the back. I lift my hand to protect myself and manage to get a hold under her armpit. I drag her forward, flipping her over through a full turn, bringing her slamming down hard on her back on the passenger seat.

"Sit down!" I yell at her, the volume of my desperate voice seeming to finally have some effect. She backs away from me and moves toward the door, pulling up her knees and curling herself into as small a shape as possible. "Put your belt on, Ellis," I tell her. "Do it!"

When she doesn't react I ignore her, focusing my attention on getting as far away from the city as possible, passing a large armored transporter on the inside. There's a flash of light and a thunderous noise directly above me, and I brace myself for another missile explosion, but it's just more helicopters, their pilots and passengers fleeing from the fallen city along with everyone else. I glance at the dashboard for a fraction of a second—as long as I dare—and I see that we're doing more than ninety miles an hour. More than a mile a minute. We might be six or seven miles away now, maybe more. Is that far enough?

"We've got to get away from there, you understand?" I yell over the noise of the engine, looking over at Ellis. She cowers on the seat next to me, half naked and covered in blood and grime. Her huge brown eyes stare back at me unblinking. Poor kid's in shock, traumatized by everything that she's seen and done since we were last together. If only Lizzie hadn't taken her away from me. She'd have been better off with me there to explain everything. "Listen, we'll find somewhere safe to stop, then we'll—"

Her eyes dart away from my face and toward the windshield. She looks up, scanning the white clouds above us. I follow her gaze, then look down again and steer quickly out of the way as we almost hit the back of a slower dark green vehicle. We rumble over the hard shoulder, the tires brushing the edge of the grass verge and churning up clouds of grit and dust. I yank the Land Rover back on course, the sudden movement making us both slide over to the right. Ellis's gaze remains fixed, staring into the sky.

"What is it?"

She doesn't answer, but it doesn't matter. I can hear it now. Even over the Land Rover's straining engine and everything else, I hear a high-pitched whine. And then I see it—a single dark speck racing across the sky toward the city at an unimaginable speed. Must be a jet or . . .

Fuck . . . It can't be . . .

The accelerator pedal's already flat on the floor, but I try to push it down harder still when I realize what it is I'm looking at. With one hand on the wheel, I reach across and shove Ellis down. She yelps in pain and protest and tries to fight me off, but I ignore her cries and keep pushing. She slides off the seat, and I shove her harder, forcing her down into the foot well.

"Get down!" I scream, my voice hoarse with panic. "Get your goddamn head down now!"

She looks up again, and all I can see is those beautiful brown eyes staring back at me. She tries to move again, but I push her back.

"Don't look up, Ellis. Whatever you do, don't look up—"

Then it happens.

There's a sudden flash of intense white light, so bright that it burns. I screw my eyes shut, but I can still see everything as the incandescent light and sudden, scorching heat wrap all the way around us, filling the Land Rover, burning my skin and snatching the air from my lungs. It fades almost as quickly as it came, but the darkness that takes its place is equally blinding. I'm thrown forward as we smash into another vehicle ahead of us, and in the fraction of a second I'm looking out, I see that the highway has become a single solid mass of smashed cars and trucks.

A howling wind swallows up the Land Rover and hurls us and everything else forward again. I try to reach out for Ellis, but I can't find her. I lean over, but I can't feel her. She's not moving. The Land Rover's spinning now. Feels like it's rolling over and over, being hit by debris from all angles. I'm thrown back in my seat again, and the back of my head smashes against the window.

Try to move but I can't. Try to focus but I can't. Try to speak but . . .

40

HOW LONG? HOURS, MINUTES, or just seconds? Everything is still, much quieter than it should be. I slowly pry my eyes open, not knowing what I'm going to see. The windshield of the Land Rover has shattered, the glass crisscrossed by hundreds of tiny, snaking cracks. We're straddling another wreck, and the nose of the car has been shunted up into the air. Lying back in my seat, all I can see in front of me is a foul and angry yellow-gray sky. It's the color of bile.

Ellis moves. I try to lean across and turn toward her, but my neck's stiff. I reach up to massage it, but I stop. My skin feels moist, raw, and pliable. Must have been burned. Ellis shuffles again, and I try to twist around. Then I freeze. I feel my bladder loosen involuntarily.

The force of what just happened must have spun the Land Rover around through more than a complete half turn, and what I can see now through the passenger window is the single most terrifying thing I have ever seen. Between here and what used to be the city, almost everything's on fire. There are flickering flames everywhere, and the ground is scorched and black. The city itself—my home, the place where I lived with my family and where I worked and played and struggled and fought—is gone. A thick climbing column of dark gray smoke rises straight up into the sky from its dead heart. At a height I can't even begin to imagine the smoke balloons out and turns in on itself again and again, forming the unmistakable shape of a mushroom cloud.

Ellis climbs up onto the passenger seat next to me. Thank God I found her. If I'd been any slower or any later or if I'd waited any longer she'd be gone now, vaporized in the blinking of an eye along with so many others. Lizzie, Josh, Edward . . . all gone. I start sobbing. The apartment, Joseph Mallon, Julia . . . Don't know why I'm crying. Is it shock, relief, or sorrow . . . ? Ellis looks at the explosion in the distance, then turns and watches me, her brown eyes locked onto mine. I try to talk to her, but I can't make the words come out. My throat is burning and dry. My lungs feel like they're filled with smoke. Is she in shock, too? For the first time since I found her she's quiet and subdued.

"We'll wait here till it's safe," I tell her in a voice that doesn't sound like mine. "Then we'll find somewhere better, okay?"

She looks at me but doesn't react. Then she looks at the broken windshield.

"Snow," she says, the first proper word I've heard my daughter say in months.

"Not snow," I tell her, watching a few large gray clumps drift down and settle on the cracked glass. "It's ash. Dirty. Poison. Make you sick."

She slumps back in her seat, and beyond her I can see the mushroom cloud again. Even now after all that's happened, it's a terrifying and humbling sight. The ultimate symbol of the Hate. Who did this?

"We're going to find a house," I tell Ellis, still watching the cloud, not knowing what I'm saying now or why, "and you and me are going to stay there together. I know it's hard to understand what happened with Mummy and Edward and Josh, but one day we'll work it out, and when we do you'll—"

She springs up from her seat and throws herself across the inside of the Land Rover, leaning on my chest, shoving me back into my chair, and pressing her face hard against the glass. I can't move, pinned down by her weight. She's following something, watching it circling us. With lightning speed she jumps away again, then scrambles over the seats into the back of the car, trampling over the soldiers' still-wet corpses. She yanks at one of the door handles, trying to get out.

"Don't, sweetheart," I shout, trying to turn my aching body around and pull her back into the front. I manage to catch hold of her, but she wrestles herself free. "You can't go out there—"

She squeezes through the gap between the seats again, pushing me back and lunging for the door. I lean across and cover the lock. She shakes the handle violently and screams with frustration.

"Ellis, don't," I plead. "You have to stay here with me. You can't—"

A sudden round of gunfire from somewhere close interrupts me. I turn and look out of the window at my side and see that there are people out on the highway now. Hundreds of them. Mostly they look like our people, but there are Unchanged soldiers among them, too. Our fighters outnumber them. They're hunting them down.

Ellis lunges at me, trying to get past. I wrap my heavy arms around her waist and try to pull her closer, but she kicks herself free. I'm too tired to keep fighting. She shoves me away, and the back of my head cracks against the window. Her constant, violent movements make the precariously balanced Land Rover shake and start to slip and lurch to one side.

"Please..." I say, cautiously trying to reach for her again. She recoils from my touch, scrambling away. She pushes against the windshield in frustration. When the broken glass starts to bulge outward, she does it again. And again. I want to stop her, but I don't have the energy. There's blood on her hands now, but she goes on thumping the glass regardless, desperate to get out. Finally, with a grunt of effort and anger, she breaks through the windshield and scrambles out onto the hood of the Land Rover. My door's blocked by another crashed car, and all I can do is follow her out. I crawl over the front of the vehicle, the metal still hot, most of its paint scorched away, shards of glass grinding into my belly. I drop down onto the ground and lose my footing when it's farther to fall than I think. I get up quickly, breathing hard. The air out here is bone dry and foul smelling.

Ellis darts away, and I follow her, moving out from the shadow of the crashed Land Rover and into the open. I look along the highway in both directions. It's a single mass of stationary vehicles now. Many of the Unchanged drivers and their passengers are dead. I can see them wedged behind the wheels of wrecks, others with their bloody faces smashed up against windows. Some have survived. One of them emerges from the back of an overturned truck a short distance away. Before they've taken more than a couple of steps away, Ellis has attacked. She jumps onto a car, then leaps at the disoriented Unchanged man, landing on his back and smashing him down to the ground with incredible brutality.

A pack of fighters races past me. They've been waiting out here in the wasteland, and now they pick their way through the convoy like vultures, stripping the meat from Unchanged bones, hunting out the survivors and tearing them apart. Up ahead a Brute thunders along the road unchallenged, making kill after kill after kill. Any Unchanged resistance is quickly crushed. Even those who try to run are chased down and killed.

Ellis lunges at another one and disappears from view. I swallow hard and force myself to move. Leg hurts. I look down and see that there's blood dribbling down from my right knee. My trouser leg and boot are stained wet-red.

"Ellis, wait," I try to shout, my voice nowhere near loud enough. I find her on the ground beside a jeep, leaning down over another body. She looks up at me, and a chunk of bloody flesh drops from her mouth. Was she chewing it? I reach out and grab her wrist before she's able to get away. "Too dangerous here. Need to get under cover. Come with me . . ."

She pries my weak fingers off and crawls away, searching for the next kill. She brings down a dazed, blood-soaked woman who's already half dead. She pulls her down to her knees, grabs a fistful of hair, and smashes her face again and again into a charred car door, denting the paint-stripped metal more and more with each impact. I haul myself toward her, using other wrecks for support. Up ahead the towering mushroom cloud is beginning to fade and lose focus. That makes me even more afraid. Soon the air will be filled with poison if it's not already. I throw myself down at Ellis again and wrap my arms tight around her. The pain in my bleeding knee is unbearable, but I have to ignore it. Ellis is all that matters.

"You have to come with me. We'll both die if we stay out here."

She puts the soles of her bare feet against the misshapen car door and straightens her legs, pushing me away. Overbalanced, and with one leg already weakened, I fall back. She bites down onto my hand, drawing blood, and I let go. She stands over me, one foot on either side of my body. I look up at her, covering my eyes against the fine dust and ash, which is falling faster now. I reach up and snatch her hand again as she sees another Unchanged and tries to run. I won't let go. I can't let go. She screams and pulls and kicks at me, but I won't let her go.

"Stay with me, please . . ."

Ellis drops down onto my chest and stares into my face. What's she thinking? Does she understand any of this? Another Unchanged trying to drag itself to safety distracts her, and she starts to move. I grip her wrist even harder.

"Don't go."

She clenches her free hand into a fist and hits me. I try to stop her, but she hits me again, then again and again and again until my face is numb and my eyes are almost swollen shut. Too tired. Can't fight back.

I feel her get up.

There's so much I need to say, but I can't get even the first word out. I'm aware of her looking down at me, breathing hard, my blood on her hands.

"Ellis—" I start to say, but she isn't listening. She looks up, then sprints away. I turn my head and watch as she disappears into the maze of crashed vehicles, searching for her next kill. All I can do is watch her go.

41

C OLD.
    Body shaking.
Breathing in dust.
The fighters are long gone. Ellis is long gone.
Empty.
Everything's lost.
Still lying in the road, curled up in a ball. Stomach churning, legs and arms aching. Head pounding. Throat dry, lungs scorched. Warm wind gusting. Swirling sky black above me. Light's fading. Stench of burning meat is everywhere. Been here for hours, face-down on the asphalt.
    Heavy footsteps.
    Someone standing next to me. A soldier? Stay still. Don't move.

"Found one," he shouts, face hidden, voice muffled by a gas mask.

"Worth taking?" someone shouts back.

"Not sure."

He kicks me in the gut to see if he gets a reaction, forcing air out. I look up but don't move. I feel the Hate rising.

"Well, has it still got two arms and two legs?"

"Yes."

"And is it breathing?"

"Think so."

"Then chuck it on the truck."

He bends down, grabs hold of my shoulder, and picks me up. He hauls me across the road, feet dragging in the dust.

Have to try to fight. It's all I've got left. Everything else is lost.

With what feels like my last breath, I straighten my legs, stand tall, and wrestle myself free. Unarmed and uncaring, I shove the soldier away with all the force I can manage. Caught off guard, he slams face first into a wreck. I spin him around and rip off his face mask. I need this fucker to know how much I hate him when I kill him.

He throws me back. Much stronger than me. I fall, my injured knee giving way. I wait for him to attack, but he picks me up again.

Is this how it ends? Is he going to kill me now?

Wait. He's like me. One of us.

"Easy, tiger," he grunts, pushing me forward again. "Save it for the Unchanged."

Too tired to protest. Filled with relief, anger, and pain.

He leads me through the highway chaos, then picks me up and puts me over his shoulder like a sack of potatoes when my legs buckle again. Can't fight. Can't react.

I open my eyes and lift my head. Hard to see anything. More soldiers wearing gas masks, all of them dragging or carrying people over this way. We reach a flatbed truck, and he pushes me up. Grabbing hands reach down and help me. I scramble up, then fall back against the side of the truck, struggling to breathe. Dust and dirt grind into my cuts and burns, but I'm too tired to care. Too tired to feel the pain.

Empty.

For half a second I try to look for Ellis, but I know she's long gone. I look around at the faces of the people crammed into the back of this truck. They're all like me. They're all fighters. No longer people, just fighters. All of us conscripted into what remains of Ankin's army or another force like it.

I was stupid to believe I could sidestep this war, that I could escape from it with Ellis. What's left of the world is now entirely governed by the Hate, and I have to be ready to fight and to kill until the last trace of the Unchanged is wiped from the face of the planet. Only then will the situation change.

My daughter is gone, lost long before I found her. Now all I have left is the Hate.

Exhausted, I close my eyes and let the darkness swallow me up.

Need to rest and recover and be ready for what's still to come. No choice. No option. The hardest battles loom large on the horizon.

WARNING:
YOU WILL KILL TODAY

"A head-spinning thrill ride, a cautionary tale about the most salient emotion of the twenty-first century...*Hater* will haunt you long after you read the last page."
—Guillermo del Toro, director of *Pan's Labyrinth* and *Hellboy 1 and 2*

a novel

HATER

DAVID MOODY

The thrilling first entry in the Hater series

REMAIN CALM.

DO NOT PANIC.

TAKE SHELTER.

WAIT FOR FURTHER INSTRUCTIONS.

THE SITUATION IS UNDER CONTROL.

AVAILABLE WHEREVER BOOKS ARE SOLD

 St. Martin's Griffin   THOMAS DUNNE BOOKS

Outnumbered 1,000,000 to 1, a small band of the living face down the walking dead

Book 2 — autumn: the city — DAVID MOODY, AUTHOR OF HATER

Book 4 — autumn: Disintegration — DAVID MOODY, AUTHOR OF HATER

Book 1 — autumn — DAVID MOODY, AUTHOR OF HATER

Book 3 — autumn: purification — DAVID MOODY, AUTHOR OF HATER

"A marvelously bleak dystopian future where the world belongs to the dead."
—Jonathan Maberry, *New York Times* bestselling author of *Patient Zero*